THE TILTERSMITH

AMY HERRICK

ALGONQUIN YOUNG READERS 2022

Published by
Algonquin Young Readers
an imprint of Algonquin Books of Chapel Hill
Post Office Box 2225
Chapel Hill, North Carolina 27515-2225

a division of
Workman Publishing
225 Varick Street
New York, New York 10014

LIBRARY OF CONGRESS CATALOGING-IN-PUBLICATION DATA
[TK]

10 9 8 7 6 5 4 3 2 1
First Edition

THE
TILTERSMITH

ALSO BY AMY HERRICK

The Time Fetch

[dedication TK]

THE TILTERSMITH

PART ONE

1

Edward Finds a Cocoon

Edward was dreaming. He was trying to pick something up with a spoon. The thing, which was going to lead him to a brilliant scientific discovery, kept sliding away like a piece of spaghetti. Then, just as he thought he'd finally got it, there was a tremendous *kabooooom!* and he woke up.

He found himself in the deep middle of the night. A thunderbolt lit the sky outside his window, and in its brief flash of light, he saw that it was snowing again. *Seriously? It was March 21. Enough already with the snow.*

He lay there counting. Ten seconds and *kabooooom!* This meant, he knew, that the storm was about two miles away. He waited for the next flash of lightning, which came quickly. It tore out of the clouds and shot down behind the houses beyond Ninth Street. Snow swirled madly through the air. This time the *kabooooom!* came only five seconds later.

The storm was headed right this way.

Edward forced himself out of bed with his blanket around his shoulders. He stood in front of the window, scanning the sky. He wanted to see another bolt up close.

Perhaps thirty seconds later, the next strike happened, right up the street. This time the lightning appeared to burst out of the ground like an enormous electrified finger. It was met almost simultaneously by a bolt from the sky, followed by an enormous concussive *baaadoooooom!* The whole house shook, and the windows rattled. Peering into the darkness and the snow, Edward saw a round metal disk go flying through the air. It landed with a great crumpling noise on top of a nearby car. The roof of the car folded upward like a piece of origami paper. The disk then slid off the car and came to a stop balanced against its side.

A manhole cover! That was what it had to be. He'd read all about how these things happened. Between the flammable gases that could build up underground and the old and frayed electrical wiring down there, sometimes all it took was a little spark to cause an explosion and—*boooom!*—a manhole cover would go flying off.

His theory was confirmed when a long tongue of fire shot up from what he could see was an open hole in the middle of the street. All the streetlamps went out like the candles on a birthday cake as the tongue of flame reached higher and higher and slowly died back. He was surprised at what a short time it took before the fire department and then Con Edison began to arrive.

A few minutes later, Edward's aunt Kit knocked on the door and came in without waiting for an invitation. She was barefoot and wearing her flannel pajamas. The storm had already begun to move slowly off. She joined him at the window. "Well, did you see it?" she asked.

"Did I see what? Could you be a little more specific?" Her vagueness often drove him crazy.

"The part where the lightning shot up out of the ground."

"Well, yes, I did. That was pretty cool. But it's common, you know. There's a positive electrical charge on the ground, and it shoots upward to meet the negative electrical charge coming from the clouds. Happens all the time."

"Does it, now? Well, that's an interesting explanation."

"Isn't it?" he said and hoped she wasn't going to give him one of her crazy alternative theories.

She didn't. Instead, she said, "Well, in any case, the timing is amazing, isn't it?"

He didn't like to encourage her, but he couldn't help asking her what this meant.

"I mean with tomorrow being what it is."

"What's tomorrow?"

"Don't tell me you've forgotten. Well, you'll remember in the morning. We'd better get to bed. We're going to need our sleep."

It seemed only ten minutes later that she woke him with a loud rap on the door. She threatened to make a personal live appearance in his room if he wasn't down for breakfast in fifteen minutes. He sat up groaning.

Outside, all was quiet. A fine light snow was still falling.

His reflection in the bright windowpane revealed that his curly mop of medium-brown hair was smashed down flat on one side, while the hair on the other side of his head stood up in a tangled snarl. There was a red mark where his cheek had been resting against his hand.

He definitely would have liked fifteen more minutes of sleep, but having Aunt Kit in his room in daylight would be dangerous. He did not want her messing with any of the items in his valuable collection of stuff. There were, for instance, three meteorite fragments (Mr. Ross, his science teacher, had helped him identify these), a raccoon skull with some fur still stuck to it, a complete wasps' nest, now empty of wasps (as far as he could tell), a fish eye he was keeping in a jar of alcohol till he could get around to dissecting it, a pigeon wing dried and spread out like a lady's fan, numerous seashells, and several jars with different types of animal dung. All were kept on a special bookcase in no particular order.

And then there was his latest experiment.

For this project he had recently needed to borrow two of Aunt Kit's baking pans. It wouldn't be good if she noticed this. He was attempting to grow a mold that could successfully break down plastic.

It could take a plastic bottle over 450 years to decompose, and by 2050 there would be more plastic in the sea than fish. Edward had read that some scientists had recently discovered a new strain of mold that could break down plastic way more quickly than that. They'd found it in a garbage dump. But this mold was hard to find or produce in a lab. Imagine if Edward found something that improved upon the original discovery. That, after all, was the way good science was done, wasn't it?

The building of new discoveries on the foundations of the old ones?

He'd always liked molds a lot anyway.

As he walked into the kitchen, Aunt Kit was standing very still, watching her cuckoo clock. When he sat down at the counter, she turned and put her finger to her lips.

"Not a word," she whispered. "It's nearly time."

She was holding a wooden spoon. He knew her well; she had been his guardian since he was three. She had a belief that certain moments were more loaded with power than others, moments when luck and ripeness of time came together. Clearly, this was one of them. According to her theory, if you said or did the wrong thing at one of these points, the whole universe could go out of whack.

The air was fragrant with pancakes, but there was no sign of them. Hanging over the counter from a golden ribbon was a bronze bell. It was attached to one of the racks she hung her pots and pans and dried herbs from. She was a big one for drying stuff. "I'm hungry," he complained. "How much long—"

"Shhh!" she said in a low whisper. "Wait for it. Wait for it . . ."

He held his tongue. The minute hand on the cuckoo clock clicked forward. Seven thirty-three.

"Now," she said softly, and she struck the bell with her wooden spoon. The bell rang out. Edward liked this bell. He liked the way you could hear the wave of sound traveling outward. When the note finally traveled away into silence or wherever notes travel to, there was a pancake in front of him.

The pancake was a thing of glory—slightly crispy around the edges but light and golden in the middle. He sat down and began to eat. It was an excellent advantage to have a guardian who was a chef, even if she was missing several marbles.

"The first pancake of spring," she announced.

Edward looked out the window sharply. He had forgotten the date. It didn't look promising out there at all. It was still snowing lightly, and he could tell it was cold.

He waved his hand toward the window. "You call that *spring*? So much for your magic bell."

She looked at him with that look. "Edward! Don't play the fool with me. My *bell* doesn't bring the spring in. Spring is a meeting of the Forces That Be and the Matters That Are. It's a very, very delicate balance of things. If we humans are knocking out that balance by cutting down the forests and fishing out the seas and filling the air with carbon dioxide, then it's up to those of us who care to do what we can. And, of course, to alert the other powers out there. I ring the bell in the hopes it will be heard by friendly ears."

Ahhhh. She was in high wackadoodle gear today. Edward finished the last bite of his pancake and slipped off his stool. Now that he was awake, he was eager to take a look at what had happened with that manhole last night. But Aunt Kit was between him and the door.

"I want you to be careful today, please," she said.

"Of what?"

"Well . . ." She hesitated. "For one thing, there's trees down all over the place. And there could be more branches ready to fall. So just stay alert. Keep your eyes open and listen to the back of your mind. It often knows things before the front of your mind does. It might keep you out of trouble."

"Sure. No problem," he said and tried to step around her, but still, she blocked his way.

"And do me a favor. My next round of Wednesday bread-making classes will start tonight. Remind Danton and Franklin, please."

Edward groaned. "Look, I'll remind Danton for you, but I think you should remind Mr. Ross yourself. Text him, why don't you?"

He knew she didn't like texting—something about how it messed with the currents in the air. He, however, refused to be placed in the middle of that situation—a situation that was due to Feenix's relentless scheming and general busybodyness. She had introduced Kit and Mr. Ross at a party, and he had been coming to Kit's baking classes ever since. Ed did not like having Mr. Ross see what a featherhead his aunt was, and he knew—no matter what Feenix thought—the whole thing could end only in spontaneous combustion and disaster. Why Feenix thought otherwise was a great mystery to him.

"Fine," Kit said. "I'll take care of that myself."

"Good. Anything else?"

She leaned forward and kissed him on the cheek. "You might want to comb your hair."

He wasn't about to go all the way back upstairs for a comb. He smashed his lucky green baseball hat down on his head on his way out the door.

When he got outside, he saw she was correct about there being tree branches down everywhere. Plus, there were garbage cans rolling on the sidewalks, and an inch of snow over everything. The Con Ed truck was still there—a little ways up the hill—along with a bunch of guys wearing helmets and neon-yellow vests. They had put up ropes and orange cones around the open manhole. It was the opposite direction from school, but Ed couldn't help himself. He walked up to the busy scene.

"So, have you figured out what happened?" he asked one of the guys when he got there. Another one was just about to descend into the hole.

The guy shook his helmeted head. "Whatever it was, it burnt all the lines out up and down the whole block. Musta been a short, and the lightning just happened to be in the right place at the right time. Pure luck nobody got hurt." The worker pointed over to the manhole cover leaning up against the crumpled car. "Those things can weigh more than a couple hundred pounds."

Edward went over to take a closer look. The heavy cover had landed so its underside was exposed. The front of these things was sometimes really fancy, with raised designs going round the rims, but the underside of this one was without any decorations. It was filthy and caked with mud in some places and smelled strongly of scorched metal. He was just about to walk away when something caught his eye. Something half dangling from the caked-on mud near the rim. It looked like a bunch of dry brown leaves wrapped around each other like a cigar. Or maybe like a big old crooked toe.

Ed bent closer. The thing was wonderfully ugly. It was about an inch and a half long and slightly curved, and it appeared to be attached to the manhole cover by a fine transparent thread. Was it some kind of seedpod?

He picked up a nearby stick and gave the thing a tap. The outside gave slightly, like shoe leather might. There weren't any seams that he could see, but he spotted a small teardrop-shaped indentation near its dangling bottom. It occurred to him that he was looking at some sort of cocoon. Mr. Ross had gone off on a tangent about cocoons just last week. It was what moth caterpillars built around themselves while they went through their changes.

What a brilliant place to build a cocoon, Edward thought—right under a manhole cover. Under normal conditions it would be protected from the weather and any hungry animals. He reached out to pull it free. It would be a perfect addition to his collection.

And then, for a moment, he hesitated. Something seemed to hold his hand in place.

Keep your eyes open and listen to the back of your mind.

Was the back of his mind telling him to leave it alone? Would he be messing with nature if he pulled it loose? But if he left it here, what if some dog or squirrel ate it? And what about the terrible, cold, weird weather they'd been having? What if it froze and died an untimely death? What if it was the last of its kind?

No, he decided. It definitely wouldn't be right to just leave it here all unprotected.

He took hold of the thing and gave a tug. He felt, more than saw, how the nearly invisible thread snapped. He caught the cocoon in his hand.

2

Science Class

In science class Mr. Ross was standing in the middle of the room, greeting each student as they entered. There was a bright, floppy daffodil planted behind one of his rather sticky-out ears. Brigit was particularly struck by this, because in her dream that morning her brother had had a daffodil behind his ear, too. In the dream, he was old enough to walk, and he was holding her hand and trying to get her to climb a hill with him.

Brigit wondered where Mr. Ross had gotten the flower. He must have bought it at a fruit and veggie market or someplace like that. She hadn't seen any actual daffodils growing anywhere around here yet.

She was sitting at the high lab table that she always shared with Feenix and Edward and Danton now that they had all become friends. So far, no sign of Feenix, which wasn't unusual, but Edward and Danton were here. She glanced at them from time to time. She liked what a contrast they made next to each other—Edward so pale-faced, definitely someone who didn't get outside much, a little soft around the middle, with his uncombed hair and that look he often had of having left his body and wandered off to some entirely different dimension where he was concentrating on some fascinating scientific idea. And then Danton so brown and glowing and completely here, watching everything and poking up into the air conspicuously like a giraffe. He was already well over six feet, with long skinny legs and knobby knees and huge feet.

When he caught her looking at him, she looked away quickly.

Brigit hoped that Feenix wasn't late because she'd gotten stopped by Ms. Trevino again. Then, just as the second bell rang, Feenix made her entrance and Brigit breathed a sigh of relief.

Feenix was in full noise mode—boots clacking, jewelry clinking, coat flapping. As everybody knew, Feenix had a thing about this coat. In school, she carried around a fake doctor's note that said she should be allowed to wear it, as she was prone to something called "hypothermatics" and could have a heart attack if she got too cold. Mr. Ross laughed when he read this and didn't bother her about the coat again. Now she sat down with a flourish and slammed her books on the table. She looked around the room defiantly and shook her mane of dark, rough hair back.

One of her eyes was slightly higher than the other. It wasn't all that noticeable, but when she smiled, that higher eye seemed to lift up a fraction of an inch, and it startled people. Somebody else might have been given a lot of trouble about a thing like this, but people gave Feenix trouble at their own risk. Sometimes she inked a picture next to this eye—an animal or odd design. Brigit was pretty sure she did this to distract people from the asymmetry. Plus, she liked to see how far she could get through the day before their principal, Ms. Trevino, caught her and made her wash it off. Today she had painted what looked like a small blue lightning bolt.

The bell rang, and Mr. Ross bowed to the class and waited for silence. Then he spoke in a hushed, solemn voice. "Are you ready? Shall we continue with our courageous and daring journey down the digestive system?" When no one answered, he turned to the Smart Board and clicked on a photo of a slippery-looking and tangled pink mass of intestine. "What are we looking at?"

Feenix's hand shot up. He nodded at her. She pointed at the daffodil behind his ear. "What's with the flower?"

Brigit and everybody else knew that this was another game Feenix played. She would try to keep Mr. Ross off topic for as long as possible. Mr. Ross was a person who was easily led off onto other topics.

"Aha!" Mr. Ross answered happily. "I thought you'd never ask."

Detestable Robert groaned. He did not like when Feenix succeeded in distracting Mr. Ross. "Detestable Robert" was Feenix's name for him. Brigit didn't think this was exactly fair. Robert was irritating, but Feenix drove a lot of people crazy, too.

Mr. Ross went over and pulled a couple of things out of his backpack—a big yellow grapefruit and a bright-green apple. There was a chopstick driven through the center of the apple so it stuck out at either end. He laid these down gently on his desk. "Who can tell me what great celestial event occurs on this very day?"

Brigit knew the answer, but she wasn't about to raise her hand and have everybody stare at her. Robert lifted his arm, looking bored. "The vernal equinox," he said.

Mr. Ross nodded in satisfaction. "Magnifico!" he said. "And who can tell me what the vernal equinox *is*?"

Robert raised his hand again, but Mr. Ross ignored him. He looked around and stopped at Edward. "C'mon, Eddie, my man. I know you know this."

"First day of spring," Edward said.

"Spring?" Feenix objected. "Does that look like spring to you?" She threw her hand toward the window. How can you call that spring? It's March 21. This isn't good, is it? What if something's happened? What if spring doesn't come at all?"

Mr. Ross wrinkled his brow and pulled on his ear. "These are good answers and a difficult question. Knowing that you are thinking about these things makes it worth it to get out of my bed in the morning." He bowed to them all. "But before we can go any further, we need to take a closer look at what the vernal equinox is.

"First of all, I want you to realize that in ancient times people did not have our advantages. They had no clue. They saw that the seasons came and went and the year turned round in a somewhat predictable way, and they really wanted to know why. But they had no telescopes and not enough math to figure out what was going on.

"They reasoned that powers greater than they were must be responsible. And what were these powers, they asked? If they could answer that, maybe they could get some control over them, and maybe they could make sure their crops would always grow again and their cattle would be fertile. Well, they thought hard and started coming up with all sorts of answers. You will know some of them from studying mythology. The Pueblo Indian story about the Blue Corn Maiden. The Winter Katsina god lures her into his house because he has fallen in love with her. He seals the windows with ice and the doors with snow. There will be no more spring and no more new growth unless somebody can rescue her.

"That story might remind you of the one from Greek mythology about Persephone and the pomegranate. Persephone falls down a great crack in the ground and is held prisoner by Hades, the god of the underworld. The whole world stays winter until, at last, he agrees to release her as long as she promises to come back to him at the end of the summer. There's lots of stories with that shape, but lots of other story lines, too. There are monsters who must be vanquished and lovers who are being kept apart and must find their way to each other before the seasons can move on.

"Then humans gradually began to *look more closely* at the physical world. They began to stare at the stars and the sun and do the numbers. They learned about astronomy and geology and the scientific method. Because of science, today we know about the vernal equinox and why we have seasons.

"Let's take a look, shall we? I'm going to need a couple of volunteers so you can visualize this properly. I'll be asking these volunteers to be traveling about one hundred million miles out into space. Who's ready?"

Only Feenix volunteered. She liked nothing more than to be the center of attention. Her noisy bracelet, which she had made herself from Scrabble tiles, clinked and jingled. But Mr.

Ross ignored her. He looked around the room thoughtfully. "Brigit, you will be the earth."

Brigit froze in surprise. Generally, teachers had gotten into the habit of giving her a free pass in the class-participation department. She was pretty sure it was because of her condition and they felt sorry for her. But this was already the second time Mr. Ross had called on her this week.

Feenix leaned over and whispered to her, "You're good. You're good. Just remember to breathe and count slowly." Feenix had been giving her instruction all through the winter.

Brigit nodded at her and went to the center of the room, breathing very deliberately and counting. Mr. Ross handed her the green apple with the chopstick.

"Who will be the sun?"

Danton put his hand up. This, of course, was Danton's way. Danton took care of everybody. He was a kind person. "I'll go," Danton said. Before Mr. Ross could even acknowledge him, he had bounded to the center of the room, next to Brigit. There was some smothered laughter, but Mr. Ross squelched it with a look. Everybody watched to see if her condition would start up, but—nothing happened.

Danton was now officially taller than Mr. Ross and, of course, towered over Brigit. He bounced lightly on his toes as if gravity kept a weaker hold on him than on other people. He radiated can-do cheerfulness. Mr. Ross handed him the large yellow grapefruit. "I give you the sun." Danton accepted it with a bow. "Danton, I am going to ask you to take on a most delicate and vital task. Please kneel down upon the floor and balance the grapefruit upon your head."

"You're kidding."

"Am I a kidder?" There was another ripple of laughter. "C'mon, Sunshine," Mr. Ross said. Danton knelt down slowly and placed the grapefruit on his head. It wobbled for a moment and then settled. "And by the way, what would happen, Danton, if you dropped it? I mean, what would happen if the sun disappeared from its place in our galaxy?"

Danton thought about it, kneeling and holding the grapefruit on his head. "We'd be kaput, wouldn't we? We need the sun to hold us in orbit. If it disappeared, we'd go floating off into space and freeze to death, right?"

"Impeccable logic." Mr. Ross nodded. "Now, Brigit, hold the apple out in front of yourself so its axis"—he lightly tapped the chopstick—"is straight up and down. Walk once around the sun and come back to where you started."

Brigit did as she was told and walked once in a careful circle around Danton.

"Perfecto," Mr. Ross said to her. He turned to the class. They looked back at him.

"Perfecto, except that there is one small, vital thing wrong with this picture. Anybody know what that would be?"

Brigit could hardly believe herself, but she opened her mouth and she said, "The axis of the earth is wrong. It should be tilted."

A hush fell over the room. She could feel everybody's eyes on herself. She could feel the flicker of heat starting up under her blouse. But then Mr. Ross, as if he understood perfectly what she needed, took the attention neatly off her. "She is correct. The earth's axis should be pointed at the North Star." He looked up at the ceiling of the classroom. He pointed in the direction of a wad of blue gum. This gum had been stuck there for as long as anyone could remember.

"Yuck," called out several voices.

"Silence!" commanded Mr. Ross. "Remember what Einstein said: 'Imagination is more important than knowledge.' Or in other words, knowledge has its limits, but imagination gives us the whole world. So, let us employ ours now, please. We gaze upon the North Star, otherwise known as Polaris. Brigit, please tip the axis of the earth toward this star."

She did, and everyone saw how the apple tilted slightly sideways.

"Now I will guide your orbit around the sun." He took hold of Brigit's shoulders. "Oh, sweet Earth, mother of us all, do not waver in your fixed inclination. At all times keep your northern pole tilted and pointed at the North Star, and go in steady devotion around the sun."

Mr. Ross guided Brigit slowly around the grapefruit. He stopped her when the top half of the apple was tipped away from the sun. "Anybody know what time of year this would be?"

"Winter!" Asim called out.

"Correct! At least, it is winter in our northern hemisphere because it is the time of year when we get the least direct light. In the southern hemisphere it would be the opposite. It would be summer. Now, watch what happens next." He continued to guide Brigit forward, and as he did, he called out, "January! February! March!"

He stopped her abruptly. Brigit could see clearly how at this point the earth was getting the same amount of light on both its top and bottom halves.

"*Ta-da!* Look closely. The vernal equinox. This is where we were at seven thirty-three this morning." Mr. Ross's eyes were bright with the joy of astronomical revelation. His ears seemed to stick out a little farther, as they usually did when he was excited.

"This is the day when the northern and southern hemispheres receive equal amounts of light. After this, the light of spring will grow stronger here, and all that has slept through the cold winter will generally awaken or return. Our part of the world will grow warm and green again. If there are no major interruptions, there will be grain and grapes and flowers, and the cattle will fatten and the summer will arrive in all its plentitude. All shall rejoice." As Mr. Ross spoke, he moved Brigit along. The class all could see how the upper half of the earth tipped slowly toward the sun. He paused her for a moment. "Here is the day of the summer solstice. The longest sunlit day of our northern year. Then, of course, we continue on to another fall and another winter." He walked her slowly back to where she had started.

"Do you see it, my intrepid knowledge seekers? It is the tilt of the earth which gives us our seasons! It is further believed that without the seasons there might have been no life on earth—or very little of it. It would be too constantly hot in some places and too constantly cold in others. No tilt, and none of us would be here now. What a wonderful little gift we were given with that little twenty-three degrees off center. There are, in fact, many ways in which tilts and asymmetries make our world possible. All is in a constant struggle between balance and imbalance. Without those struggles our world and even the universe wouldn't exist as we know it. I suggest we all give thanks to the tilt." He put his hands together and bowed his head for a moment.

There were some giggles from around the room.

"Hooray," Danton said. "May I get up now?"

Mr. Ross nodded at him. Danton tipped his head forward so that the grapefruit rolled off into his hands. Then he stood. Mr. Ross looked up at him thoughtfully. "I think you grew again last night. Did you know that people do more growing asleep than when awake? You two may sit down now." Brigit sat down feeling greatly pleased with herself.

Now Feenix stuck her arm up in the air and waved it back and forth so that her bracelets made a big racket. "You still haven't answered my question! Your vernal equinox has come. But there isn't a single sign of spring. What's going on?"

Robert groaned and raised his hand.

"Yes?" Mr. Ross asked.

"It's just weather!" Robert exploded. "Weather is very changeable. It's what happens day to day. Hundreds of other things affect the weather besides the tilt of the earth, and we don't have time to talk about them all now. The important thing to know is that Feenix is scamming us. She's trying to make sure we never get back to the subject of digestion! We have a citywide test coming up, and she doesn't give two flying flarts about it, because she knows she's hopeless anyway."

Mr. Ross put his head to one side and studied Feenix. "Is that possibly true, Feenix? Do you really not care about the citywide exam?" It seemed to Brigit that Mr. Ross must know about Feenix and that he enjoyed her game. That he liked the way her mind went wandering around.

"I want to know what happens if spring doesn't come," Feenix insisted stubbornly.

Edward raised his hand.

Oh, oh, Brigit thought. Edward didn't raise his hand very often.

Mr. Ross called on him. "Something you want to share on this question, Edward?"

Edward said, "If spring doesn't come, it would be a major disaster, similar to what happened in 1816."

"Tell us," Mr. Ross prompted. "What happened in 1816?"

"Well, in 1815 there was a major volcanic eruption in Indonesia, and so much dust was thrown into the air that a lot of the earth's sunlight was blocked out. There was no spring and no summer the next year. Everything froze and crops couldn't grow. There were food shortages and famines all around the world. The famines caused typhus epidemics, and thousands of people died. There was actually snow until August in a lot of places."

"Excellent answer and example."

Feenix jumped right back in. "Well, okay. That sounds nasty. But I don't see any major volcanic eruptions going on right now, do you?" She waved her hand at the window. "So nobody's answered my question."

Mr. Ross sighed. "Well, I understand your concern. It *is* unusual weather. But as Robert suggests, *weather* may be all that's going on, and things may soon change for the better. My suggestion is that we give it some more time, and then we'll revisit the matter. In the meanwhile, let's return to our adventure down the small intestine, shall we?" He looked around at the class and pointed at Beatrice the Poisonous Toadstool (Edward had named her this). "Beatrice," he said. "Would you tell us what you had for breakfast, please?"

Beatrice very reluctantly admitted that she'd had a strawberry Pop-Tart. Brigit almost felt sorry for her. Mr. Ross was undoubtedly going to follow that Pop-Tart all the way down her digestive system.

3

Edward Forgets and Edward Remembers

Edward hurried up to his room that evening, wanting nothing to do with what was going on in his aunt's kitchen, and threw his jacket on his bed. But then he couldn't find his phone. While rooting around in his pockets, he happened upon a stiff leathery-feeling object. He pulled it out, puzzled, and then, with a shudder of excitement, recognized it.

The cocoon. He had forgotten all about it. It was still shiny, brown, and repellent looking. He put it down on his desk and examined it closely. Perhaps if he created the right conditions, he could get the moth to hatch out.

Edward dug around in the back of his closet, where he stored items that might come in useful one day, and found a small glass-sided terrarium. It was dusty but empty. He considered. Aha! Right down at the bottom of the stairs was one of his aunt's vases of dried grasses and old tree branches. Tiptoeing down the stairs in his socks, he grabbed a few of the cattail stems from the vase, along with a branch that maybe had once held autumn leaves.

Before he turned to go back, he peered around in the

direction of the kitchen. The space down here was one big open area of living room, dining room, and then kitchen. They all ran into each other, but you could divide them up, if you needed to, by closing the pocket doors. Which they rarely did. Today he could see seven or eight people standing around the center granite-topped counter in the kitchen. Edward recognized several of them. Aunt Kit had a large number of loyal followers.

Including Danton, who was up near the front. Cooking was Danton's latest fixation. He had many of them. His fixations could be very tiring, because he always wanted to shared them. But Edward was getting used to this. Danton loved soccer and basketball, but he also loved jazz and food carts and Coney Island and movies. Now he had gotten it into his head that he needed to learn to bake. Since he loved to eat, this actually made some sense. He had not missed one of Aunt Kit's classes all winter.

And then there was Mr. Ross, who stood at the work counter, kneading his dough. *This*, Edward simply could not get used to. When Mr. Ross came to their house for a baking lesson, Edward, if he could, stayed out of the kitchen. Today, he was just about to make his getaway when he heard his aunt talking about "how to make friends with your dough." Edward's first reaction was to get back upstairs quickly. His second reaction was to stay hidden and hear what Mr. Ross had to say about this.

His aunt stood at the head of the counter in her flour-dusted pink apron, her hair pinned up behind her head. Possibly, she looked pretty and rosy, but it wasn't a thought Ed had much interest in. "It is of the utmost importance that you be confident and quick. You do not want your dough to suspect that you are unsure of yourself. If you are unsure of yourself, your dough will become unsure of itself, too, and lose its liveliness."

Mr. Ross had paused in his kneading and was staring at her. He opened his mouth and then closed it. Then he opened it again. "I assume you're speaking . . . well . . . poetically? You don't really mean that the dough can feel your feelings?"

She laughed. "Why not? You don't think dough can feel things?"

"Well, since it isn't alive and it doesn't have any sensory equipment, I don't see how it could."

"What makes you think it isn't alive? This one, particularly. It's full of yeast, isn't it? You were the one who pointed out last time that yeast is a one-celled organism in the fungi family. One cell, but very much alive and picking up on our messages, loud and clear."

"I don't think yeast cells are capable of picking up on my confidence or lack of it."

"That's the front of your mind speaking, Franklin. Which is perfectly fine as far as it goes. But then there's the back end of your mind, which sends out all sorts of communications and picks up all sorts of messages."

Mr. Ross frowned and seemed to consider an answer. Before he could find one, Danton jumped in. "Isn't that kind of like what you're always saying, Mr. Ross, about how the whole earth is one living body and that every little living system on earth is part of the bigger living system? That everything is always talking back and forth even though we don't actually *hear* it going on?"

Edward found himself deeply annoyed with Danton. Why was he sticking his nose into this? But Mr. Ross only laughed. "Well, I'm not sure *what* Kit is saying, but hers is the best bread I have ever tasted. Therefore, I am confident that she has something to teach me."

Edward turned quickly and hurried back up the steps. When he was safely in his room, for a moment he couldn't remember why he was holding a bare tree branch and a bunch of dried-up cattails. He stared at them, puzzled. Then he saw the cocoon waiting on his desk.

Again it had slipped from his mind. He felt his own forehead. Maybe he was coming down with a cold or something? What was with his memory today? Well, whatever. He worked quickly, setting up the terrarium with nice soft cattails on the bottom. The cocoon had a little sticky sort of button on one end of its cigar-like shape. Ed, who had read that it was possible to move a cocoon if you were careful, knew about this button. It was where the thread had hung before. He put a drop of rubber cement on it to make it a little stickier and held the button end of the cocoon onto the dry branch till it stayed stuck. Then he leaned the branch up against the glass wall of the terrarium. The cocoon rocked gently from the branch and then stayed still. He found a pencil under an empty bag of Doritos (his aunt would have three-alarm heart failure if she knew he was eating these) and took some careful notes describing the cocoon's color, size, and shape. He also took some photos. When all was done, he put the screened lid over the terrarium and looked around for a safe place to keep it. He certainly did not wish for his aunt to come in here and start busy-fingering around with his new treasure. In the end he placed the cocoon on top of a bookshelf, behind a stack of books, and sat down to do his homework.

About an hour later Danton barged into his room. He was holding out a plate of warm yeasty-smelling bread slathered with butter and raspberry jam. "So, were you nice and confident with your dough?" Edward asked him sweetly.

Danton's mouth was full, and he didn't seem to catch Ed's sarcasm. "Try thum. Ith delithous."

4

A Passage of Time

The weather did not improve. There were no volcanic eruptions, but wherever spring was, it stayed stuck. Nevertheless, Danton rose every morning full of hope. Winter had to end soon. Danton was an incurably optimistic person. Usually, his mother and his brother would be gone already when he came into the kitchen. His mother would have taken Mikey off to school, and then she'd have gone to the gardening store she owned in downtown Brooklyn. Danton would have breakfast with his father if he was at home (his father was a musician and often away on tour). After breakfast he'd go bounding out the front door with his head full of plans.

If it was snowing or sleeting, he would just ignore it. Often his jacket was wide open. He would keep himself warm by jogging along and thinking about what they would all do when the weather finally warmed up. They could go roller blading in Prospect Park and watch a movie there under the stars in the summer. They could go to Coney Island and see a baseball game and ride the Cyclone. He wondered if Brigit liked roller coasters. And there was going to be that new show about black holes at the planetarium. Ed would love that.

If he wasn't thinking about the end of winter, he was thinking eagerly of what lay ahead in the day. He would always slow down when he got to the fountain in Grand Army Plaza. Just in case he ran into Brigit. Somehow, either by luck or by some other invisible force, they often seemed to run into each other there. If not, they met on the steps of the school with the others. Then there was science class to look forward to and lunchtime and maybe Kit's bread-baking class later in the day. You never knew what might happen. And he felt like he was friends with the whole world—the lampposts, the cat watching him from behind a front window, the mailbox at the corner.

Danton had many commitments and responsibilities, of course. His father always said that to live a good life, the second most important thing was bravery. The first was kindness. Danton let the bravery part take care of itself, but he made it his first rule of business to be kind. He always watched in the hallways to see that none of the younger kids were getting pushed around (a habit from watching over his younger brother, he supposed). He visited his grandmother every week and helped his mother in the store when she needed it. He tried to make sure Edward didn't drift too far out into space when he was supposed to be paying attention in class.

If he had any worries at this time, the first of them was probably Mr. Ross. Mr. Ross was Danton's favorite teacher, and he had always walked into the classroom fizzing and popping like a bottle of soda ready to go off. Until lately. Lately, something seemed to be keeping him tied to the ground. There was a look in his eye of troubling thoughts or maybe sadness. Danton wished he knew what it was and how he might help him.

The second worry Danton had was Feenix. The worry was how to keep her out of trouble and make sure she didn't end up in summer school. As it was, Feenix got called into the principal's office at least once a week. There was, for instance, the day she stuck a blob of peanut butter into each toe of the French teacher's running shoes. (She stored them under her desk during the school day.) And the day she hit Detestable Robert in the back of the head with the dodgeball during gym. (She was sure it was he who had snitched on her about the peanut butter.) And there was the occasion upon which she called Mr. Armand, the security guard on the second floor, Mr. Armpit. Each time Ms. Trevino let her off with a warning. But no one knew when Ms. Trevino would run out of mercy.

In spite of Danton's incurable optimism, the weather continued to be cold and sleety and sometimes snowy all through April. Every time Feenix tried to bring this up in class and ask why, Robert would raise his hand in indignation and point out that the citywide test was nearly upon them and maybe Feenix was deliberately trying to sabotage the rest of the class since she could probably never pass the test herself. And then Feenix would slowly rise to her feet, shooting nearly visible lightning bolts from her eyes, and suggest to Robert that he go somewhere and sit down on a spiny sea urchin. The class would explode into hoots and cheers of excitement. Mr. Ross would have to step in and regain control of the class, and Feenix's question would be forgotten.

Mr. Ross finished up with human and animal digestion and moved on to how plants produce their own food through photosynthesis. From there he introduced the wonderful world of food chains and tried to impress upon them the very delicate web of interactions that the whole earth depended upon. He had them draw food chains and act out food chains and write poems about food chains. Everyone was going half-mad with listening to the radiators clank and steam and having been cooped up inside for so many weeks.

"All righty, then," Mr. Ross began one morning. "We've talked about food chains on the savanna and food chains in the desert. We've talked about food chains in the jungle and food chains in the sea. But how about in cities? Let's think about a city park, like our own. Any food chains in Prospect Park that you can think of?"

There was a long silence. "Oh, c'mon, guys. Who's a photosynthesizer up the hill there?"

Danton felt sorry for Mr. Ross. He raised his hand. "Well," he offered, "the grass photosynthesizes its own food."

"Okay. There's a good starting point. Now, who eats the grass in a city park?"

"Grasshoppers?" suggested Danton.

"Oh, splendiferous guess! They do indeed. In fact, many insects eat grass. But let's stick with the grasshopper for the moment. Who in Prospect Park would eat grasshoppers?"

Tessa raised her hand and suggested robins.

Mr. Ross was now perking up. You could see his ears sticking out just a bit more. "Now we're getting somewhere. Robins love 'em. They love worms, too, of course. Chock-full of vitamins and nutrients. But here's a tricky question. Who in a city park would eat a robin? Any predators big and quick enough?"

Robert raised his hand, but before he could get his mouth open, Feenix interrupted indignantly. "Excuse me! Why are we still talking about this? There aren't any robins up there now! There isn't any grass, either. And forget about grasshoppers. And if there's anything in the park big enough to eat a robin, it's about to starve to death. *That* chain is broken. What's going on? Why isn't there any spring?"

Robert sank back in his seat and groaned.

"All right, all right," said Mr. Ross to him. "We respect your dedication to preparing for the citywide exam, but I think we've been avoiding this question for too long. At least, I know I've been avoiding it. It is, after all, a question that concerns all of us, isn't it? Clearly, Feenix is wondering about something that many others are wondering about as well. What are these unusual weather patterns? Why's it freezing cold here, and on the other side of the country half the forests are on fire? There are explanations being tossed around out there, but they're complicated and far from well understood. I'm sure some of you must be listening to the news and the meteorologists? Anybody want to share any thoughts?"

Robert kept his mouth stubbornly closed. Edward sighed and raised his hand. Mr. Ross looked relieved and pleased. "Edward? Tell us what you know."

"Global warming," he said. "Global warming's throwing everything off."

Feenix looked at Edward with outrage. "But that's ridiculous. Why should global warming make the spring so cold?"

Mr. Ross nodded. "Sounds ridiculous, doesn't it? But he's probably right. Or, at least, it's one piece of the mystery. Anybody know why global warming might cause a big freeze in the weather here?"

Kseniya put her hand up. Kseniya knew an awful lot, but she tended not to speak a great deal. Danton figured she was probably a little shy because her English wasn't so perfect. Mr. Ross smiled at her and gave her the go-ahead.

Kseniya cleared her throat a little nervously. "It is because the global warming makes leak in polar vortex. This is very bad in Europe last year. Now it is here."

"Very good," said Mr. Ross. "Although it's certainly not good news. Tell us what else you know. Tell us about this leak in the polar vortex."

"Please. I can show you on the globe?"

Mr. Ross brought the globe to her table.

She held it still with one hand, and with the other she drew an invisible circle around the top and then around the bottom of the earth.

"These are two vortex. One over North Pole. One over South Pole."

Mr. Ross was nodding his head. After all, he loved stuff like this. "Picture them like yarmulkes," he told the class. "One is sitting on the Arctic, one is sitting on the Antarctic. Go on, Kseniya. And what do they do?"

"They go round and round. Spinning. Very cold wind. They make a wall, and wall holds cold air like prisoner at poles. But when the earth grows too warm and ice it is melting, wall starts to make leak."

Here, Kseniya used her fingers to pull apart the invisible edge of the Arctic vortex. "Sometimes very big cold weather comes down through leak. Maybe now. Maybe here." She dragged her fingers down the globe, into the northeastern coast of Canada and the United States. She looked around at the class. She pointed out the window.

Mostly, there was a long silence while everybody thought this over, but Feenix did not bother to raise her hand. "Wait a minute! Am I understanding this right? This is a disaster! Why didn't you tell us this before? How long will it last?"

"Well, Feenix, it's good that you're upset. You should be. But we don't know the answers to all these questions. The size of the leak in the vortex has never been this big before. Global warming is growing. It's setting loose so many different forces. That's why it may be more sensible to call it climate change rather than global warming. The seasons are getting out of sync, the ice is melting, the seas are rising. Every year we see more and more extreme weather events—storms and cyclones and droughts and even . . . freezes. At times these forces work hand in hand and amplify each other's effects. At times they fight each other. Some people think we can figure this stuff out, how these forces work, and get some control over them. What do *you* think?"

Feenix stared at him. She shook her head slowly. "You know what I think?" Since everybody, including Mr. Ross, knew very well that she was going to tell them one way or another, they just waited. She sure did love to have everybody's attention.

"It's like we're going back to where we started," she said. "Just like in those days with the gods and the goddesses and the monsters. They're fighting with each other, and they're more powerful than us, and we don't understand them."

Robert groaned.

Mr. Ross didn't seem to have noticed. "Well, I think you might be right in a way. There are certainly things to be learned from the old stories. Our new stories will evolve over time, but they'll always retain some of the old shapes. That's how scientists go forward, too. They overturn old facts and build new ones on top of them. It's going to be hard work. You people better get ready."

That night, Aunt Kit held a biscuit-making class in her kitchen. Ed was in his room, working on his mold experiment, so he did not have the satisfaction of hearing the disagreement between Mr. Ross and his aunt. But Danton heard it all.

As they were all pouring their buttermilk into their flour mixtures, Mr. Ross said to Kit, "Did you ever consider using food scales for your measurements instead of measuring cups and teaspoons? Food scales would be much more exact."

"But that would be a fool's errand," Kit laughed.

Mr. Ross looked surprised. "What do you mean? If an experienced cook goes to the trouble of recording accurate measurements and writing them down in a recipe, wouldn't it make sense to follow them exactly? Surely, doing this increases the chances of making the recipe successful."

"Not necessarily," Kit answered. "When you measure something, what does it guarantee? Measuring doesn't stop a cup of flour from being in a constant state of change, does it? After all, things constantly push and pull on one another. All things change with the moon and the time of day, the bright and the wet weather. And in cooking, all things change according to who is doing the measuring and who is doing the stirring and how gently or forcefully the dough is mixed together. One way or another, everything touches everything else."

It reminded Danton of what Mr. Ross had been going on about with the food webs.

"A good cook must rely on his own senses," Aunt Kit went on. "He has to stay alert and use his eyes and his nose and his hands." Here, she stopped to put her hand into her bowl. She lifted out a clump of dough and squeezed it and dropped it back in.

Danton saw the way Mr. Ross watched her.

"Well then," Mr. Ross asked, "what's the point of measuring at all?"

"Measuring is fine," Aunt Kit explained. "But it's just one of many things that must be considered in shaping the outcome of your recipe. You've got to read the signs. You've got to pay attention to all the other influences that might not be visible. And asking for exactness can kill the spirit of anything. Don't forget that."

"I won't," said Mr. Ross. He gave an uneasy smile. He

couldn't seem to take his eyes off her, but he let the discussion drop. Rather wisely, Danton thought.

Later, however, while they waited for the biscuits to rise in the oven, Danton saw something that left him shaken. He was on his way to wash his hands at the sink when he caught sight of Mr. Ross and Aunt Kit standing in her little pantry space together. Mr. Ross had Kit's hand in his own.

Hellamenopee, Danton thought (this was one of his mother's favorite expressions). *Feenix was right about them.* Mr. Ross was looking into Aunt Kit's eyes. Danton could have sworn he was about to kiss her, but before anything could happen, she shook her head. A little cloud of flour flew out from her curly hair. She often had flour in her hair.

"This is not a good time, Franklin," she said firmly.

Mr. Ross let go of her hand, a look of such sorrow on his face that Danton longed to comfort him, but of course there was no way to do that under the circumstances. "What is it, Kit? Have I offended you in some way? Is it because of what I said about using a food scale?"

"No, Franklin, it's not because of what you said about using a food scale. I know how dearly science holds exactness, and I know I shouldn't minimize its importance. It's just that . . . well . . . there are things on my mind. I need to concentrate right now. This is a very important time. I have a great deal to do, and I must keep my focus. It wouldn't be safe to allow myself to be distracted."

"Distracted from making biscuits?" Mr. Ross asked.

"It's the little things which hold up the world sometimes," she answered.

The next day Mr. Ross looked pretty bummed. He talked about sea algae and phytoplankton. How all the other life in the sea depends upon them. And how, as they float around doing their photosynthesis thing, they give off nearly half of the earth's usable oxygen. Then he had the students do a dramatic reenactment of an Arctic food chain.

The clump of sea algae was played by Alberto, who was devoured by zooplankton (Cecilia). The zooplankton was snacked down by a codfish (Alison). The codfish was taken down in a single bite by the seal (Ivan). The seal was ripped to pieces and gruesomely devoured by a polar bear (Feenix). This did a pretty good job of waking everybody up.

"As long as each part of the food chain does its bit, the chain stays alive and well. But what happens if one piece of the chain disappears or grows too big or becomes poisonous?" Mr. Ross asked. He lifted the classroom thermometer off the wall. They watched him carry it over to the radiator and hold it there for a minute.

"Two degrees warmer," he announced. He held the thermometer up in the air. "Imagine that I am the spirit of global warming and here is a sea full of thriving phytoplankton." He walked slowly around the empty area in the front of the room, waving the thermometer through the air.

"Can you see what happens to the phytoplankton? Close your eyes. They're doubling overnight because of the warmth. This is what's called an algae bloom. It's happening all over the earth right now. Use your imaginations! Picture it! They take over the surface of the water and become poisonous. When the zooplankton feed on this bloom, the zooplankton die. The codfish below are weakened by the lack of oxygen and lack of food. They die quickly or are eaten by the seals. Soon there are no codfish left for the seals to eat. The seals become slow and weak and turn into easy prey for their predators. When the polar bears have finished them off, *they* have nothing left to eat. They die a cold death out on the ice. Which, don't forget, is melting rapidly. Sometimes it's the little things which hold up the world."

PART TWO

5

The Juggler

A morning arrived in late April after there had been sleet pinging and spitting against the windows most of the night. Half-asleep, Feenix was trying her best to ignore the voice calling from somewhere far away. Her door flew open with a bang. She peeked through her mostly shut eyelids. The mother person stood there, steam shooting from her nostrils. Her mother was small but capable of swelling up and filling an entire doorway when it suited her. Feenix quickly shut her eyes tight again. She had been having a dream, a dream that the bronze panther statues in the park had come alive and were chasing her. But now the dream slid back to wherever things like that came from.

She could feel her mother not moving, ticking like a time bomb. Mr. Perlmutter jumped off the bed and slunk away. Big fat traitor cat.

Her mother exploded. Eighteen directions at once: lateness for school, laundry still not put away, life-threatening stickiness on floor in kitchen, back door left unlocked, email from math teacher about late homework . . . *summer school.*

Feenix was not worried about summer school. Summer was apparently never coming.

"Answer me! Do you hear me?"

Feenix didn't open her eyes. "Wait a sec. Let me put my hearing aid in."

"I'm not tolerating this, Edith. If you are not up and out the door in the next ten minutes, you are grounded for the weekend."

"Stop calling me that. You agreed."

Her mother made a strangled sound, like she was choking on a chicken bone. "*Feenix.* You have ten minutes to get yourself dressed and ready to go. This afternoon you are to come straight home and get all this stuff done instantly, right away, do not pass Go. You hear me?"

"Yeah, sure."

Her mother stomped off. Feenix counted to twenty to make certain her mother wasn't coming back with some new complaint or command. Then she rose from her bed and checked her face in the mirror to see if it had improved in the night. She brought herself close to the glass. Better? She stepped back and looked again. She sighed. How can you look at the same face in the mirror day after day and know after a while?

Time for some face art. She opened her ink box and sketched a delicate vine of green leaves growing up from the corner of her left eye. At the top of the vine she perched a tiny bird. Not bad. A few finishing touches and then she brushed her teeth. On with her skirt, her Hello Kitty fuzzy sweater, her boots. Then her earrings, her nose rings, her bracelets, and her backpack. She cracked her door open and listened.

Yes. Her mother was in the shower.

Feenix knew how to move in perfect stealth when it was necessary. She silenced her clinks and blings, slipped down the stairs, and hurried into the kitchen. She grabbed a PowerBar, snatched her coat from the hook in the hallway. Her hand was already on the front doorknob when her mother yelled "Stop!" from the top of the stairs, draped in a towel.

Not good if her mother saw the face art. "I'm late!" Feenix yelled back and flung the door open and leaped forth into the morning.

The sleet seemed to have stopped for the moment, but there was no sign of the sun, and that nasty sharp wind dashed straight for her. Good thing she had her coat. She didn't stop to button it up. If her mother came out on the stoop to yell after her, she needed to be out of hearing range, but she was a tall and strong girl and a fast walker.

It wasn't till she felt safely far from home that she saw she was going up the hill toward the park. This was not the right direction for school. How this sort of thing happened to her, she was never quite sure. Things pulled upon her. And she always had a lot on her mind. Today, for instance, how to get past Ms. Trevino without being spotted.

She tore open the wrapper of the PowerBar, gobbled several bites, realized she was thirsty. Really thirsty. Like walking-in-the-desert thirsty. But no way she was going to go back in that house and risk running into her mother. Anyway, out of the blue, she knew she needed water-fountain water. From the park. The perfect, most delicious water in the world.

Perhaps she had just enough time if she really hurried. She wouldn't go into the park itself. She'd just take a drink up by the Ninth Street entrance. There was a fountain there, wasn't there? She was pretty sure there was. She'd hardly be late at all. Which she really could not afford to be.

She picked up speed and didn't stop until she got all the way to the Ninth Street entrance. And there was the big bronze memorial to General Lafayette, and there, beside it, was the water fountain. But what if it hadn't been turned on yet?

Edward's aunt Kit said that the world was full of currents and energies that people weren't, in general, able to see or hear. They weren't equipped for it. The currents looped and twisted around and through people. Mostly, the currents danced to their own music and ignored people. But every now and then, one of them might pick someone up and carry that person along for a joyride. And very rarely, if someone was in great need and asked very nicely, one of them might lend a helping hand.

So Feenix asked nicely.

Please, please, oh invisible and magnificent ones, grant me my wish and I will gladly pledge myself in service to you. I don't know what exactly I could do for you, since you're probably not interested in my puny powers. But whatever—you've got them. All I ask is that there be water in this water fountain before I die of thirst.

Feenix closed her eyes. She felt it. She was sure of it. A quick, bright sensation rushing playfully around her head. She opened her eyes and bent over the fountain. Pushed the big brass button. Water flooded into her mouth. Oh joy. Oh bliss. It was the sweetest water she had ever tasted.

Of course, that might have been because she was so thirsty.

When she finally stood and wiped her mouth, she was facing the park. Not far away, off to her left, rose a small hill. Its top was guarded by a little wood of mostly evergreen trees and a thorny clump of brambles. As she watched, something fell down, down through the branches up there, something red and gold. It landed on the ground outside the trees and then rolled down the hill in her direction. It didn't roll far but came to a slow bumpy stop in a drift of crumbly leaves.

She was late. She should turn around. She should speed up and get herself to school semi on time.

Not that she really considered this alternative seriously.

She took a step forward and then another. And then she was in the park. She didn't follow the path but headed over to the hill and the mound of leaves. Farther than she thought, but she reached it at last, and the object gleamed up at her brightly. She bent over it, not touching. Staring.

The ball fields weren't far from here, and this was about the size and shape of a baseball. But it wasn't a baseball. Its cover was made out of diamond-shaped pieces of red fabric stitched together with a fine gold cord like you'd get around an expensive box of chocolate.

She picked it up. Squishy. Its weight shifted in her fingers as if it were filled with rice or sand. But where had it come from? She stared up toward the brambles and trees. Kids, maybe, messing around up there? "Hello?" she called out. "Somebody lose a weird ball?"

There was no answer except the wind sighing through the

evergreens. She climbed higher. She called again. "Anybody looking for this?"

Nothing. Right here the woods were still skimpy, with one of those nice-smelling blankets of pine needles on the ground. But then came the thorny brambles, and after that the trees grew closer together, and the brambles got bramblier and thornier. She didn't see how she could get through without ripping her coat to shreds. She peered in. What was on the other side of this little forest? She couldn't remember.

"Hello?"

Still no answer, but this time, once again, she caught sight up ahead of something in the trees. Something flying up and then falling down. Red and gold. The same as what she held in her hand.

"Hey!" she called out. "Somebody in there? I got your other ball!"

No sooner were these words gone from her mouth than she noticed a narrow passageway right in front of her. But half hidden by the brambles. Just wide enough that if she pulled her coat tight, maybe she'd be able to pass through. And up ahead it definitely looked lighter. Like there was an opening.

Carefully, she worked her way forward, the red-and-gold ball clutched in her hand. Several times she had to stop to untangle her hair. And the thorns stabbed and tore at her hands. But then it got lighter. And lighter. She stepped out of the trees.

She was in a large rectangular space with crumbling brick pathways and overgrown hedge bushes and empty flower beds. There was a sundial, as well as a lily pond without any lilies, just muddy rainwater.

Feenix had known there was an old-timey garden place over on the other side of the park, but she'd had no idea there was one in this area. Once it must have been beautiful, but obviously no one took care of it anymore.

It was so quiet. No birds. No wind. The trees and thorns made a silent protecting wall all around. Not a sign of anyone else. What fun it would be to bring the others here and surprise them.

She stepped onto the brick pathway. Even her boots were quiet. Like they were holding their breath, too. She walked toward the pond. "Hello?" she half whispered. "Anybody here?"

When she reached the pond, she stepped up on its rim. The water was murky and full of fallen leaves and branches. She walked along the border, which was made of neatly cut blocks of something—marble, maybe. No sign of anything alive anymore. But there might once have been frogs and goldfish. Around the edges, there were some weird-shaped evergreen bushes. One looked like a rabbit. Another like a fox. On the other side of the pond there was a small tree standing off by itself. It had crooked bare branches, some of which almost swept the ground. Gray-green ivy grew up its trunk. It would be a great climbing tree.

Just as she was thinking this, there it was again, that flickering movement. Right there in the branches of this very tree. Another red-and-gold ball, flying up and then falling. Huh. She stood very still. She watched. The ball vanished. She called again, but still no answer.

She'd had enough of this fooling around. She jumped down from the rim of the pond and marched to the other side. "Who is that?" she called out. "Who's here? This is your last chance, otherwise I'm out of here."

She stood in front of the tree. She saw how some of its roots had pushed up out of the ground. These were just as twisted and gnarly as the branches. The ivy went around and around the trunk in thick ropes. But there was no one there.

And then there was. A boy. No, not exactly a boy. Someone more than a boy but not exactly a man, either, leaning up against the tree. He wore a silvery-green jacket almost the same color as the ivy. His hair was the same color. He must have dyed it. Which must have been why she hadn't seen him in the first place. At first glance his pants might have been green sweats, but she liked fabric and knew something about it. These looked they had maybe been woven by hand, maybe from wool. And his boots were dark suede and very soft looking. "I love your outfit," she told him. "Are you a thrifter?"

He was staring right at her. In fact, he was leaning forward to get a closer look.

"It's rude, you know, to stare at people like that," she said.

His eyes were like dark watery stones and were set far apart. It was almost hard to look at both of them at the same time. She wondered if people gave him a lot of grief about this. Like they gave her. He had a wide red mouth. "You can see me?" he asked.

"You'll have to hide better than that if you don't want people to see you."

He took a step toward her. Before she could back up, he reached out and touched the corner of her eye, right where she had painted the green vine and the little bird. She felt a shock, like what you got in the winter when you touched somebody else after walking across a carpet. "Did you draw this yourself?"

"Yes."

"It's exactly right. Tell me your name."

She wondered if this was a good idea, but almost before she knew what she was doing, it slipped from her mouth. "Feenix."

He appeared to think this over. "Ah, well, then you may call me Jack, and I wasn't hiding. I was waiting for someone to come and let me out. You people have certainly made a fine mess of things, and I've gotten locked in. Did you bring the key?"

"The only keys I have are my house keys."

"Well, why did you come looking for me, then?"

"I didn't come looking for you. I was on my way to school, and I just ended up in here by accident."

"You must be mistaken. You can't just find your way in here by accident. Perhaps you haven't remembered yet. It happens, you know, when you cross. Some memories will go missing. I seem to have forgotten most everything myself on the way over."

"No. I don't think I've forgotten anything. I was on my way to school, and I happened to find this ball or whatever it is." She held out the red-and-gold beanbag.

"Ah," he said and smiled. "Well, there you are. Clearly, you're meant to take this other one, then. You'll have to carry it to the Lady, since I am stuck here." And he held up another ball exactly like the one in her hand. "We're running far behind ourselves, and there is so much work to do. These balls will get things started."

"This is some sort of game, right?" she asked him. "One of those role-playing things?"

"Would that it was a mere game. You must take them and bring them to her. If there is dire need or emergency along the way, you will use them yourself. All you have to do is juggle them. The whole balance will go out if we do not act quickly."

"What kind of dire need, and what are they supposed to do?"

"You don't know? Well, I suppose not. Why should you? But they'll show you themselves if they choose. Here." The ball practically leaped into her hand. It was a perfect weight, like the first one, and felt almost alive against her palm. "Unless they call upon you to use them, you should keep them well hidden. And as long as you keep them on your person, no one else may use them without your agreement."

Feenix decided that, all things considered, it would probably be best to simply do as he asked. She slid them into her pocket. And then, to humor him, she asked, "How am I supposed to know who she is, this lady?"

He frowned. "Well, I'm not sure . . . It's been so long. But she'll be nearby somewhere. She may be a little hard to look at. You know, like the sun in your eyes. But I'm certain you'll recognize her."

Before Feenix could ask how she was going to recognize this lady if she couldn't look at her, the fellow took a step closer. There was a strong earth scent coming off him. Sort of muddy and leafy, as if he had been sleeping on the ground. "Please allow me to kiss you. You're less likely to forget."

What? Seriously? Kiss him? What kind of kiss was he talking about? She shook her head. "That's okay. I have an excellent memory."

Clearly, he was disappointed. Which was flattering. Because, actually, for someone with such an odd face, he was very nice to look at.

"Well then . . . it is your choice. But it will certainly make things more difficult. And all the more reason that you should hurry. Now go quickly. Any doorway that lets your kind in won't stay open for very long. You wouldn't want to get stuck here with me, would you?" There was something about the way he asked the question that she didn't like. She looked around quickly, and then she spotted it, over on the other side of the pond. The little dirt path that she had come in by. She hurried over and stepped onto it. It wasn't until she had gone a few steps that she thought to look back.

There wasn't a sign of Jack. He must be playing his hide-and-seek game again, disappearing into his ivy. She ran forward along the path, and then she tore her way out of the brambles and hurried down the hill.

She was going to be very late to school.

6

Edward Is Reminded

Edward was awakened by a thunk and then a loud crash. He sat up slowly and gazed around. A pile of books lay tumbled on the floor at the foot of his bookcase. Huh. How had that happened?

There was another thunk and then another. His eyes traveled upward to the top of the bookcase, where the noise seemed to be coming from. There was a small terrarium sitting up there. One corner of it was sticking out—slightly over the edge of the shelf. Still half-asleep, he sat there watching in fascination as with another thunk, the terrarium moved forward an inch, as if on its own. It wouldn't be long before it would reach the point where it would overbalance and nose-dive to the floor.

Possibly they were doing construction in the building next door? Although he didn't hear anything.

Or, more interestingly, maybe it was an earthquake?

He threw the covers back and put his feet on the floor. Nothing that he could detect. He looked back up at the terrarium.

What was it doing up there, anyway? Another thunk and it

moved forward another inch.

Edward pulled a chair over to the bookcase and peered up into the terrarium.

Wait. What? There was something inside it. Something swinging through the air. A big shiny toe-like thing, brown and gray. It was banging—thunk!—against the glass.

Edward remembered, and the remembering was like getting punched in the stomach. All the air whooshed out of his lungs. It all came back to him in a rush. The storm. The flying manhole cover. The cocoon stuck to its underside.

But how *could* he have forgotten?

Another thunk and the glass tank began to tip over. Edward took a breath, reached for it in the nick of time, and caught it in his hands. He climbed down from the chair and carried the terrarium to his desk. He stared down through the mesh screen at the cocoon. It had fallen loose from its branch and now lay innocently on the floor of the terrarium.

Was it bigger than when he had seen it last? He was sure it was. And hadn't its color changed? But it must have been several weeks since he had hidden it up there. You couldn't rely on your memory for this kind of thing. That was why a scientist took notes.

He grabbed his observation book from where he had left it on the radiator, and opened it up. There were all the experiment notes he'd taken in the last year, including, most recently, his mold notes. So far, none of the molds had been the slightest bit interested in eating plastic. He was going to have to try some new forms of mold or perhaps begin experimenting with other types of fungus.

But he was getting distracted. This was not what he was looking for this morning.

Where were the notes he'd made on the cocoon? He was certain that he had made some. But all he could find were the torn ends of some pages that might have been ripped out by someone. Had he done this? He didn't think so.

Suddenly, he remembered that he had taken some photos. He grinned to himself. How smart he was! He grabbed up his phone and rapidly started scrolling backward. He stopped when he got to some blurred images of what looked like a half-smoked cigar.

That was it? The photos were so out of focus they were worthless.

What rotten luck. He sat down at his desk and stared at the cocoon again. It didn't move now. It just lay there. How could he have forgotten all about it? He took the screened lid off the terrarium and picked up the cocoon carefully. He examined it from all sides, and now he noticed the little teardrop-shaped indentation on the very bottom. The shell of the cocoon seemed thinner there, and he could have sworn it was pulsing faintly. Was it getting ready to open up? If he hid it once more, he had a distinct fear that he was going to forget it again.

There was a loud rap on his door. "Edward! Are you awake?"

"Sure am, Auntie!" He knew it annoyed her when he called her Auntie.

"Do not play with me this morning, Edward. There are some disturbances, and I have to run out. I want you to be very careful today."

"Whaddaya mean? What kind of disturbances?"

"Mrs. Chaduary has the fire department over at her house right now." Mrs. Chaduary was one of Kit's students. "She says her bin of pistachio nuts self-combusted in the night and there's been a small fire. She wants me to come. And then Mari called just a minute ago from her bakery. She has a large catering order for this afternoon, and none of her bread doughs will rise. I'll stop at Mrs. Chaduary's first, and then I'll go over to the bakery."

"Seriously?" Edward laughed. "Mrs. Chaduary's pistachio nuts self-combusted?"

"Don't laugh. Pistachios happen to be very flammable. You need to be very careful how you store them. Look it up. I'm leaving your lunch outside your door here."

He waited, listening for her to walk away. When he heard her footsteps recede, he opened his door and picked up the brown paper bag. He brought it into his room and put it down on his desk next to the cocoon. The moment he had done so, an excellent idea came to him.

A way to make sure he remembered.

7

Feenix Visits Ms. Trevino's Office

Feenix was sure she was going to be late, but when she bounded up the school steps and opened the door, she saw, to her astonishment, that she was right on time. It was not Feenix's habit to go around looking gift horses in the mouth, so she thought about this no further. Everybody was milling around in the front hallway. Ms. Trevino was wide awake and in high gear, personally greeting all who passed her by, directing traffic, watching for signs of unlicensed fooling around. She spotted Feenix immediately.

Oh, rat burps.

"Good morning, Ms. Trevino," Feenix said brightly. "It's always great to see you."

Ms. Trevino gave one of her snorts. She was famous throughout the school for these and was known behind her back as Snorty.

"Right," she said. "Just stand there and don't move an inch. You know about the eye in the back of my head." She turned again to the rush of traffic.

"Buenos días, Caesar. Good morning, Elena. Let's go, people, let's go. No time to waste. The world is going to need you. I promise. Get educated now before it's too late. Coats in lockers."

Where were the others? Oh, there they were, passing by now. Edward at the rear, naturally. Looking like he was lost in perhaps an entirely alternative dimension. Danton glared at Feenix. She would get a lecture from him later on for not meeting them on the steps. He liked to plan things early in the day. Plus, he was always worrying about her getting in trouble with Ms. Trevino.

Brigit smiled at her.

"Good morning," Ms. Trevino said to them. "Edward, this is not a snail parade. I love the way you are always thinking so hard, but pick up your feet. Remember, I'm expecting great things from you."

When they had passed out of sight and the hallway was clear, Ms. Trevino turned to Feenix.

"All right, you know the drill. Go spit out the gum and wash off the face art. Let's have a little heart-to-heart, shall we? Meet me in my office in two minutes. Make it snappy."

Feenix lifted her left eyebrow and hoped her vine and her birdie spoke all her feelings for her. "You got a tissue or something? You know, for the gum?"

"No, I do not have a tissue or something."

Feenix smiled and shrugged.

"Let's move along, please," Ms. Trevino said. "Girls' room. Go."

But Ms. Trevino wasn't there when Feenix got to her office. Feenix wandered around, fingering the tchotchkes. She had spent a lot of time in this office. Ms. Trevino had a big high-backed interrogation chair that was quite comfortable. But Feenix liked to see what was new when she came to visit. Ms. Trevino had a thing for little glass animals. They were all over her bookshelves. There were real animals and some imaginary animals—centaurs and monsters and a long ivory-colored serpent with wings. Apparently, she traveled a lot and brought these back. But there weren't any photos. Were there other people in her life? Feenix wondered. Anybody to bring her flowers at the end of the day? Anybody to tell her that she needed to loosen up a little bit? She could be a real pain in the neck, but Feenix felt a certain responsibility toward her. Just then she heard the footsteps in the hallway. Quickly, she slipped into the interrogation chair.

Ms. Trevino entered the room and took her place behind her desk. She examined Feenix in silence. Feenix readied herself for the big lecture—self-control, self-respect, not wasting one's potential, big picture, consideration for others. Blah, blah, blah, blah. But Ms. Trevino didn't waste her breath. She just held her thumb and her first finger about an inch apart. "You are this far from summer school. Imagine the good times we're going to have together."

Much as she felt a responsibility to keep Ms. Trevino's day interesting, Feenix really didn't want to spend the summer with her. Feenix launched into apology mode. Sorry. Really. It was just a stupid mistake. She had painted the vine and the bird on there last night and then forgotten about it this morning because she was in such a rush to get to school on time. And she was sorry about the gum. She'd had no time for breakfast, and it made her stomach feel better. But next time she would grab a protein bar. She wouldn't let it happen again. She was trying. She really was.

You couldn't tell from Ms. Trevino's face what she was thinking. Was she wondering how much of this was true? Feenix was never very sure herself when she made her apologies.

"Listen to me, please," Ms. Trevino said. "I've asked you before to leave off the face decorations. It's a distraction in the classroom. You're a very gifted artist, but you don't need to hide your real face. And in general, I'd suggest you just tone it down a notch. Lose some of the bling. You're a very stand-out, shiny person all on your own."

Feenix felt this was really inappropriate, Ms. Trevino giving her fashion advice. She, with the little pixie haircut and her eternal black trousers and those boring gold knot-shaped earrings. And anyway, wasn't she also the one who was always going on about imagination and freedom of expression and accepting everybody in all their various rainbownesses? But Feenix nodded and kept her face in blank politeness mode.

Ms. Trevino was watching her like she was trying to make up her mind whether to say something else. At last, she spoke. "I've got one more piece of advice this morning. You're probably not going to appreciate this, either." Feenix waited, listening with interest.

"You're a risk taker, and you love to stick your nose where it doesn't belong. Take it from me—these can be very rewarding qualities but also dangerous ones. By all means, go exploring. Just remember that if you go looking for the world in back of the world, you may well find it. And if you do, proceed with caution. You don't want to get stuck where you don't belong."

On one hand, Feenix had no clue what Ms. Trevino was talking about. On the other, her words seemed to ring a distant bell.

"All right. You'd better go," Ms. Trevino said. "Let us try not to run into each other again today."

Feenix stood up. As she walked out of the office, she shoved her hands in her pockets. For a moment she couldn't think what the warm squishy things were under her fingers. Then, with a jolt, the strange meeting in the park came back to her. How could she have forgotten?

8
Science Class

Feenix had decided it would be best to keep at least one hand in her pocket so she wouldn't forget again. Of course, this was easier said than done. In general, Feenix's hands were almost always busy. For instance, today, as soon as she sat down in science class, she pulled out her notebook and began to doodle. She was famous for her doodles, some of which were very rude. But it's not that easy to doodle with one hand, since you often use the other one to hold the paper. She decided she'd write herself a memo instead.

At the top of the page where she was supposed to be taking notes, Feenix wrote, *Check pocket*. Then she took her hand out and continued with her cartoon of Edward, which emphasized his trendy hairdo. Kind of like a muffin that had risen only on one side.

After a bit she let some of Edward's hair grow out and turned it into a vine of ivy, which eventually went climbing around a crooked, leafless apple tree. She wondered where she had seen something like that lately.

Mr. Ross was going on and on this morning about greenhouse gases and how they added to global warming. Boy, he was a downer lately. He was getting more depressing to listen to than the school marching band. She tried to think of some new way to interrupt him but wasn't coming up with much.

Mr. Ross launched into a lecture about how producing electricity and heating resulted in high amounts of fossil fuel emissions. Then he went on about cars and trucks and planes and how everyone needed to use their bikes more. "After transportation, manufacturing is the worst offender, but does anybody know what the fourth-worst culprit is in creating greenhouse gases?"

Robert's hand—of course—shot up. "Meat production," he said in that way he had, like only a bunch of ignorant fools like the people in this class wouldn't already know this.

Mr. Ross nodded. "Good. But why? Can anybody else tell us why?"

Apparently, Edward couldn't resist. He raised his hand. "Cow burps and farts," he said. "They produce a huge amount of methane gas."

The class, of course, went crazy laughing and making farting sounds. When they calmed down, Mr. Ross said, "But they're both right, you know. It's absolutely true. Has to do with the way cattle, particularly, digest grass. So, what do we do if we want to produce less cow burps?"

Tessa raised her hand. "Everybody eat less meat?"

"Give that contestant a golden shekel!" And Mr. Ross took a gold chocolate coin from a bowl on his desk and handed it to Tessa.

Feenix had a brilliant idea. "I know, I know!"

"Yes, Feenix?"

"Wouldn't it be better if all the living things on earth were photosynthetic? I mean, we'd all have to be green, of course, but that way we wouldn't need to eat meat. And also how could food chains go out of whack if everybody could just go outside and sit in the sun whenever they got hungry? The whole world would have enough to eat. There wouldn't be any famines or children starving. And think about all the time it would save since we wouldn't need to go shopping or do any cooking."

Feenix could see that she had perked him up a bit. A little color had come into his cheeks and the tips of his ears.

"Okay, what does anybody else think of Feenix's idea?"

Millie raised her hand. "Well, another good thing would be that animals wouldn't have to eat each other anymore, so there wouldn't be any killing. Humans wouldn't need to kill animals to eat. There wouldn't be any polar bears eating seals. No lions eating baby elephants. No hawks eating rabbits. Everybody would be at peace."

"Back to the Garden of Eden! Peace! It sounds wonderful," Mr. Ross exclaimed. "Anybody else have any thoughts on this suggestion?"

Robert raised his hand. He looked like little wisps of smoke were about to come out of the top of his head.

"Oh, oh," Mr. Ross said. "The voice of reason. Go for it, Robert."

"The whole idea is ridiculous. You can't just change something like that overnight. If you change one thing, it affects everything else in the ecosystem. It would be a disaster if all the living things were photosynthetic."

"Tell us more. I can see you're bursting with good news."

"Well, first of all, if animals higher up in the food chains weren't eating what was lower down in their food chains, everything would go completely out of whack. Birds eat five hundred million tons of insects every year. Imagine if the birds stopped eating insects. Insects can lay hundreds of eggs at a time. The insects would probably take over the world in just a few weeks."

"You got more?" Mr. Ross prodded him.

"Well, even worse, there would be no more pollination, because the bees and the butterflies and the bats wouldn't be looking for nectar anymore. If there was no pollination, all the plants and flowers and trees that exist now would die off."

"Hmm," Mr. Ross said. "Anybody have any counteroffers to make?"

Edward raised his hand. "Well, what if we could be partly photosynthetic—you know—like hybrid cars? It sounds crazy, but maybe someday with genetic engineering we could figure out a way to make it happen. Maybe you'd only use the ability if you got stuck in the desert or there was nothing good to eat in the refrigerator."

Mr. Ross laughed, and they all realized they hadn't heard him do this in a while. "Oh, my beloved seekers of knowledge! Do you see? Do you see how we need all of you with your irrepressible imaginations leaping out of the box and your necessary objections and your fast-forward experiments?" He bowed to Feenix and then to Robert and then to Edward and, finally, to the whole class. "You've made me think of a nice little surprise I'm going to bring in for you next time."

When the bell rang a few minutes later, Feenix started to stand, and Edward must have noticed the doodle she had made. Before she could stop him, he reached over and tore out the page, ripping it into several pieces. He dropped the pieces into the wastebasket on his way out the door.

9

The Cocoon Opens

By lunchtime, it was sleeting again. Danton had put out the word that it would be better if they all stayed in. They met at their usual table in the back of the cafeteria. Feenix, Brigit, and Edward all sat, while Danton put his stuff down and said, "I'm gonna go get some lunch. Anybody want anything?"

"I'm good," Edward said. "Kit gave me something."

"Get me one of those pizzas, would ya?" Feenix asked.

"You want something, Brigit?" Danton offered.

"No, I'm good." She gave him a quick smile. Then she pulled out her book and her sandwich.

Edward opened his backpack and took out the lunch bag that Aunt Kit had packed for him. He opened it and was puzzled to see an old gym sock inside. It was tied up with a rubber band and bulged slightly. He lifted it out and laid it down on the cafeteria table. He stared at it. He knew he knew what it was, but what was it?

"Kit's putting your lunch inside your socks now?" Feenix asked.

"Very funny." Edward had stuck the sock in his lunch bag himself, hadn't he? But why?

Feenix grabbed the sock and undid the rubber band.

"Hey! That's mine!" he protested.

"Ewwwww!" Feenix yelped. "What is it? What is with you? Where do you find this kind of stuff? It looks like a somebody's cut-off toe."

He grabbed the sock back out of her hand. He peered inside. Now he had it! And it had gone exactly as planned. He'd put it in his lunch bag knowing he'd find it at lunchtime and be reminded.

He shook it out onto a paper napkin very gently. They all stared at it. "Well?" Feenix said. "What is it, Ednerd? And why is it in your sock?"

"*A*, I think it's a cocoon," he replied, ignoring the "Ednerd" bit. "And *B*, I think it might be about to open."

"Whatever it is, it's maximally creepy," Feenix informed him.

Edward tapped at it lightly with one finger. He noticed it was cold. Had it been that cold this morning? He hoped that it was still all right.

"Where'd you find it?" Brigit asked.

"I found it near my house." Edward touched the cocoon again. The cold was worrying him. How could he warm it up? He wondered if it would help if he breathed on it. He leaned over and exhaled gently.

"What are you *doing*?" Feenix asked.

"I know," Edward said. "I know what we need." He looked up toward the front of the room, where the steam table was. Good. There was Danton chatting up the lunch ladies. The lunch ladies had hair-netted heads shaped like big cauliflowers.

They loved Danton. He was a flirt and a flatterer, and when it came to food, he was a bottomless pit. Edward watched them loading up his tray with this and that.

When Danton arrived back at the table, he was beaming. "Look what I got. Two chocolate puddings. Two personal pan pizzas and a tuna-noodle casserole. And there's a new lady. She wanted my opinion on the tuna-noodle casserole. She put chives in it, I think. Adds a little bite. Hey, what do you think you're doing, Eddie? Hands off!"

Edward had taken one of the pizzas and flipped it upside down on the paper plate so that its bread side was up. He carefully lifted the cocoon and laid it on the warm bread. Then he whipped the plate out from under Danton's other pizza and used it to make a snug little cover for the cocoon. "Perfect," he said with satisfaction. "That should warm it up."

"But my pizza!" cried Danton. "What did you do to my pizza?"

"This is science, Danton—science! Sacrifices must be made."

"But what is it? Is this another one of your finds?"

"Yeah. Another of my finds. I've got to keep it warm."

Danton shook his head and picked up the remaining personal pan pizza. He offered a bite first to Feenix, then to Brigit.

Feenix took a bite. Brigit ducked her head shyly. Edward decided to make himself wait at least fifteen minutes before checking the cocoon again. From the bottom of the bag, he took out the hummus-and-olive sandwich on fresh-made anadama bread that his aunt had given him. His aunt was a dedicated vegetarian. There was a bunch of red grapes, too.

Everybody sat eating quietly for a while. When perhaps ten minutes had passed, Danton nudged Feenix with his elbow. "Ook oo's 'ere," he said with his mouth full. They all looked around and saw two of Feenix's old crew coming their way. Beatrice the Poisonous Toadstool and Alison the Hangnail.

"Crudlies," Edward groaned. Feenix had once been their queen. Which was weird to think about. But that was way back last year.

"And how are you today, my lovelies?" Danton asked.

It was amazing, Edward thought, how Danton would make friendly conversation with pretty much anybody—crossing guards, lunch ladies, toothless grandmas, drooling babies, even toxic mean girls. "We're good," said Beatrice.

After Feenix had stopped hanging around with them, Beatrice had become their new queen. Feenix tended to stay quiet now when they were around, an unusual thing for her. Edward assumed she felt sort of guilty for dumping them, even though they were radioactive.

"And to what do we owe this pleasure?" Danton smiled.

"Well, we heard something," Alison the Hangnail said. "Something, you know, that we thought maybe we should warn you guys about."

"Tell us," Danton said. "We're all ears."

"I'm not," Edward said under his breath.

"Well, we've heard that Robert . . . you know . . . has got . . ." Beatrice and Alison broke down into giggles.

"All right, already," Feenix interrupted impatiently. "Just spit it out, whatever it is. Robert's got rabies?"

"Nope. Even better. He's got a crush on one of you," Beatrice said.

There was a long silence, which Edward broke. "Do you people seriously have nothing better to do with your time?"

"Don't you want to know who?" Beatrice asked innocently. She smiled and reached out a hand for the paper plate covering the personal pan pizza. "You don't mind if I have a bite, do you?"

What happened next happened quickly. Edward tried to grab her arm but instead caused her to bump into the table and send the entire pizza and plate flying. There was a grand commotion. The cocoon fell and rolled along the floor. Did Edward see something fluttering away? He cursed and was down on his knees in a second, trying to see what had happened. "Where'd it go?" he yelled. "Where'd it go? Be careful. Don't step on it!"

It took a while to find the cocoon. It had landed up against somebody's book bag. He knew immediately that he was too late. The cocoon felt too light and hollow, and the tissue-thin covering over the exit hole had been torn away.

He stowed it in his hoodie pocket and stood up, looking all around. "Anybody see a moth or a butterfly go by?" he asked the kids sitting nearby. He got a lot of blank looks and some laughter.

The doors to the hall stood wide open. Edward knew it was a long shot, of course, but if the moth had taken off, there was no other exit it could have left by. He went along the corridor quickly, searching in every corner. When he reached the stairs at the end—the only other open passageway—he climbed these, still looking all around himself with fierce concentration. *Blastoids and crud buckets.*

It was only a matter of minutes before he came out in the front hallway. His heart sank. If whatever had escaped from the cocoon had gotten up here, he'd never find it. Too many turns and twists and classrooms.

Then, just as he was about to give up in despair, he was sure he saw it, a lopsided gray moth, one wing bigger than the other. It fluttered through Ms. Trevino's open office door. The hallway was silent. He tiptoed up to the side of her door and peeked in.

Empty.

He stepped into the room and looked up at the ceiling and around at the walls. Ms. Trevino's interrogation chair was parked, as always, in front of her desk. He went over to the chair and bent to peer under it, just in case. Then he looked under her desk. Nothing there, either, except for Ms. Trevino's pointy pink shoes, which she wore on assembly days.

When he stood up, there was a man sitting in the interrogation chair, his legs crossed.

The man smiled at him as if he knew just what Edward was thinking.

"Oh, sorry!" Edward said and began to move back toward the door. "I didn't realize there was anybody in here. I didn't mean to disturb you."

"Stop where you are, please." The man got up from the chair. "You haven't disturbed me at all. I was looking for somebody to come and show me around, but perhaps you can help me."

Now that he was standing, Edward noticed that the guy looked a little off balance. One shoulder was higher than the other. Edward also noticed the guy's feet. He was of regular height, but his feet were tiny. He wore a gray suit and a red vest and little polished black boots. Edward wondered if he'd had to get the boots specially made.

"Well, if you're looking for Ms. Trevino, maybe I could find her for you."

"Ms. Trevino?"

"Our school principal. This is her office. She's probably somewhere nearby." Edward took another step backward. As he did, a cold draft must have come in through the window, because the door blew shut.

"Ah, I see," said the man. "Yes, yes. I was seeking her. And you, young man, what was it you were looking for?"

Edward met his eyes uncertainly. "I *was* chasing a moth, or maybe a butterfly. But I couldn't find it."

The man laughed. When he did, Edward noticed that the guy's skin seemed to stretch too tightly over his bones, as if it didn't quite fit properly.

"An entomologist!" the man exclaimed. "Well, that's a funny coincidence. One of my own great enthusiasms, actually. Requires great powers of observation, doesn't it? You're probably just the sort to help me find what I'm looking for."

Edward was curious in spite of himself. "What are you looking for?"

"Well, I've been hearing rumors that there are some students in this school with great . . ." He paused, perhaps to find the right word. "*Gifts*," he finished. He lifted his eyebrows, which were dark and shiny like his hair. "Perhaps you're one of them?"

Edward shrugged and didn't say anything to this.

"Naturally, I am most eager to interview your Ms. Trevino, but my experience has taught me that it is always preferable to speak to a person on the ground. You look like a most intelligent and observant young fellow. Even better, I'm guessing you are a man of science. Maybe we can be of service to each other."

Before Edward could think of a reply to this, the door to the office flew open. Ms. Trevino stood there staring at the scene in front of her. On the general principle that it was better to avoid principals, Edward usually stayed out of Ms. Trevino's path, but at this moment he was glad to see her.

"And to what do I owe this little surprise party?" She looked first at Edward and nodded. Then she turned to the stranger. "And you are?"

"Why, I'm Superintendent Tiltersmith. Weren't you expecting me?"

"I was not."

"Well, I know who you are. You are Ms. Trevino. What a pleasure to meet you." He held out his hand. She took it reluctantly, and he bowed from the waist. "What an honor it is to find myself in your celebrated presence."

It looked like maybe he was going to kiss her hand, but she pulled her fingers away and gave one of her snorts. "Well, thank you, but I don't know about the celebrated part, and I am not aware of having made any appointments for this hour."

"Well, I must apologize," the man said. "I went to a great deal of trouble to find my way here, but it is true, I had no time to make an actual appointment. I am from the Central District Office."

She shook her head, frowning. "And which Central District Office would that be?"

"The Accreditation and Licensing Office. Naturally, we don't give notice when a school has risen to the top of the list."

"What kind of list is this that you are referring to?"

"Well, the review list, of course."

"May I see some identification, please?"

"Certainly, certainly." Here, he took out a card case and flipped it open to show her.

She looked back up at him. "Again, I don't understand why I wasn't notified of your coming. Is there a problem that brings you here?"

He laughed. "On the contrary. There's no problem at all. We're hearing some astonishing things about you. *And about your students.* But surely, you'll understand that it would be difficult to make truly accurate observations if we let schools know when we were coming. It is far more useful to inspect an institution in its—shall we say—natural state?"

"It is not an institution," she corrected him. "It is a community of learners."

"Yes! Yes. Exactly. One of the fascinating things we've been hearing. Your extraordinary methods have caught our attention even from this distance. Rumors have reached us of how some of your students are beginning to reveal most exceptional talents."

"Well," she said, sniffing, "we're a magnet school. Of course we attract motivated young people. And once they walk through the door, naturally we do everything we can to help them make the most of their potential. Nothing out of the ordinary. Just exactly what we're supposed to be doing."

"Perhaps," Superintendent Tiltersmith said, smiling. "But I'm sure there's more here than your modesty is admitting to. And you and I both know that some of the greatest *treasures* are often right under our noses in the most ordinary and unexpected of places. It's just up to us to discover them. I would *love* to take a look around if you could spare me a bit of time."

Ms. Trevino's cheeks had turned a little pink.

"Perhaps this afternoon?" the superintendent asked. "If it is at all convenient? A little tour of the school? I am most anxious to visit your classrooms and see what there is to see."

She still seemed uneasy, but Edward could tell she was thinking it over. "Well, as it happens," she said at last, "I have a bit of unscheduled time."

"May I suggest that we begin at the top and work our way down?"

Edward used this as his cue and started to slip out the door, but the superintendent took hold of his shoulder as he went by, and held it tightly. "It was a pleasure meeting you," the man said. "And if you don't find your moth, perhaps you'll find its carrying case, which would help us identify it. If you do, bring it to me. I believe we can be of service to each other."

10

Feenix Juggles

Math was the last class of the day. Feenix arrived late. She had spotted Ms. Trevino up ahead and thought perhaps it would be best to stay out of her path. Especially because she appeared to be giving a tour to a man in a very sharp suit. Ms. Trevino could be particularly prickly when giving a tour.

So Feenix hid in the girls' room and waited until they were past.

When she got to class, the door was open, and Mr. Albers was wandering around the room, peering over people's shoulders. Mr. Albers was short and stubby with practically no neck. He looked a lot like an evil Mr. Potato Head. He could be quite dangerous. Everybody was already working on the Do Now problem. There was an empty seat next to Edward, but Feenix would have to get to it without being seen. To her deep surprise and gratification, it was Brigit who saw her difficulty and came to her rescue. Brigit called out to Mr. Albers.

She was so shy that her voice, when you heard it, was startling. It was clear and musical. "Mr. Albers, there's something I don't understand here. Could you help me?"

Mr. Albers went to Brigit and bent over her desk so that his back was to the door. Feenix turned her clackings and clinkings to silent mode and slid across the room to take the empty seat next to Edward. He shook his head to show his disapproval but didn't look up.

She opened her notebook and stared up at the Do Now problem on the board. It was a toughie. Mr. Albers liked to get them good and frustrated before the class really got going.

Mary is 24 years old. She is twice as old as Ann was when Mary was as old as Ann is now. How old is Ann?

She fiddled with it hopelessly for a few moments, then her mind drifted off. She was trying to remember something but couldn't think what it was. When Mr. Albers finished helping Brigit, he lifted his head and looked around the room. His gaze stopped short at Feenix. "Edith Rivera," he said. "Where's your late pass?"

She gave him her best look of surprised innocence. "Late pass? Why would I need a late pass?"

Mr. Albers shook his little blip of a head in tired amusement. He had threatened that if she was late again, he would send her on an express train to Ms. Trevino's office. Why didn't she think about stuff like this earlier—when it would be more useful? "You do remember what I said would happen if you were late again?"

"I've been sitting in this chair since the first bell." She held his gaze without flinching. "I'm nearly done with the Do Now.

If you send me to the front office, I will lose this valuable learning opportunity."

"Tell you what," Mr. Albers said. "I'm in a generous mood. I will give you a chance to redeem yourself. Go up to the front board, and if you can give us the correct answer, I will allow you to stay. If not—well." He smiled and shrugged.

She looked up at the board. "No problem." She didn't have a clue. She got up. She made her way to the front of the room. She went slowly, as if she had all the time in the world. Her boots clacked against the wooden floorboards. At the front of the room she found the marker. Held it up for the class so all could see. They laughed.

She read over the problem slowly. Nodded like she got it. Looked again at Mr. Albers. Looked meaningfully at Edward, like he might signal her the answer, but he shook his head. He had this crazy thing about honesty.

"Get on with it," Mr. Albers said. Anyone could see that he was growing eager to close in for the kill.

"You know I'm very visual," she said. "That's my learning style. You don't mind if I draw some pictures?"

"Edith, you've got two minutes."

Swiftly, Feenix drew several drawings of Mary and Ann in different outfits and sizes. First Mary twice as big as Ann, wearing a nice little feathered hat. Then the other way around. Then a picture of a giant grinning Mary chasing a tiny terrified Ann, who was screaming, *Help!*

There was a lot of snickering.

Feenix was, as all knew, a good artist. She stood back, examined her work, put her hands in her coat pockets, and at that moment instantly remembered what she had been trying to remember all morning. The juggling balls.

"And the answer is?" queried Mr. Albers in his hungry voice of doom.

And then she remembered the fellow in the garden. She had forgotten about him, too. Hadn't he said something about using them in case of dire need? Well, wasn't this dire need? And the juggling balls certainly seemed to agree with her. It felt like they were practically trying to leap into her hands. Might as well go out with a bang.

"Let me try one more thing," she pleaded. "I have a new technique. Helps my brain turn over. Let me try it."

"Edith! Enough!" he said sharply.

But she had already taken the two red-and-gold juggling balls out of her pocket. She threw one in the air and then the other. To her surprise, she found that it was easy. The juggling balls seemed to be showing her exactly what to do. Up and down they flew, their diamond patches of red and gold color weaving and crossing through the air.

Mr. Albers opened his mouth and then shut it. The class laughed and clapped. In the corner of her eye, she saw that someone going by in the hallway had stopped suddenly and was watching her. It was the man in the excellent gray suit with the red vest (she did love fabric). He appeared to be riveted. In the next moment Ms. Trevino was standing beside him.

Well, that was it. Now she was done for. She ought to stop, of course. But it was totally against Feenix's guiding principles to ever do anything halfway. She smiled at her audience and continued juggling.

Ms. Trevino stepped into the room, looking grim as Death with a toothache.

All hell broke loose.

As the balls flew up into the air, a startled bird with a bright-red breast dropped from the ceiling. In a panicked burst of feathers it went careening around and around the room, seeking an exit. Feenix kept juggling, and another bird appeared and then another. Soon there must have been a dozen of them.

Perhaps they had been perching up on one of the overhead lights.

Some of the kids jumped out of their seats and started chasing the birds around the room, waving their hands at them. Others stayed where they were and yelled directions at the hand wavers.

"What is going on in here?" Ms. Trevino demanded. "Feenix, what did we discuss this morning? Stop this circus performance right now!"

Feenix bowed to the inevitable. She let the balls fall back into her hands. Plunk, plunk. Without missing a beat, she dropped them into her pocket.

"Everyone freeze!" Danton ordered. Everyone froze. Danton leaped to the window and pushed it all the way up. Then he grabbed someone's spiral notebook, and in long-legged leaps and bounds, he shooed the birds across the room and out the window. Everyone applauded madly. Danton bowed modestly and sat down.

Ms. Trevino had her hands planted on her hips. She looked at the math teacher accusingly. Mr. Albers tried to speak, but his mouth merely opened and shut.

Ms. Trevino turned to Feenix. "What on earth? Can't you get through a single day without riots and mayhem? Where did those birds come from?"

Feenix bristled. "I have no idea! I was just trying to figure out the Do Now problem."

The man in the suit was now standing beside Ms. Trevino. He had his eyes fixed on Feenix, and she returned his gaze boldly. Then she looked at Ms. Trevino, who was taking slow, calming breaths. Perhaps she was visualizing a distant summer meadow. She was big, as they all knew, on calming breaths and visualization of beautiful scenery. "Class," she said at last, "this is Superintendent Tiltersmith from the Central District Office. I had hoped to impress him with some of your hard work and progress, and what do I find—"

But before she could go any further with her scolding, the superintendent guy interrupted. "But, indeed, Ms. Trevino, don't you see what's going on here? Right under our noses? A perfect demonstration of those very methods you try so boldly to cultivate." He spun about to point at Mr. Albers, and now Feenix noticed how dainty his feet were. "This courageous, free-thinking teacher allows his student to use her own methods to find an answer, and there—voilà!" Now he twirled around to point at Feenix and then at the Do Now problem on the board. "Does anybody know? Is she correct?"

Everybody looked at all the little pictures of Mary and Ann jumping around and changing sizes. There at the bottom, where the answer was supposed to go, was written in bold numerals *18*. Where had the number come from? Feenix hadn't a clue, but she had great hopes that it was correct.

"Well?" Superintendent Tiltersmith pressed. "Does anybody know? Is she correct?"

Detestable Robert raised his hand but didn't look at her. "Yes," he said. "That's correct." The man in the excellent suit bowed to him.

Who was this guy? Feenix wondered. How did he get his hair like that, black and shiny as shoe polish? The man turned to Ms. Trevino. "As you yourself have said, 'We each have to find our own path through the woods.'"

"I said that?"

"No? Well, perhaps not in so many words, but I'm sure it's what you meant."

"Yes, well," Ms. Trevino said, "in any case, I'd certainly like to know how those birds got in here." She looked doubtfully at the answer on the board once more, then she turned her attention to Feenix. "All right, Feenix. March straight to my office and put those balls in the Confiscation Basket."

Once again, Feenix realized too late that she'd boxed herself into a corner. She drew in a sharp breath. "I . . . can't!"

"And why not?"

"They're . . . not mine."

"And whose are they?"

"Well . . . I . . . I'm not sure."

"That's enough nonsense, Feenix. You made your choice. Now you must live with its consequences. Be grateful it's not summer school. Into the basket they go. And they'd better be in there when I get to my office. Go."

As Feenix passed the superintendent, he bent close and whispered in her ear. "You owe me."

11

Danton Finds a Toad

At two fifty-five Danton was nearly to the front exit when he remembered his Spanish book. It was in his locker. He skidded to a stop and about-faced. He usually got to the front steps first, but he knew the others would wait for him.

He had to run against the rush-hour crowd, and then Coach Baptista stopped him to talk about the next soccer practice. By the time he had retrieved the book and started back for the exit, the hallway was nearly empty. Passing by the principal's office, he happened to glance through the partially open door. Someone was inside the room. Not Ms. Trevino, but the superintendent guy who had come into the room during math class. He was standing by the Confiscation Basket, looking down at it. It was a straw basket with a lid—round and colorful and tightly woven. Ms. Trevino, who liked to travel, had brought it back from India.

At this moment, Ms. Trevino came through the inner door that connected her office to the front office. She caught sight of the superintendent, and she stopped where she was. He turned and faced her.

"Superintendent Tiltersmith. I have been searching all over for you," Ms. Trevino said coldly. "Where have you been?"

He looked surprised. "Why, I've been waiting for you, of course. Did we not agree to meet here?"

"I don't believe so."

He shrugged. "Well, in any case, here we are. Let me say how impressed I am with all I have seen. Everything appears to run so smoothly, Principal Trevino."

Danton was glad to see her look him up and down suspiciously. "Perhaps. But after all, they're middle schoolers. Ticking time bombs set to go off at any moment."

He nodded. "Have you considered dungeons? I find them most helpful myself."

She snorted. "Very funny."

"Yes, but seriously, yours is a job for only the bravest and most sturdy of hearts. I am filled with admiration for your patience. That young lady, for instance, the one who was juggling. Such an interesting case study she would make. In fact, just the sort I am looking for in my research. So imaginative and full of promise, but difficult to manage, I am sure. I was curious to see if she had followed your instructions regarding her juggling toys, or if she had chosen to go along her own path. You will not mind if I take a look?"

She came toward him slowly and stood across from him on the other side of the basket. She narrowed her eyes. "Actually, I would," she answered. "I never think of my students as 'cases.' They are individuals, each unique and full of possibility. And I always respect their privacy. I think, properly speaking, it should be between Feenix and me whether she put those things in the basket."

His face tightened. "A woman of great principle."

"Yes, that's me," she said without a smile. "Now, I have a great deal of unfinished business to attend to. As you know, you caught me by surprise today. I have taken almost an entire afternoon to give you this tour, and I hope that what you have seen will be of some use to your fascinating research, whatever that may be. I regret to say I need to bring this visit to an end. I *must* return to my school."

The man shook his head sadly. "Of course, of course, I do understand. We each have our own paths to follow, don't we? Myself, I believe I am close to finding what I have come to find. I simply need to take a little peek into this basket. There must be some way we can reach an agreement here."

He had a fountain pen clipped onto his jacket pocket. Normally Danton wouldn't notice what kind of pen somebody had, but this one was unusual, midnight blue with gold decorations that seemed to lie just beneath its smooth enameled surface. The man pulled the pen out now and began to jiggle it between his fingers as if this would help him think.

"I don't think so," Ms. Trevino answered.

"Goodness," he laughed. "This is like pulling teeth. Third offer is the charm. It's the last one that the rules permit me to make. Are you sure you wouldn't like to help me out?"

She crossed her arms. "Whose rules are we talking about here?"

Danton, watching her, felt a thrill of admiration. She wasn't a big lady, but with her chin out and her feet firmly planted, anyone could see she was an opponent not to be messed with.

The superintendent gave a half smile and pointed the pen at her as if to emphasize something he was about to say.

However, before he could open his mouth, something flew into the window with a loud smack, and Danton turned his head sharply. *A robin*, he thought, watching it struggle briefly. Then the bird dropped from sight.

He turned his attention back to the standoff by the Confiscation Basket. He was startled to see that Ms. Trevino was gone. He looked around. The connecting door to the front office was still open. Had she gone out that way?

The superintendent stood there for a moment, staring, for some reason, at the floor. Then he slid his pen back in his pocket and squatted down by the Confiscation Basket and began pulling things out: a set of windup plastic chattering teeth, two cell phones, a rubber snake, a rubber spider on an elastic cord, a pair of toy handcuffs, a whoopee cushion, a lifelike puddle of rubber vomit, a green kazoo, and many other interesting objects. The superintendent, however, did not seem happy. He was muttering angrily to himself. Possibly cursing. Danton couldn't make out what he said, but the sounds were very unpleasant.

At last, the basket must have been emptied, because the man sat back on his heels and turned his face to the ceiling. He closed his eyes. He might have been thinking. He might have been taking three long calming breaths. Although Danton doubted that one. The superintendent opened his eyes and tossed all of the junk back into the basket. When he stood up at last and turned around, Danton quickly retreated, taking a few steps over to a nearby bulletin board. He pretended to read what was posted there.

A moment later, the superintendent came out of the principal's office, into the hallway. He shut the door behind himself and walked right past Danton without any sign of recognition and disappeared around a corner.

But where was Ms. Trevino? Danton went over and peered into the busy front office. No sign of her there. He went back to Ms. Trevino's hallway door and pushed it quietly open. The room was empty. All was quiet. No sign of the principal. Unable to help himself, Danton tiptoed over to the Confiscation Basket and peered in. Maybe because he was so distracted by all these inexplicable events, it took him a moment before he could remember what it was that the superintendent had been looking for. Then it came back to him. Feenix's juggling balls.

Not a sign of them.

As Danton turned away, his eye was caught by a small object on the floor, something the superintendent must have missed. A little green-and-brown rubber toad, not much bigger than the pit of an avocado. Danton bent down to reach for it, and the rubber toad gave a little hop.

Huh! Not rubber at all. But where had it come from? It must have escaped from one of the science rooms. Danton managed to scoop it up in his hands. As he did so, the toad gave out a sound—half croak, half snort. A crazy thought came to him. Which he immediately dismissed. He would have to think what to do with the little creature. For the moment, he put the toad into his jacket pocket and zipped it most of the way closed.

When Danton reached the front steps of the school, the others weren't there. They must have gotten tired of waiting. Ed would already be at home and up in his room, conducting science experiments. Feenix and Brigit would be at Ed's house, too. They had agreed to help out at Kit's baking class today. Danton bounded along the avenue and turned up the hill. The rain had changed to a drizzle, but a cold wind was barreling down at him. As he stopped to zip his jacket, he became aware of a feeling that he was being watched. He turned and saw a scraggly branched tree loaded with wet robins. They sat silently, their feathers all puffed up, staring at him as if they thought he might have something edible on him. He felt around in the pocket that didn't have a toad in it, but found nothing there.

"Sorry," he said, holding out his empty hands. He wondered if any of them were the same ones from math class. He'd never seen so many in one place before. Then he hurried onward.

When he reached Edward's house, Aunt Kit was the one who opened the door. The smell that wafted out of the house and into the cold, damp afternoon was irresistible—warm and buttery and beckoning.

"Ohhhh," he sighed. "I know what this is. I know what this is. I can almost recognize it. Give me a second." Now, Danton had an excellent sense of smell. He inhaled deeply several times, then his eyes lit up. "Challah bread? Could we be making challah bread?"

"Right on the nose," Kit said, laughing.

He loved challah, with its satiny brown crust and airy, moist inside and a little sweetness. "Hooray!" He grabbed her up and swung her around. "When are you going to marry me?"

"Put me down. You have some growing to do before you marry anyone. And I, myself, do not plan to marry until the moon turns blue and the socks start matching themselves up in the laundry basket. Now come inside. You're late. Feenix and Brigit have been here for some time."

"Where's Eddie?"

"You know where Eddie is. He is visiting his mold kingdoms."

"You're not supposed to know about those."

He hung his jacket on one of the hooks in the hallway. Carefully. Next to Brigit's green one. He made sure no one was looking, and leaned in to sniff at it. It smelled of rain and the shampoo she used. And maybe tea, he thought. Did she wash her hair with tea?

He went into the kitchen.

12

Edward Examines the Cocoon Again

When they reached the house that afternoon, Feenix and Brigit had gone into the kitchen, but Edward had tiptoed straight up the stairs.

His aunt caught him as he hit the landing. "Stop right there."

He stopped. He looked at her. "How goes it, Auntie?"

"That remains to be seen," she said. "You tell me. How was your day?"

He shrugged. "Oh, you know."

"No. I do not. Give me a highlight or two, and then I will release you."

"Uhhh . . . Okay . . . I know! Feenix got a Do Now answer correct in math. In front of everybody."

"Was she pleased?"

Edward shrugged. "She looked more surprised than anything."

Kit smiled. "Okay, another highlight."

Edward sighed. "Well, let's see. There was an unannounced visit from some superintendent guy. From the Central District

Office. He said his name was Tiltersmith. Ms. Trevino was not happy."

Aunt Kit put her hand down very gently on the banister. "Oh yes?" she said. "What did he look like?"

Edward lifted his eyebrows. "Actually, he was sort of weird looking. Really black shiny hair and he had eensy-beensy feet. Why do you ask?"

She drew in a sharp breath and then let it go. "No reason. Did he say what he was doing here?"

"Some sort of research. You know him?"

"Why would I know him?" She sounded offended.

"I have no idea why you would know him. Can I go now?"

"What's that on the back of your hand?"

He looked at the back of his hand, puzzled. There was something written there in black marker. But the words had run in the rain.

"Don't know. Must have written a note to myself, but I can't read it now. Anyway, I gotta go. Homework. You said you would release me after two highlights."

She had just opened her mouth to say something else when Feenix called from the kitchen. "Kit! Where are the mixing bowls?"

Feenix had no interest in cooking, but sometimes she came along to assist. Edward did not like to imagine what it would be like to have her as a teaching assistant.

"All right, then," Kit said to him reluctantly. "Come down later and get some challah bread."

In his room, he took off his jacket, and before anything else, he checked on his molds. The *Penicillium* and the *Cladosporium* had not changed, but the mystery red mold had sprouted several new spots of furry blue. He made some notes.

As he wrote, he again noticed the blurry message written on the back of his hand. It looked like two words. He could make out the last letters in the first word and the first letter in the last word:

$$--eck \ s--$$

Eck? What could that word have been? Deck? Neck? Dreck? Check?

Check the s . . . ? Had he been reminding himself to check something? The sandwich he never ate? His schedule? His science notebook? He hadn't a clue. Odd that he couldn't remember. He opened the main section of his backpack and looked inside. There were his notebooks and texts. He unzipped the front pocket.

A sock.

A little ding went off in the back of his mind like the ding in a pinball game. Was he supposed to check the sock? He pulled it out and opened it.

The cocoon.

What was going on here? He had almost forgotten again, hadn't he? About finding the cocoon at lunch and Beatrice knocking it onto the floor. How it had been empty when he picked it up. About searching for the moth and meeting that

Tiltersmith guy in Ms. Trevino's office. This must be what he'd meant by a "carrying case." Edward wondered if the guy would really be able to identify it if he brought it to him.

He also wondered if it was possible that it was giving off some chemical that was disturbing his memory. He would have to be very careful about touching it or breathing in when examining it.

Carefully, he turned the sock upside down over his desk and shook the cocoon out onto a piece of paper. He wanted to see if he could get a closer look at the thing now that it was empty. Rummaging around in his equipment drawer, he found his magnifying glass and a pair of lab tweezers.

The cocoon was lying on its side, still brown and leathery looking, still about the size and shape of a big toe.

He opened his observation notebook to see what he might have written down before, and then remembered that his notes had been torn out.

Well, all right. He'd have to start fresh. He would take some new notes.

He tapped at the thing with his tweezers, and it seemed to him that it was a little drier and tougher than when he'd last examined it. He turned it over. Where the thinner tissue of the indentation had been, there was now a teardrop-shaped opening. Clearly an exit hole. Inside was black as midnight.

Using his magnifying glass, he tried to see farther, but still, all he observed was darkness. He angled the desk lamp over it and tried again. But still—nothing. It was like trying to look down the pipe in the bathroom sink.

Squeezing the prongs of the tweezers together, he lowered them toward the hole. As he did, he was startled to feel a sucking pull, a forceful magnetic tug. He let go, and the tweezers vanished into the cocoon.

Twenty minutes later he had lost numerous paper clips, several pennies, a quarter, a favorite jumbo marble, and an old Lego fireman. How the bigger things had been able to fit through the small hole, he couldn't fathom. He didn't dare touch the cocoon with his bare fingers now, but he spotted a spatula he had "borrowed" from Aunt Kit to use with his molds. He lifted the cocoon with extreme care. It felt light as a feather, and when he laid it on his scale, indeed, it weighed next to nothing.

So where did the coins and the marble and the other objects go? How did they all fit in there together? Why did they now weigh nothing? He had only a moment to contemplate the possibility that he had made a discovery that would change the entire future of scientific inquiry before there was a loud rap at his door.

"Eddie, you in there? We brought you some challah." Without waiting for his answer, Danton pushed the door open. He bounded in, Feenix and Brigit bringing up the rear.

Edward stood against his desk, blocking the cocoon from view.

"And guess what, Edsel?" Feenix said. "Your auntie invited us to spend the night here before the big picnic on Sunday.

We're all gonna help her bring everything over to the park, including the Maypole."

"Oh, joy," he said. He turned casually, still blocking their view, and picked up his lucky baseball cap and put it down over the cocoon.

13

Brigit in the Park

That night, Brigit dreamt of her brother again. The dream felt important, but in the morning all she could remember of it was that they were climbing Weaver's Hill together in Prospect Park. He brought her to an old wooden bench on the top of the hill, and then she woke up.

After a few minutes of lying in bed, she got up and looked outside her window, searching for any signs of spring. All she could see were some robins jabbing their beaks into the hard earth. It didn't look like they were coming up with anything. She hoped they weren't too hungry.

Downstairs her grandad was at the kitchen table, drinking his tea and reading the newspaper. This could be either a good sign or a bad sign. Some days he was neither here nor there. Reading the paper meant he was here, but the news often put him into a state.

"What's the news, Grandad?"

"Och—the devil is still riding round and round on his merry-go-round," he said sadly. "The temperature is rising, and the ice at the top of the world, it goes on melting. And it's not just the bears and the seals and fish who are losing their homes, but they say the plagues that have been sleeping fast in that ice are waking up now and will be soon coming this way. And do the governors and the bankers and the prime ministers open their eyes? No. They are all for standing around and laughing it away while they go on filling their own pockets."

Brigit walked to him and kissed the top of his head. He looked surprised, as if he hadn't realized she was there at all. His face softened. "What are you after, then, today, Birdie? You have that look upon you."

Birdie was what they called her in the family, but not many other people knew this.

"What look?"

"That look your Gran used to have. That one that was upon her when she had some great notion. I'd recognize it anywhere."

She smiled at him. "I don't have any notions upon me, Grandad."

"Sure, and maybe you just don't know it yet. Dress warm, Birdie. There's another storm coming later or sooner. I can feel it in my knees."

When Brigit reached the plaza across from the park, she looked around for Danton. It was here that she sometimes ran into him, but this morning he was nowhere to be seen.

He had walked her home yesterday evening. He usually did after they spent the afternoon at Edward's. Partly because they lived in the same neighborhood. But also, she suspected, because he felt sorry for her. It was just the way he was. He was a protective sort of person. He knew how her baby brother had died in his crib last year and how brokenhearted her family had been. There were other things, too, smaller things, that kept him watching over her. The way she had hardly spoken a word when she first came to this new school. And, of course, everybody knew about her embarrassing condition. There was no way to hide it. He believed she was weak and defenseless and needed watching over.

Once upon a time Brigit had had an idea that he might be thinking of her in some other way. There had been that night at Kit's holiday party when he had stepped so close and had looked down at her from his six-foot-threeness. She had thought maybe he was going to kiss her. But the problem was, she had no idea what you were supposed to do if someone kissed you. What if she made a mess of it? So she had pretended she heard someone calling her, and she had ducked and turned away.

This was possibly the most mortifying thing that had ever happened to her.

Especially mortifying because after that it never happened again. He had realized what a feeble puddle of a person she was. Now she hurried across to Prospect Park West and headed along the sidewalk. As she drew close to the Third Street entrance, her attention was drawn to the two bronze panthers who flanked the wide entrance, standing way up high on their stone pedestals. For some reason, they were often in her dreams, too. Sometimes they appeared as protectors, sometimes as bloodthirsty hunters. There was no way of knowing which they were today. She lowered her gaze and took in a sharp breath. Standing in front of her were the two head Crudlies, Beatrice the Poisonous Toadstool and Alison the Hangnail.

Brigit could see right away how glad they were to get her alone.

When she had first arrived at the new school in the fall, they had made her life a lonely misery. This was back when Feenix was part of *their* crew. Then something had happened, or a series of things had happened. And Feenix had left the Crudlies. Nobody seemed clear what it had all been about, but as Aunt Kit liked to say, a sneeze at one end of the universe can change everything at the other end.

Brigit knew that the Crudlies somehow blamed her for Feenix's desertion. And now Beatrice the Poisonous Toadstool was smiling at her. Brigit thought about how a smile could be an invitation or it could be like a shiny knife sliding between your ribs. She didn't say a word but forced herself to look Beatrice straight in the eye. This was one of the things Feenix had recommended. Feenix said it was best to look directly at the things you were afraid of. When you looked at things from the corner of your eye, they were more frightening.

Beatrice threw Alison a little glance, and Brigit could tell that they had some sort of plan. She took a breath. She heard Feenix's voice. *Breathe deeply and don't fight it. Just go with it.* Here was her chance to practice. She stood up tall (which wasn't all that tall) and pushed her hood back so her face was there for all to see.

"Everything okay? Where are your . . . friends . . . this morning?" Beatrice moved the word "friends" around in her mouth as if it were a little pebble or something she was trying to get rid of.

"I suppose they're on their way to school. I should be, too. They're probably waiting for me." Brigit tried to walk around her, but Beatrice reached out and grabbed her jacket sleeve.

"Wait, wait," she said. "What's your hurry? We want to talk to you."

Brigit tried to pull away, but the Toadstool gripped tighter, and Brigit heard a little ripping sound.

"Oops, my bad," Beatrice said. "Sorry about that. But you know, maybe it's time for a new jacket anyway. This green is kind of weird with your hair. In fact, we could help you with some suggestions if you'd like."

"That's okay. I think I'm good."

"You know, me and Allie and some of the others were so worried about you when you first got here, the way you never talked. We thought you might have, like, some sort of disability. But we were glad to see you made some friends, right? Even if they're sort of, well—you know."

Brigit remained silent.

"Listen, I hate to say this, but with you not really knowing your way around yet, we wanted to just give you a word of warning about Feenix. She used to hang with us, but she was such an embarrassment to herself, we were always having to cover for her so she wouldn't get in trouble. We just had to cut her loose. She can't stand not being the center of attention, and she takes advantage of people to make herself look big— especially with shy, mousy people. You should watch your back is all I'm saying."

Mousy? Was that it? Was that the way people saw her? Brigit felt a surge of resentment at this description. She was surprised to find herself opening her mouth to speak. "It's nice of you to worry about me, but me and Feenix are okay. And I think you've misunderstood about her. She was just needing a change. People need to change things up sometimes, don't they?" This was a very long speech for Brigit. She was rather pleased with herself, but she could see that Beatrice was very annoyed.

"Well, of course that's the way *she* tells it. I'm sure you know by now what kind of a storyteller she is. She'll say anything to make herself look good or make somebody else look dorky." Beatrice paused. "You know what she says about you, right? She says you've got it really bad for someone. But you're clueless what to do. I'm sure that's not true, is it?"

This, unfortunately, caught Brigit by surprise. The blush came on fast, and there was no stopping it. It flamed up her neck, onto her face, scorched her cheeks and her forehead, and turned the tips of her ears scarlet. She knew that when it felt like this, the skin around her mouth and her eyes stayed white, which gave her the look of a deranged clown.

Beatrice started laughing and pointing. Brigit tried to turn away to hide, but there was Alison, with her phone practically in Brigit's face, getting ready to take a picture.

"Quick, Allie! Get it!"

"Say 'cheese'!" Alison cried. She held the phone up a little higher and was just about to snap a photo when a large whitish-green glob dropped through the air and landed with a splat all over her hand.

Alison let out a screech. She looked up. They all looked up. There was a tree right inside the park whose branches hung out over the wall. On every branch sat a rusty-red-breasted robin. There must have been twenty or thirty of them.

Another robin let loose, and a splat of poop landed right on Beatrice's upturned face. "Uuuuugh!" she cried and tried to swipe it off, spreading it everywhere. "Gross!" As if this was the signal, another greeny-white bomb fell and then another and then another. Some landed harmlessly on the ground, but many of them exploded on the heads and shoulders of Beatrice and Alison.

"Move!" Beatrice yelled. She pushed Alison, who was standing there as if glued to the sidewalk, looking up at the tree.

"Where'd they all come from?" Alison wailed.

"Who cares where they came from, you pinhead! Move!" She turned angrily toward Brigit. "I don't know why we even bothered with you. Go run and find your little gang of weirdos."

Brigit watched them go with relief. She looked down at her own shoulders and jacket and wondered how it was that the birds had missed her. "Thank you," she called up into the tree. The robins perched there, watching her silently. They looked so hungry. She wished she had something to feed them, but her pockets were empty.

It was as she began to turn away and head to school that she realized she was really thirsty. Maybe it was from the stress of her encounter with the Crudlies. She turned toward the water fountain, which was usually right here under the panthers, but it was gone. She looked around and saw that it had been moved. There it was, up the path a little ways.

How long had it been since she had gone into the park? She nodded nervously to the panthers and passed between them. Then she walked quickly up the little winding path until she reached the fountain.

She took a breath of surprise. This was not the same old fountain. It had a wide bronze basin. All around its rim were bronze ivy vines and leaping fish. Looking at it, she was thirstier than ever, and she hoped fervently that it had been turned on. She leaned over and pressed the button. What a relief when the water came leaping merrily out. She took a long drink. The water was icy cold, as if the pipes were being fed from a distant mountain stream. When her lips were numb and her thirst quenched, she lifted her head. She saw that the dirt path forked here. One way led into the brambles. The other way led toward a clearing in the pine trees. Although she couldn't catch more than a glimpse from here, she thought she saw a bench in there and maybe some sort of statue. Her curiosity got the better of her. She'd just take a quick look.

She hurried through the soft carpet of pine needles and soon found herself in an old untended garden space with crumbling redbrick pathways. There were flower beds full of withered stalks and weeds, and a nearly empty rectangular pond that held only some rainwater and old leaves. How had she never known this was here? Around the sides were bushes that had once been trimmed into animal shapes but were now overgrown and scraggly—a fox, she thought, and a squirrel and a bear.

In the middle of the pond a stone boy all green with moss knelt on a pedestal and gazed down into the muddy water. On his head of curling hair, he wore a bird's nest.

Brigit stepped onto one of the worn brick paths and approached the edge of the pond. She felt a strong desire to get a closer look at this statue. She could see that he was dressed in loose stone pants and shirt, everything green with moss, his curling hair green, too, but she couldn't really see his face from this angle. She took a step up onto the marble rim of the pond. No sooner had she done this than a robin flew out of the nest sitting on the statue's head. Brigit had thought the nest was part of the statue, but as she looked at it again, she saw that it was an actual, real nest, though a very messy one. It seemed to be constructed of dried grass and twigs, mud and string, feathers and bits of cellophane candy wrappers. The bird settled on a nearby branch and watched her.

"I didn't mean to disturb you," she said softly. "If you have eggs, please go back to them. It's very chilly. I should be on my way to school, anyway."

The bird didn't move, but something else happened. The statue stood up. It rose, not stiffly, but with a graceful slowness, like a leaf unfurling. It turned toward her and then stopped and stared.

She wondered how she could have thought he was a statue. Or that he was a boy. He was older than that, and he looked twice as alive as everything else around them, more alive even than the bird watching them from its branch. His eyes were like dark underwater stones and very far apart. His face, unlike the rest of him, was a smooth polished wood color, though his cheeks were quite rosy. His mouth was very wide, too, but sensitive and delicate at its corners. He stood lightly on his pedestal in the middle of the pond.

"Hello," she said, realizing she was staring and not wanting to be rude.

"You can see me, too?" he asked.

What did he mean? "Well, yes. I mean, I can see you now. At first I mistook you for a statue."

He thought about that. "Well, perhaps that's what I was. It's hard to remember. I keep falling asleep. Did you come to bring me the key?"

Brigit looked at him, puzzled. "No, I didn't bring anything."

"Why were you looking for me, then?"

"I'm sorry, I wasn't looking for you. I just found my way in here by accident."

He shook his head. "That's what the other one said. But it's not possible, you know. You can't get in here by accident."

"What do you mean? Which other one?"

He lifted his arm and jiggled it as if he were showing off a bracelet. He paused and thought again. "And she had a High Eye." He touched one of his own eyes.

"You mean Feenix?" Brigit asked, startled. "Was she here? She didn't say anything about meeting you."

"Yes! Feenix!" He smiled now. His wide mouth lit up his whole face. "You know her! Of course you do. You are tied together in some way. Don't be frightened. I must look at you more closely."

It happened so quickly she had no time to be afraid. He leaped from his stone perch onto a tree limb that had half fallen in the water and took a few effortless steps along the limb. From there he jumped nimbly ashore. He stood before her, just a few steps away. His head cocked to one side.

"That red hair is awfully conspicuous," he said.

She could easily have pointed out that his green hair was even more so, but thought it might be rude.

"And you remind me very much of someone," he said, frowning. Then he snapped his fingers. "Wait, wait—it's coming to me. Brigit from Far Land. I believe that was her name?" He smiled, as if remembering something. "She was a Nor'easter, she was. You're not, by chance, related, are you?"

"You can't mean Brigit McFarland, can you? She was my grandmother. I was named after her. Did you know her?"

He smiled a half smile. "Grandmother? How fast the time goes here. But since it often runs in families, that would explain a lot, wouldn't it?"

Now Brigit felt she'd really gone down a rabbit hole. "No," she said. "It doesn't explain anything. Who are you?"

"Why, I'm called Jack, of course."

"I'm sorry. I don't remember her ever mentioning anyone named Jack."

He laughed. "Well, she wouldn't have, would she?"

"Why not?"

"That would be a long story. And we don't have that kind of time now. You people have made such a mess of things. This is likely our last chance. My lady will be awake and looking for me everywhere. Did your Feenix have any luck, do you know?"

"Luck with what?" Brigit asked.

He hesitated. "Did she use the—" Here he paused and made a juggling motion.

It took Brigit a moment and then she remembered. "Yes," she answered. "But how did you know?"

He ignored the question. "And did the Cheeryups come?"

"The *cheeryups*?"

Now he did a wonderful thing. He closed his eyes and pursed his lips and gave such a perfect imitation of a robin singing that he might as well have been a bird himself. The robin who had been sitting on the branch nearby sang back to him in delight.

Cheeryup, cheeryup, cheery-cheeryup!

"Yes," Brigit laughed. "They did. You're right, you're right. But they're hungry, I think. It's colder out there than it is in here. Maybe the ground is still too hard for worms. The spring just won't come."

The happiness went quickly from his face. "Of course. That would surely be the case. That's why we must find the Lady. Brigit from Far Land, we're running out of time. I must trust you with the second of the Vernariums. There is only one left after this."

She watched him lift a little red bag hanging from a gold cord around his neck. He pulled it over his head. "It is my task to guard these during the dark months. I gave your friend the first one. You must get this to the Lady, but along the way it will signal you in case of dire need. Don't use more than a little pinch here and there. It's very powerful." He held it out to her.

Brigit took it and stared at it nervously. "But what's in here and how do I use it?"

"Don't worry. It will show you if it chooses. Put it in your pocket for now, where you can reach it easily. Best not to let it be seen. But no one may take it off your person unless you agree."

She did as he said. "And what does this lady look like?"

At this, he blinked and shook his head. "It's been so long since I last saw her, I couldn't say. I don't think she ever looks the same, although she usually has her bees about her. I'm sure it will be clear when you meet." Now he took a step closer to Brigit, and his face, which was so open and honest, turned sly. "Allow me to kiss you. It will help you remember what I have told you."

Oh, she was tempted. In spite of his being so odd looking, there was something beautiful about him. It would be a great chance, wouldn't it? She stood quite still as he bent toward her. Then, from the back of her mind, she remembered a warning her grandad had once given her: *You must never accept food or kisses from the Ones on the other side. I believe 'twas that which took your gran so young.*

Was Jack one of those? She moved away. "It's all right," she said. "I'm sure I'll remember, and I'd really better go now. I'm going to be very late to school."

He looked disappointed and sighed. "Well, hurry then. Before your path closes up."

Brigit looked behind herself, startled at these words, but saw with relief that the same dirt path was still there waiting for her. Without another word, she hurried over to it and stepped back into the trees.

Before she was even out of the park, she noticed a change in the little red sack. She had kept her hand in her pocket, so she felt it quite clearly. The sack, made from some sort of rough woven material, had begun to grow warm against her palm. And then warmer. She looked around. The ground where she stood was cold and bare and hard. What was she supposed to do? Was there some sort of dire need here? She pulled the sack out and held it in her palm. Immediately the drawstring around its neck loosened, and the bag opened up. There was, she could have sworn, a faint humming sound coming out of it. She peered in.

What she saw looked like fine red earth mixed here and there with a glint of gold. She reached in, took a pinch, and dropped it into her palm to get a better look. She sniffed at it. It smelled strong and peppery. In the next second, she gave a loud and forceful sneeze.

The stuff blew into the air in a red-and-gold cloud of dust and whispered down to the ground.

Everything grew very quiet. Even the nearby sounds of street traffic stopped. Then, in the bare-branched tree over-head, a bird called out a note of inquiry. Brigit looked up and saw a robin sitting there watching her. "Cheeryup!" Brigit called, trying her best to answer.

The robin was apparently not impressed and made no reply.

When Brigit looked again at the ground, she drew in a sharp breath. Fanning around her in a half circle were a dozen delicate spears of green.

Wait. Had they been there all along, or had they just appeared when she looked away? She couldn't be sure. She crouched down to look more closely. They rose just a little way above the earth, the slender spike-nosed beginnings of something. Daffodils maybe. When she turned her head to the right, she saw another half circle of green. These were even taller than the first ones, and they were beginning to pop into yellow buds. She had the most peculiar sensation that these spikes were watching her, just as she was watching *them*. Just as the robin was doing. Everybody was watching everybody else. It was ridiculous, she knew, but she couldn't help herself. She closed her eyes and counted slowly to twenty.

When she opened her eyes again, she rose with a nervous gasp and took a step away. The buds had opened into full-fledged daffodils, and in a half circle around these, new sharp tips of green were already breaking through. Was it possible? Had the pepper, or whatever it was, done this? Had there been a dire need for daffodils in this spot?

When Brigit lifted the bag with excitement, thinking she would try again, she found it had gone quite cool and silent. Uncertain, she stood there for a long moment, then drew the string tight and slipped the bag back in her pocket. With a start, she realized she was going to be late to school. The others would have given up on her by now. Down the little hill she hurried and then out the exit between the two stone panthers. She didn't look up them, but she was sure she felt them watching her back as she crossed the street.

14

Feenix Stares Down the Tiltersmith

Feenix actually arrived first on the front steps of school that morning. She stood there trying to understand the thing in the air. It felt like a lining up of electrical forces. A battle? A storm? The crowd on the front steps seemed to feel it, too. Everyone was restless, and those crazy robins were everywhere, trippety tripping, stabbing at the ground with sharp beaks. Though she couldn't tell if they were actually finding anything to eat yet.

But where were the others? There was no sign of Ms. Trevino, either. Well, that was good, right? Ms. Trevino often came out in the mornings to greet her adoring public, but Feenix would have to find a way to slip around her if she did. She would not appreciate the excellent skunk in the corner of Feenix's eye. The flippy tail lifted high. As if it were about to do its thing. One of her best efforts yet. How long could she keep it before someone told her to wash it off?

Now she spotted Danton galumphing down the street. He took a running leap and left the ground to whack at a low-hanging tree branch. When he reached the school steps, he took them two at a time. He leaped the final ones in a single bound. Then he stopped abruptly and looked around, frowning. "But where are Ed and Brigit?" he demanded.

Feenix looked at him. "Seriously? Why would I know the answer to that question?"

"But she's always on time," Danton said with a note of irritated impatience, as if this were somehow Feenix's fault. "Why don't you text her? See if everything's all right."

She gave him a pretend sweet smile. "Why don't you text her yourself, if you're so worried? But look, here comes Dweebo. Faster than a speeding glacier."

Edward obviously didn't notice her or Danton. His shirt was half untucked, hair stylishly arranged like a bear just coming out of hibernation. Where was his lucky hat, she wondered? He almost never left his house without it. Edward started up the steps. Frowning. His mind was clearly several light-years away. When he reached the top of the steps, Danton grabbed him by the shoulder.

"Hey," Edward said, startled.

"You seen any sign of Brigit?"

Edward looked around as if only now waking up to where he was. He shook his head. "She's not here yet?"

"You think we should worry?" Danton asked him.

Edward looked puzzled. "About what?"

"Well . . . I don't think she's ever been late," Danton said.

"Don't be such a dundersnap," Feenix told him. "You think she doesn't know her way to school yet? And *what* is that weird noise?"

"What noise?" Danton asked.

The noise came again. *Snorrrk!*

"Is that coming from your pocket?" she demanded. "I heard that last night during baking class."

Danton looked puzzled for a moment, then he froze as if he was trying to remember something. "Oh . . . yes." He unzipped his pocket and reached in. "I meant to show you guys this. I found it in Ms. Trevino's office at the end of the day."

"You? What were you doing in Ms. Trevino's office at the end of the day?" Feenix demanded.

But Danton made no answer. He just pulled his hand out of his pocket, his fingers curled around something. There was another *snorrrk*.

"What do you have in there?" Edward asked with interest.

Danton cracked his fingers open so they could peer inside.

"A toad!" Ed exclaimed. He loved stuff like this.

"You're carrying a toad around in your pocket? Seriously?" Feenix laughed.

"Well, yes. I mean, I'm not sure. You see—"

"No, I *can't* see," Ed interrupted impatiently. "That's the problem. Let me hold it for a second. Maybe I can identify it."

Danton hesitated and then dropped the little brown-and-green creature into Ed's cupped palms. Ed examined it carefully. "*Bufo americanus*," he declared. "Common toad. But it's a nice one. Where'd you get it?"

"Well, actually, here's the thing. I was walking by Ms. Trevino's office, and I saw—" He broke off because the double front doors of the school had opened up at last.

Everybody turned to look. Silence fell over the crowded steps. It wasn't Ms. Trevino. It was the superintendent guy

Ms. Trevino had brought with her to math class yesterday. The one with the shiny tiny boots and, today, a different three-piece suit. Tweed, brown and black. Perfectly pressed but not stiff. It hung really well on him, even considering the slightly crooked shoulders. He was quite the dresser. And that blue pen! It shone out from all the way up there.

Superintendent Tiltersmith stepped out. All the poor robins looking for something to eat in the frozen front lawn rose up and flew across the street. A big mess of them landed in the trees around the playground area. There was something about the way the superintendent watched them that made Feenix shiver. At last, he turned to the crowd of students buzzing and bouncing around in front of the school.

"Quick," Danton whispered. "Put that toad in your pocket and be careful! We'll all be very sorry if something happens to it."

Edward blinked, then did as he was told.

Feenix had a bad feeling about what was going to happen next. "What's he still doing here?" she whispered. "And why does he have such tiny feet?"

"He's coming this way," Danton said. "Be careful. I'm not kidding."

The superintendent approached them and came to a stop. His eyes flicked coolly over Edward and Danton and then turned to Feenix. She didn't flinch. She was a master at staring contests. It was a creepy face to look into, though. His skin was too gray and too tight looking. His hair was that oily, shiny bluish black.

He pointed to the skunk she had drawn near her eye. To her surprise, he smiled. "Don't tell me you do these yourself?"

"I do."

"What an impressive array of skills you have," he said. What, exactly, did he mean by this? Not that she was going to ask. "That was quite a show you put on yesterday," he continued. Show? What was he talking about?

He watched her face and waited. Then it came back to her.

"You almost forgot, didn't you?" he asked.

"No, of course I didn't." But she had. The juggling balls. Math class. How was that possible? In a panic, she thought back, trying to think what she had done with them.

He smiled. "Where are they?"

"Where are what?"

"The items that you were to have placed into the Confiscation Basket."

"Oh! You mean those beanbag things. Uh . . . isn't that where they are, in the basket?"

"No. They are not. I believe you failed to do as you were instructed." He waited.

She said nothing.

"Well, I shall tell you what," he continued. "Your school principal—the admirable Madame Trevino—has not yet become aware of your neglect. Now, it is to my great disadvantage, I suppose, but I have a reputation for a soft heart. You will hand the juggler's balls over to me now, and I will put them where they belong and I shall keep your secret. I would not wish you to suffer the full wrath of your headmistress for such a small offense."

Instantly, she was sure of it. He wanted them for himself. She had no idea why, but she knew it wouldn't be a good idea to allow this to happen. "Well, that's awfully nice of you," she answered, "but I can't do that."

The skin around his eyes pulled even tighter. His nose seemed to sharpen. "And why can you not?"

Feenix had been thinking fast. As luck would have it, Detestable Robert passed by on the steps just then, hunched over under his heavy backpack. He was dressed, as usual, in corduroy pants that were too short. His hair was in his eyes.

"Well, listen," she whispered to the superintendent. "To tell you the truth, that guy who just walked by? Robert Westover? He offered to take the beanbags to the basket. Such a sweet guy. He's kind of got a thing for me, and I was in a hurry, you know. I didn't want to be late for our baking class, so I gave them to him. If they didn't end up where they were supposed to go, maybe you should talk to *him*."

The superintendent eyed Robert's retreating back. Then he looked at Feenix again. "I'll have a word with him," he said. "Let's hope you are not so young and foolish that you would try to *misdirect* me." He gave a little laugh. "Although, truth to tell, I do so love a little treasure hunt. Off with you, then."

With relief, Feenix turned to go, Ed and Danton right beside her.

"Oh, one more thing—" the superintendent said.

His voice caught at the back of her neck like steel pincers. She turned around and waited.

"May I inquire where you got them?"

"Where I got them?" She stalled.

He watched her.

Where *had* she gotten them from? It was going to come back to her in a minute. "Well," she answered at last. "I don't really know. Somebody must have given them to me a long time ago, when I was a kid. I think I've always had them."

"Ah, is that so?" he said. But he pursued the question no more. He stood in silence and watched them as the threesome passed by and entered through the front doors.

15

Worms

From where she stood at the red light on the corner opposite the school, Brigit could see the last of the students disappearing through the front doors. There was no sign of Edward, Feenix, or Danton. She pictured them sitting down at the high table in science class and looking at her empty seat. Would they worry? Danton, she was pretty sure, would. He worried about the mousy ones.

The red light seemed to last forever. Her hands were freezing. She put them in her pockets to look for her gloves, and as she did, she felt something soft and warm under her left palm. What was that, she wondered? Whatever it was, it grew warmer and then warmer yet. She pulled it out, and the little sack lay there, hot against her palm.

She laughed. The sack! How could she have forgotten so quickly? She was going to get to see them again! The bright-green stems piercing the earth. The garden area around the playground would be the perfect place.

The moment the light changed, she crossed swiftly over, and passing through the gate, she headed toward the winter trees and the empty flower beds. The bag hummed in warm approval.

It was easy to follow its directions. The bag got colder when she wasn't going in the direction it wanted, warmer when she was getting it right. It drew her inward until at last she came to a stop under a tree. On this cold morning that winter refused to let go of, there wasn't a child or a parent in sight. The tree trunk went smoothly upward to a height just over her head. There it forked and forked again into a hundred crooked, hopeful branches.

Again, the drawstring around the neck of the bag loosened itself. She reached in and took out a pinch of the red-and-gold dust. She bent over to breathe the peppery stuff in, and again, she gave a loud, forceful *"Achoo!"*

The dust blew upward into the tree and then floated down. Some of it got caught in the branches. The rest drifted down and scattered across the ground. She waited, watching closely.

Nothing happened. What had she done wrong?

Wait! Was she supposed to close her eyes?

She closed her eyes and counted to thirty. She opened them again, then nearly wept in frustration. Not a single green stem showed itself. Had she imagined it? Had it been only wishful thinking the first time—that the dust had caused the green spears to appear?

She closed her eyes again and began to count: "One Mississippi, two Mississippi . . ." She was going to make herself go all the way to sixty. But before she got close, she felt something under her foot, a little collapsing inward of the soil.

Her eyes flew open and she stepped back. A worm, a slick pink bit of muscle no longer than her pinky, was slithering cautiously out of the ground where Brigit had just stood. As it slid quickly through the scraggly grass, her eye was caught by another one emerging from the cold soil.

And then another one! And then another.

In a moment, everywhere Brigit looked the soil was crumbling and collapsing. Hundreds of tiny earthquakes. Worms everywhere. Some half out of the ground, pushing the earth aside. Some all the way out already, sliding through the old leaves and scrabbly grass. Now there were two of them crawling over her sneakers. She didn't mind worms, not at all—she knew they were good for the soil and the plants—but there were so many of them. What if they took over the whole park and chewed up everything? What if they started leaving the park and crawling out onto the sidewalks? What if they choked the sewers and ate all the little green stems in the gardens before the gardens could even begin? Maybe the whole balance of things would go out, like Mr. Ross talked about. Was this Brigit's fault?

She looked around, searching for some sort of answer, and when she turned her face upward, she drew in an astonished breath. On every branch of the tree, pale-pink buds were just beginning to split open from their cases. Next to every bud there sat a robin. Right over her head. When had they arrived so silently? Every branch had three or four birds sitting and watching. They were waiting for something.

Oh! What a donkey head she was! They were waiting for her to get out of the way. No sooner had she retreated a few paces than the birds began to drop to the ground. In a few moments, they were everywhere, a starving invasion of robins. Once on the ground, they stabbed at the worms and wrestled with them and danced about with them in their beaks. Darting and stopping. Darting and stopping. An all-you-can-eat earthworm-breakfast jamboree. Some of the worms were fat gladiators who wrestled and whipped themselves about and managed to escape back into the ground, but more than many were slurped down like spaghetti.

Brigit stood there riveted, watching the scene of slithering carnage. When the last worm was eaten, the robins scattered among the trees, tuk-tuk-tukking cheerily to each other. And now the petals of the new buds began to unfurl. A delicate blush of delicious scent filled the air. Brigit turned slowly, breathing it in, and as she did, she happened to glance up at the school.

She froze. There was a figure watching her from one of the windows.

As she stood there in dismay, her first thought was about how late she must be. Her second thought was to wonder what he was still doing here.

It was only a couple of minutes before she was hurrying up the side steps of the school.

16

Venus Flytraps

Danton was puzzled about the front hall. Something seemed off, as if the floor had tilted slightly sideways. But that made no sense. And where was Brigit? He kept looking behind himself, but there was no sign of her.

"Stop doing that," Feenix said. "You're rubbing my nerves the wrong way. She's fine. She's probably just caught a cold or something."

"She never catches cold," Danton said. Feenix just rolled her eyes. Eventually Danton had to admit they couldn't wait for Brigit any longer, and they went to class.

In the science classroom, there were eight boxlike shapes that hadn't been there yesterday lined up on the low bookshelf. Each one was covered by a green cloth. A cardboard sign propped in front of them said *NO TOUCH!!*

Danton, Feenix, and Edward sat down on the stools at their high lab table and waited. Mr. Ross was in the back of the room, feeding his jar of fruit flies or something, so he didn't see Brigit when she appeared in the doorway. She looked at no one but entered the room in that quick, skimming-over-the-water way she had, like a small one-person sailboat, her shoulders held high, her braided red hair carrying its own light as always.

Danton felt a confused mix of feelings. First, relief. Second, that he wanted to get a close-up look at her face for just a few seconds. Third, that he didn't want anybody else to notice him staring at her face.

Brigit sat down, and before Feenix could open her mouth and start interrogating her, Mr. Ross announced that he had brought in the surprise he had promised them. "I'm going to give each table one of these." He pointed to the bookshelf. "Don't uncover till I say the word, please." One by one he carried the boxes over to the lab tables. When each group of four had one, he gave the nod. "Okay. Go ahead."

Feenix took hold of the cloth on theirs and pulled it off. Beneath was a small glass terrarium containing some kind of plant with long cactus-looking needles around its leaves. Danton knew what it was right away. His mother sometimes sold these as novelty items in her gardening store.

"Anybody know what we've got here?" Mr. Ross asked, and Danton raised his hand.

"Venus flytraps," he said.

"And what is it that makes this plant so unusual?"

"They trap and eat bugs."

"And what's so unusual about that?"

"Well—like we've been talking about—plants mostly just make their own food. They photosynthesize their food from the sun. They don't catch and eat stuff. Venus flytraps are sort of hybrids, like Ed was talking about."

Mr. Ross gave him a two-handed thumbs-up. "Right. These plants live naturally only in a very small region of North and South Carolina. They evolved in poor, boggy soil which does not give them all the nutrients they need to thrive. They have adapted to this problem by developing a backup system to get supplements. They trap bugs and digest them to make up for what they cannot get through their roots. Now, just so you know, there are many different types of carnivorous plants like this. Some use tentacles to trap their prey, some drown them, some have sticky flypaper-type leaves. The Venus flytrap is one of my favorites. Let's take a look at how they do their thing." He was holding one of the potted plants in his hand. "Danton, you want to come up and point out which part of the plant is the trap?"

Danton accepted the invitation and walked around showing how the plant had several stalks and at the end of each stalk was a double-leafed shape. These were the traps. Each one looked like a folded but half-open taco waiting to be filled. The inside of the taco was a bright red. The outside was green. Fringing the outer edges of the taco leaves were the long needlelike teeth.

"Okay," said Mr. Ross. "Now look at the plants inside your terrariums. You each have one plant, and each plant will have around four or five stalks with traps. You see them?"

There was a rumbling chorus of "yeses."

"I will tell you right off the bat that all these plants are hungry. This is their feeding time. I feed them once every two weeks. Now, I'm going to give each table one of these." He held up a clean baby-food jar with a cricket inside it. "Then

I'm going to count to three, and you will let your crickets go into your terrariums and observe what happens. Here's the question I'd like you to keep in mind as you observe: If one of the traps closes, what do you think triggered it to do so? As always, remember to try to keep your minds open. Don't jump to conclusions. There's a trick here."

Mr. Ross now walked rapidly around the room, distributing the cricket jars, till every table had one. "Okay. Ready? One, two, three—release them!"

The cricket jar was in Edward's hand. Feenix lifted the lid off the terrarium, and Edward shook the cricket in. They all bent close to the terrarium and watched, holding their breaths. The cricket fell to the bottom, next to the plant. It didn't move. "Oh wow," Feenix said. "Look at it. It looks terrified. Like when the Romans sent the Christians into the arena with the lions."

"Shhh!" Ed said. "Just watch." Everybody watched. The cricket took a tentative hop.

"Look. It's starting to move!" Feenix announced.

"Shhh!" Ed snapped. "We're not blind."

Mr. Ross was moving around the room, watching and listening.

Their cricket began to circle with a little more confidence around the base of the plant. It appeared to be checking the situation out. At last, it took a short leap and grabbed hold of a pea-green plant stalk. It climbed slowly upward, stopping now and then, perhaps to listen for trouble. When it reached the top, it peered into the motionless watermelon-colored booby trap. Then it slipped through the rubbery-looking spikes that surrounded its rim, and landed inside.

"Waiiit for it! Waiiit for it!" Feenix whispered, her voice choked with excitement.

"*Will* you be quiet?" Ed whispered.

For a few moments their cricket didn't move, then it took a hop and froze. Then it hopped again and froze. It took another hop and brushed against one of the sharp-looking hairs that grew out of the moist pink surface.

"I bet that's it," said Edward. "I bet that's the trigger." They all watched, holding their breaths. But nothing happened. The cricket took a few more jerky steps and then hopped safely out the other side of the trap.

"Must be a dud," Danton said.

"Wait," Feenix told them. "It's crawling up another stalk. Maybe this one will take it."

They all watched as the cricket slowly edged its way up the new stalk. Then, without any messing around, it jumped right into the trap at the top. It bumped into one of the hairs. But again, nothing happened. The cricket stayed inside this one, wandering cluelessly around, oblivious to the danger it was in.

"Maybe they're all duds," Feenix said.

At this moment the cricket brushed up against another hair. The trap snapped shut. Feenix gave out a little scream of excitement.

Brigit, Danton, and Edward had seen it, too.

In a silent, deadly second, the spiky teeth around the sides interlaced neatly and formed a cage. They could see the cricket inside suddenly realizing its predicament. It banged and slammed against the bars. Apparently this was happening all around the room, for there were cries of surprise and excitement coming from all corners.

"Whammo! Did you see that?"

"It was so fast!"

"Zap! That thing didn't stand a chance."

Kseniya raised her hand. "I see the trick! It must be two! Two times to make the closing!"

"Bravissimo!" cried Mr. Ross. "She is correct. The traps will not close until two or more hairs are brushed." Mr. Ross was practically dancing with excitement.

Danton was relieved and happy to see Mr. Ross's spirits so refreshed.

"But why?" asked Mr. Ross. "Why would the trap wait for the second trigger?"

There was a very long silence. At last Edward said, almost more to himself than to the class, "There must be some survival benefit to doing it this way, but what?"

It was Kseniya who spoke out. "It does not wish to close on something too small or too quick! A raindrop. An ant or a—"

"Right!" Robert interrupted. "It wants something big and juicy. By waiting, it makes sure it's not wasting its time. But how can a plant know how to count?" Robert had forgotten all about the rest of the class. He seemed to be speaking directly to Ed and Kseniya now. They were in their own little world.

"Could it be some kind of electrical charge?" Edward asked.

"That's got to be it!" Robert agreed. "Each time a hair is brushed, a charge gets stored somewhere until there's enough to make the trap close!"

"Oh, brave new world that has such smarty-pants as these to walk upon it!" cried Mr. Ross. He bowed to the class. It was at this moment that two interruptions occurred. The first came from the back of the room, where Padma began to cry. "Oh, the poor, poor cricket. What happens to it now?" The second was that a screech of static from the PA system crackled into the room.

"Greetings and good wishes, young scholars," boomed out a rumbling voice. *"Forgive me for the interruption."*

Feenix looked around at the others and mouthed the word "Tiltersmith."

"Allow me to introduce myself," the voice continued. *"For those of you who have not yet met me, I am Superintendent Tiltersmith from the Central District Office. I have been hearing the most interesting things about your school. Yesterday, I arrived here after a rather long and arduous journey. I was welcomed by your most remarkable principal, Madame Trevino, and she offered to give me a tour of your classrooms. I quickly saw some signs of what I have been looking for, and I was even more impressed than I expected to be. Unfortunately, we had not gotten very far in our walkabout when, as the banana peel of ill luck would have it, Madame Trevino had a small accident—a collision with an obstacle she did not see coming. She will need to take some time off to recover herself."*

There was a stirring and whispering throughout the classroom, and the superintendent paused for a moment, almost as if he could hear them from where he sat. Danton noticed that Mr. Ross hadn't moved. His eyes had an oddly glazed look.

"Meanwhile, I have volunteered to step in as acting principal. For me, a wonderful opportunity. Every dark cloud has its

silver lining, does it not? My nose tells me that I have come to the right place to tip the balance toward a major breakthrough in my research. I believe one or more of you may have a critical piece of the treasure I'm seeking, and while I'm searching for it, I expect we will have some fun together. I trust you will not disappoint me. I will be conducting a few interviews, and I will begin by asking Robert Westover to report to the office immediately. In the meantime, all of you keep your minds alert and your eyes open. That's what you're here for. And if any of you observe any unusual events worthy of my attention, please be sure to report them to me. You'll find yourself amply rewarded."

The loudspeaker gave out an abrupt screech and then went dead. Mr. Ross, who had not moved all this time, now opened and closed his mouth like a goldfish. He frowned and gazed uneasily around the room.

Robert was looking rather pleased with himself. This worried Danton. How could a person be so smart and so clueless at the same time? Surely he should have noticed that there was something not right with this Tiltersmith dude. Robert bent to pick up his backpack and then stood.

"You're leaving us, Robert?" Mr. Ross asked.

"Uh . . . yeah. I'm going to the principal's office?"

Mr. Ross looked confused, but he said no more.

From the back of the room, Padma, who had been crying quietly, spoke up. "But what will happen to the crickets?"

Mr. Ross frowned at her as if he wasn't quite sure what she was talking about. Then he perked up. "Yes, yes! The crickets. What's going to happen to them now? Once they're caught in the trap, you can't see them anymore, right? The trap is now shut in such a way that it is airtight. Soon it'll begin to release digestive enzymes. These, along with a lack of air, will kill the insect. Then the enzymes will slowly break down the soft parts of the insect's body. Think of it as a kind of melting process. Your crickets will be liquefied. This will allow the plants to feed on the nutrients they need. The whole process will take about a week to twelve days."

"They're going to suck on the crickets for twelve days? Can't we get them out before that starts to happen?" Padma pleaded.

"Well, yes, we could force something between the leaves and break the trap open," Mr. Ross answered. "But that would injure the trap, probably cause it to die. And even if we could do it safely and let the cricket out, the plant would lose its meal and would not get the valuable nutrients it needs to thrive. I can understand this is upsetting to watch, but it *is* part of the food chain. What do you people think? Shall we take a vote? Raise your hand if you think we should open the traps."

There were only three yeas.

All this time Danton was worrying. "I don't think this is good," he said softly to the others.

"You mean about the crickets?" Edward asked.

Danton whispered to Feenix. "Feenix, didn't you tell this Tiltersmith guy you gave your juggling balls to Robert? Was that true?"

Feenix shrugged sort of guiltily. "Actually, I can't exactly remember *what* I did with them."

Danton glared at her. It wasn't that Danton particularly liked Robert. Robert could be insufferable, as his mother would have said (she liked this word). But Danton didn't think Robert was insufferable on purpose. He probably just didn't know how to be any other way. On the other hand, Danton was pretty sure that whoever or whatever the Tiltersmith guy was, he was dangerous.

Danton raised his hand and told Mr. Ross that he needed a drink of water. Once released, he bounded down the hallway and then the stairs, hoping to catch up with Robert before he got to the principal's office.

He arrived just in time to see Robert disappearing inside.

17

The Tiltersmith Interviews
Detestable Robert

Danton glanced around. It was very quiet in the hall-way. He walked softly up to the door and found it open a crack. He peered in. Robert was standing in front of Ms. Trevino's desk, looking at the Tiltersmith, who sat behind the desk, idly playing with his fancy pen and talking.

"I called you in here because you, Mr. Westover, appear to be made from rare stuff. How tickled I am to meet you. I have taken a look at your records. They are most impressive." He patted a file folder that was sitting on the desk. "If the reports are true, you are gifted with a mind that drives home like an arrow. In particular, your memory and calculation skills are exceptional. You are just the sort we watch for down at the Central District Office. I have a feeling we may be able to be of great help to one another. You could, perhaps, even help me to improve your school." The superintendent gestured grandly to the air around him.

Danton could see how Robert puffed up, like a rooster look-ing pleased with itself. "Yes," he replied in his stiff-necked way. "I do sometimes think that Ms. Trevino doesn't put enough importance on the academic side of things. We could use some changes here."

"Well, I am very interested in *your* organizational methods. Perhaps you'd let me have a look inside your schoolbag to see your notebooks and how you order them."

Robert hesitated, then he said, "Okay. Sure." He put his backpack down on the desk in front of the superintendent. The superintendent unzipped the main pocket. "You might be interested in my color-coding system for each subject," Robert said. "It helps me put everything in its proper place. I can explain it to you, if you'd like."

"Yes, that sounds like it might be very useful. But first, let me just take a quick look myself, if you don't mind."

There were several loud clunkings and clatterings as the superintendent turned Robert's backpack upside down and shook it out on the desk. "Hey," Robert objected. "Be careful. Everything is alphabetized."

"Oh, dear, dear. So sorry," the Tiltersmith said without sounding sorry at all. In fact, he sounded annoyed and impatient.

"Were you looking for something in particular? Would you like to see my last math exam? I received the highest grade because I was the only one able to answer the extra-credit problem except for Edward, but he had gotten question nine wrong. It wasn't all that difficult, really."

The superintendent said now, in a rush, "No, no. I know exactly how you did on your last mathematics exam. But I would like to see what you keep in these other pockets." He unzipped the one in front.

"Hey," Robert said. "There's no schoolwork in that one. Just personal items."

"Indeed, indeed, and your personal items are fascinating to me. I would like to see what such an able scholar considers important to carry with him." Again, there was the sound of numerous small objects falling onto the desk.

The superintendent didn't seem actually all that interested in Robert's keys and phone and junk. He turned impatiently and looked Robert up and down. "What about the pocket of your trousers?"

Robert was beginning to look less puffed up. Danton could see that he was starting to understand that something wasn't right here. Reluctantly, he pulled out a pack of chewing gum and a handful of coins and put them down on the desk.

The superintendent stared at these for a long moment. He seemed to be trying to make up his mind. "Where are they?" he demanded sharply.

"Where are *what*?"

"I think you know what I mean."

Robert shook his head. "I don't, actually." He moved nervously toward the desk and started collecting his stuff. "Look, I probably should get back to class."

The Tiltersmith didn't move, just sat there watching Robert put his stuff away. When Robert was done and he started to turn, the Tiltersmith said, "Stop," and Robert stopped.

"The juggling balls. What have you done with them?"

Robert stared at him. "Juggling balls? What do you mean?"

"You know what I mean."

"What? No. I don't . . . Oh, wait, you're talking about those stupid things Feenix was distracting everybody with yesterday? I have no idea. Why would you think I knew anything about them?"

"I was told she gave them to you."

"Who told you that? Why would she give them—"

"*She* told me," the superintendent said, interrupting him. "She said you were a very sweet fellow and that you were going to put them in the basket for her."

"She said that—" he asked in disbelief. "I mean, that I was a sweet fellow?" He shook his head, as if to organize his thoughts. "That seems very unlikely. Perhaps you misunderstood her. But if she did say that, then she was lying. She makes up stories all the time. She might have been trying to confuse you."

"Why would she want to do that?"

"Who knows why Feenix does the stuff she does?" Robert took a step backward. "I'd really better get going. I have a quiz coming up in my French class."

The superintendent ignored this. "An alternative explanation might be that *you're* trying to confuse me."

"But why would *I* want to do that?"

"Because those juggling balls are actually quite valuable."

Robert stared. "Well, they're not valuable to me."

"Do you know what? I think I'd better have you stay here for a bit while I go sort this out."

"I can't do that," Robert protested. "I have a quiz coming up in my French class."

The Tiltersmith laughed. "Oh, no need to worry about a thing. I'll take care of it." He came around the side of the desk. "You just stay right here."

Danton backed away from the door, fearing the Tiltersmith was going to catch him peering in. He ducked into the library across the hall and hid himself in the bookshelves. He counted slowly to sixty and then tiptoed back out into the hallway, looking both ways. No sign of the Tiltersmith. He walked back to the principal's office and listened. No sound. He pushed the door open quietly and peeked in.

The room appeared to be empty. He stepped inside. "Hello? Robert? You in here?"

There was no answer. Danton did not have a good feeling about this. What was it, exactly, that had happened last time he came into this office? He had found that toad! He had nearly forgotten. But where was it now? What had he done with it? Oh yes, hadn't he given it to Edward on the front steps? He hoped Edward was keeping it safe.

Danton took a breath. It seemed ridiculous, but he checked under the desk. There were Ms. Trevino's high-heeled assembly-day shoes, but, of course, no sign of Robert. Danton wasn't sure why, but he opened the Confiscation Basket and peered inside. Same old rubber vomit and electrified handshake buzzers. Nothing new.

Now he stood in the middle of the room and turned around slowly, looking for some clue to what had happened. His eye was caught by Ms. Trevino's collection of blown-glass figurines. There were several dozen of them—birds and animals and miniature houses, a cherry tree with tiny pink blossoms.

There were some imaginary creatures there, too. A sad-looking dragon, a three-headed dog, a winged sea serpent. Some were clear glass, but many were brightly colored.

Danton started to turn away when another one of the figures caught his eye. What the Hellamenopee? Standing behind a spotted giraffe was a glass boy. The boy's mouth was open as if he was going to speak. He was about four inches high, and his hair was half over his eyes. His brown corduroys were too short, and his navy-blue glass sweater-vest too baggy. He had a backpack over his shoulder.

18

Two Places at Once

Language period was one of those times of day when they sometimes lost track of each other. Danton and Ed were taking Spanish. Brigit was taking Italian, and Feenix was in French.

As soon as Brigit walked into the classroom, she spotted him.

He was sitting in the back corner, taking notes on a yellow memo pad with his fancy blue pen. Nobody else, including Signora Moretti, gave any sign that they noticed him. Brigit pretended that she did not, either. But once she sat down, it was almost as if she could feel his gaze roaming around the room. Like a searchlight. Once or twice she even felt the skin prickling at the back of her neck, as if he had seen the gold cord from which the little red bag now hung like a necklace. She stared straight ahead.

When the bell finally rang, she leaned down to pick up her backpack, and there were his shiny little booted feet. He was somehow sitting in the chair right beside her.

As she stood up, it was impossible not to look at his grinning face.

"Did I startle you?" he asked.

She just shook her head and walked out of the classroom as fast as she could.

The others were waiting in the hall. "Don't let's wait here," she said in a low voice and went right past them without looking back. She hoped they would follow. Danton was beside her in a moment.

"What's wrong?" he asked. "Are you all right?"

She didn't answer until they had turned the corner and headed up the stairway to Health and Safety class. Then she paused on the landing, by the window, and watched the passing crowd nervously. "That Tiltersmith person. He was already sitting in the back of the room when I came in. There's something wrong about him. I could feel his eyes the whole time. He was looking for something. Then, when I got up to leave, somehow he was sitting right next to me."

"That's not possible," Feenix said sharply. "He was sitting in the back of *my* room. At least for some of the time. You must have just missed him going in and out somehow."

Brigit just shook her head. She didn't see how this could have happened.

"Well, he's certainly not in either of your classrooms now," said Danton. He pointed out the window. "Look. He's right over there."

From here they could see the playground and the park right across the street. The sky was still covered in clouds, but Superintendent Tiltersmith was standing under a small tree that seemed to give off a light of its own. Brigit had forgotten about this tree until now. It was in full pink blossom. The

Tiltersmith was watching the robins that flitted to and fro in its branches. After a moment he bent down and scraped up some soil with his fingers. He examined the soil closely. He sniffed at it and then brushed it off his hands.

Then—before they had a chance to do anything, to move back or look away—he stood up sharply, like a jack-in-the box when the lid pops open. He seemed to be staring straight at them. He had a grin on his face.

Brigit shuddered, and Danton ordered everybody away from the window.

19
Gym Class

"**C**'mon. Let's get to class," Danton said. "I don't want us to be standing here when he comes back in. What is it with that guy? What do you think he was doing out there?"

Brigit kept her thoughts to herself, and nobody else answered, either.

"Well, let's all stick close together today," Danton said. "Maybe Ms. Trevino will be back by tomorrow."

Brigit was glad to do as he suggested. For the next couple of periods, the hair on the back of her neck stood up every time a shadow passed by a doorway. As it turned out, however, there wasn't a sign of the Tiltersmith all through Health and Safety, and the most exciting thing at lunch was that Danton broke up a fight between two sixth graders who were throwing chicken nuggets at each other.

By the time they got to the gymnasium, Brigit had begun to relax a little.

The walls were echoing with the sounds of yelling and balls bouncing and feet stomping. Several classes on the same grade level were joined together for this period, and there was a general sense of rejoicing and mayhem since there didn't seem to be a gym teacher in sight. Ms. Abbott was often late for this class, so this wasn't unusual.

Brigit watched the handball players for a while and then walked over to the game of double-Dutch jump rope that was starting up. Tessa went in first:

> *Old Mother Whittlehouse*
> *had a big fit.*
> *First she did the merry-go-round*
> *and then she did the split.*

Tessa was really good. Once upon a time, Brigit had been really good, too, but she hadn't jumped since before her brother had died and she'd left her old school. She stepped a little closer now, just to watch the show. She could feel the irresistible rhythm of Tessa's feet against the floor.

> *Old Mother Whittlehouse all dressed in yella*
> *went downstairs to kiss a fella.*
> *Made a mistake and kissed a snake.*
> *How many doctors did it take?*
> *One, two, three, four . . .*

Tessa went out on the twelfth count. Brigit never did find out who it was, but somebody put a hand on her shoulder and gave her a push. She stumbled awkwardly in the direction of the spinning ropes.

"That's it, Red Mouse! Go for it!" *Red Mouse? Did they*

mean her? And yet it did not seem like an insult here, but a friendly gesture of being included.

"Go, go, go, Brigit! Your turn!" In that split second, she saw it was too late to escape. She could either let herself get tripped up by the ropes and be laughed at forever or hop in now and take the jump.

She hopped. *One, two,* and in she went, smooth as warm butter, her knees high, side to side, the ropes slap-slapping the shiny floor. Millie, who stood facing her and turning the ropes, looked surprised for a moment to see Brigit, but then she smiled and nodded in encouragement.

A little crowd was gathering to watch, but Brigit was going too fast to remember to be nervous. Her knees and her head had clicked right into the zone together, working in perfectly oiled harmony. Someone began to chant:

One, two, buckle your shoe.

Brigit bent down and tapped her shoe.

Three, four, knock on the door.

She knocked on the air.

Five, six, pick up sticks.

She bent again and swiped at the floor.

Seven, eight, here comes your date.

There was a long pause, and then, out of the corner of her eye, she saw someone take a few steps forward. Someone all legs and arms and bounce, someone waiting on the sideline for just the right moment. Brigit nearly stopped breathing, which is fatal to do when you are jumping. But she managed a gulp of air and righted herself just as Danton ducked his head, hopped in, and made a perfect landing in the middle of the two spinning, floor-slapping ropes. He kept his knees high and jumped easily from side to side as he grinned at her.

Lots of boys at this school did it, but Brigit hadn't realized Danton was a jumper, too. There was a spattering of whistles and catcalls and also some applause. Danton had on his biggest, happiest *aren't we lucky to be alive* grin. It was too contagious. Brigit grinned back. Someone began a new chant:

People, people turn around.

They both spun neatly around.

People, people hands to the ground.

They both flat-handed the floor and then shot upright and resumed jumping.

Turn to the east and turn to the west.

They did as they were instructed, but now the chanter paused to let the watching crowd get a little bigger. The ropes kept going round and round. As the crowd began to clap, Brigit realized, a little late, what was about to happen. Did Danton know? He was still smiling, never missing a beat, knees and head high. Brigit could make a run for it, but that option would be more mortifying than staying.

So she stayed.

Now kiss the one you like the best.

Brigit saw how Danton nearly froze, how he must be thinking about running, too. But then he met her gaze and raised his eyebrows a little in a question. How polite he was. She nodded. He nodded back and jumped toward her. She jumped toward him. When he was close enough, he tipped his face downward. She lifted hers up. And then the ropes stopped turning.

In the tangle that immediately followed, Brigit threw out her arms to catch her balance. Danton hopped sideways. In that moment, the little red bag, which she had hung around her neck on its gold cord, slipped free from under her T-shirt. It was now on view for everyone to see. She had almost forgotten all about it. Quickly, she slipped it back inside. When she looked up, she saw Feenix watching her, but in the next second Feenix was distracted by something else. Brigit followed Feenix's gaze and understood why the turners had stopped. Superintendent Tiltersmith was standing in the doorway. He was still wearing his sharp three-piece suit, but he had changed into little sneakers. He came forward into the middle of the room and gazed around smiling. "Well, well. Am I interrupting something?"

Naturally, no one answered this.

Brigit snuck a look at Danton, who was sneaking a look at her. She turned away and felt the heat starting in her neck. It got as far as her chin, and then she managed to get it under control.

"Where is your teacher, I wonder?" Again, there was silence. "Hmm. Well, what fun. I certainly cannot leave you here unsupervised, can I? Why, what would the Central District Office have to say about something like that? But—wait!—I have an idea. Let us play a game together." He appeared delighted with the thought. "All of you against me. If you win, you will be allowed to leave school for the rest of the day."

Shouts of excitement went through the room.

"But—" he interrupted, one finger held up. "Of course, if *I* win, you'll stay right here." He let out a sound halfway between a laugh and a giggle.

To Brigit's relief, Danton spoke out. "Tell us what the game is before we agree."

The superintendent put his head to one side and examined Danton. "You again? I notice you keep turning up quite regularly, don't you? Well, how about a nice old-timey one that everybody knows? I call it Thunder, Rumble, Turn to Stone."

"We don't know that game," Danton said.

"Of course you do. In some places they call it Grandmother's Footsteps. I think you might call it Red Light, Green Light. Come along. Let's play. It will be a great treat for me. What do you have to lose?"

Before Danton could answer that question, the room erupted into shouting.

"Let's do it!"

"I'm ready!"

"Me too!"

Brigit saw that there was not going to be any stopping the Tiltersmith guy, and in just a few moments, all the kids were lined up against the far wall.

"Now," said the superintendent, "I see you already know what to do." His voice bounced in a confusing way against the gymnasium floor and walls. "My rules are probably a wee bit different than yours, so let me go over them. I will stand here at the front of the room. You will start over there at your home base. As soon as I turn and I cannot see you, you will all move toward me as quickly as you can. The idea is for one of you to tag me when my back is to you. However, I am free to turn around whenever I choose. I will give warning by yelling, *'Thunder, rumble, Grandma's here!'* but anyone I catch still moving will be turned to stone. And as stone they must stay, until someone still in the game manages to tag me. If I turn you *all* to stone before that happens, I win. However, if one of you does successfully tag me, I will chase that person back to home base. Should that person reach home base safely, the game goes to you. But—" He held up a warning finger here. "If I catch that person, the game is mine. What say you?"

There were murmurs of excited agreement.

"There's something about this I don't like," Feenix whispered.

Danton nodded. "Be careful."

"Are you ready?" the superintendent asked. Then he turned his back on them.

Most people ran forward quickly, including Feenix. Danton, however, took one big step and stopped. Then he took another. He covered an amazing amount of ground this way because of the length of his long legs, but he could also brake quickly. It was a good strategy, Brigit thought. She tried to stay right behind him, but he had gotten quite a bit ahead of her when the Tiltersmith yelled, *"Thunder, rumble, Grandma's here!"* and whipped around. Everybody froze. Where was Edward, Brigit wondered?

The superintendent had pulled his blue pen from his pocket. "I saw you, you, you, and you," he called, pointing the pen at Rohan, Beatrice, and a couple of kids from another class. He clicked his tongue each time he pointed. "You are now stone."

Beatrice was caught with one arm flung dramatically up in the air.

Superintendent Tiltersmith turned his back again. In this round he allowed a little more time to elapse without turning around. As Brigit passed Beatrice, she accidentally bumped her elbow. The elbow didn't move. It felt hard and cold as stone. Brigit glanced at Beatrice's face and saw that her mouth was wide open and her eyes were fixed in a stare of panic.

"Thunder, rumble, Grandma's here!" On this try the Tiltersmith caught five more people, but Brigit saw that none of them were part of their foursome. Danton was in the lead. She didn't dare to turn around, but she thought she saw Edward out of the corner of her eye. He hadn't gotten very far from home base at all. Just taken a few steps.

The third time the Tiltersmith turned, it seemed he couldn't find anyone to point to. He knit his brow and made a thinking face. "Well . . . hmm, let's see if we can speed this up a bit." He stepped forward into the crowd of kids facing him. "No moving," he warned.

From off to the side, Feenix yelled out, "Hey! You're not allowed to leave your spot like that. It's not in the rules."

The Tiltersmith whipped around to see who had spoken, but Feenix had shut her mouth tight and wasn't moving. "Oh yes. Sorry," he said. "I forgot to mention. In this version, Grandma is permitted to walk amongst you. You may move if you think I won't see you. But, of course, if I catch you— well . . ." He tick-tocked his pen back and forth in warning.

Now he walked over to Jorge, who had not yet been caught. The Tiltersmith leaned forward and stared right into Jorge's eyes. "No blinking," the Tiltersmith said. "Blinking counts."

Brigit was positioned where she could see the whole thing. A staring contest. She sent Jorge encouraging thoughts. *You can do it. You can do it.*

But he couldn't. At least not for long. "Out!" the superintendent called gleefully. Jorge took an angry breath, and then he froze, his face and his body growing stiff and still.

The superintendent turned again and searched for another victim. He came up behind Tessa and poked his finger in her armpit and began to tickle her, smiling as he did. Tessa made a valiant effort to stay still but in a few seconds yanked herself away from his hand. Half laughing, half pleading, she cried, "Please don't do—"

He pointed at her. "Out!" he called. Tessa stopped pleading in midsentence.

Brigit could feel the realization going through the room. If you moved on your own, he would almost certainly spot you. If you didn't, he would make you move. Feenix was keeping her mouth shut, probably because he was so close to her.

"Oh, this is more fun than I remembered," the Tiltersmith crowed. He swiveled on his little sneakers and grabbed hold of Asim's nose and pinched it.

"Ow!" Asim yelled, and then he, too, fell abruptly still as stone.

The superintendent turned again slowly, searching for a victim. Brigit quickly looked away. She certainly did not want to meet his eyes. A peppery taste of fear came up in the back of her throat. She knew suddenly that he was actually looking for *her*. She breathed as slowly and deeply as she could, and in the silence, she was sure she could hear everyone else's heart beating. He came toward her without haste, working his way around the other kids rooted to their spots.

When he was standing in front of her, he waited for a long moment, maybe trying to decide what would be the most fun way to make her move. Brigit waited, too.

The Tiltersmith leaned forward. "No blinking," he said. The irises in his pale-blue eyes grew unnaturally dark and dilated. Brigit gritted her teeth. She tried to imagine that she had toothpicks between her eyelids, forcing them open. But it was agony, and she knew she couldn't last. A moment later, she blinked.

But he didn't say, "Out." Instead, he laughed and reached toward the gold cord around her neck. "Tell me you agree to let me take this."

What? For a moment she didn't understand, and then she did.

"Tell me you agree, and I will let you go."

She thought of the slender green stems rising up toward the light. She thought of the worms and the robins and the blossoming tree. "No!" she said stubbornly.

A look of cold fury passed over his face. "Perhaps I can help you change your mind. Let us try this." He pointed his pen at her.

A shape moved into Brigit's peripheral vision, slipped up behind the Tiltersmith, and whapped him on the shoulder.

"*Race me, Granny!*" yelled Danton as he sprinted past. He stretched his legs and ran full-out toward the home base at the back wall.

The superintendent let out a hiss like a balloon releasing air, but it took only a second for him to begin the chase. Still, Brigit took a great breath of relief. No one was as fast as Danton when he went full-out.

"Run, everybody!" Danton yelled. "Run, Brigit!"

She began to race toward the back wall, too. She was actually pretty fast when she put her heart into it. Her heart was into it.

All around her the other students had turned and were racing back toward home base. The stone ones, too, were waking up and joining. Only Edward, who hadn't gotten far to begin with, stood where he was—not too far from the wall they were all heading toward—watching the scene.

The superintendent was catching up with Danton. Brigit didn't like the way he moved. He didn't seem to be making any effort at all, and yet he was covering far too much ground. He was going to catch up.

"Run, Danton! Run! He's right behind you!" she yelled.

Danton did not turn to look behind himself, but he must have heard her, because he jolted forward and his stride grew longer and faster.

Even this did not seem to help. The distance between Danton and the Tiltersmith shrank a little more. The superintendent reached out his arm toward Danton, and Brigit took a breath to let out another cry of warning, but before she could, Edward, who was still just standing there like a stuffed bunny, seemed to come awake.

"Hop to it, Danny man!" he called as Danton passed him.

Then Edward stuck out his foot. Or maybe he was just shifting his weight. The superintendent tripped and went flying to his knees. For a moment he knelt there, watching Danton as he put out his hand to touch the wall.

"Oooops, so sorry," Edward said.

20

Puzzle Pieces

"That was pretty brilliant, Ednerd," Feenix admitted as they went down the steps together. "That look on his face when he fell on the floor was priceless. I assume you tripped him on purpose, right?"

"Tripped who on purpose?" Edward asked.

She stopped and stared at him, trying to decide if he was serious or not. Then she noticed something else. "Hey! What happened to your hat?"

He frowned and patted his head and then froze. "My hat," he whispered. "Hat, hat, hat."

"You haven't had it all day," Danton told him.

"Maybe you left it at home?" Feenix suggested.

"Home?" Edward stared at her. A terrible thought seemed to cross his mind. "Oh no! I gotta go!" He took off practically at a run as they all watched in surprise.

"Wow," Feenix said. She turned and looked at Brigit and Danton. "What's happening today? Do you have the feeling there's an epidemic of weirdness going on?"

At these words, Brigit reached up and touched whatever it was that she had under her sweater.

"And you! What's that thing you're hiding under your sweater?"

Brigit looked at Feenix almost stubbornly and said nothing.

"Brigit, don't be such a little box of fairy farts. What is it? Aren't we your friends? Show us."

Slowly Brigit drew the red cloth bag out.

"What is it?" Feenix demanded. "What's in there?"

Brigit looked uncertain. "It's just, you know, a good-luck thing."

"What do you mean, a good-luck thing? Where'd you get it?"

"I don't know, exactly. Somebody must have given it to me, but I can't remember when. Maybe I've always had it."

Feenix stared at her through narrowed eyes. "He was trying to get it away from you, wasn't he? The Tiltersmith guy. Back there in the gym. Just like he keeps trying to get my juggling balls."

Danton spoke up abruptly. "Hey! You told the superintendent that you gave those things to Robert, but that wasn't true, was it? What *did* you do with them?"

Feenix looked around for some clue. The steps were almost empty by now. The sky was cold and gray, but across the street by the playground, the daffodils were blooming and more pink buds were opening on the trees. "I don't know," she said at last. "I keep thinking I'm forgetting things. Important things."

"Me too," said Brigit. "It's really frustrating, but let's do what Kit says, just stay patient and alert and keep listening to the back of our minds. I have a feeling it's going to come to us. It's like we have to get all the puzzle pieces in one place."

"Or maybe we're just hungry," Danton said. "Maybe it'll help if we go get some pizza. I wonder what happened to Robert, anyway," he added as they started up the hill.

21

Ed Goes In

When Edward got home that afternoon, he hurried up the steps to his room as quickly and quietly as he could. *Hat, hat, hat,* he repeated to himself over and over again. He could hear his aunt clattering around in the kitchen. It wouldn't do to have her stop him. He didn't want to get distracted, because what if he forgot again?

In his room he shut the door with a faint click. He saw with relief that his green baseball cap was sitting on the desk, right where he'd left it. He pulled off his jacket and threw it on the bed. Then he went over to the desk and, holding his breath, lifted the hat up by its brim.

Ahhhh. It was still there.

The cocoon looked just as it had yesterday. Leathery and big-toe shaped. Had that been only yesterday? It was ugly and very still. It lay as he had left it—with the exit hole facing up. He had been in a terrific rush to get home and check on it, but now that he was here staring down at it, he felt a funny unwillingness to get too close to the thing.

He picked up his observation journal again, but any notes he might have taken were still nowhere to be found. Well, this time he would be sure to keep them where he could find them.

First the measurements. He took his ruler, and being very, very careful to avoid the exit hole, he measured the thing's length and width. He wrote these numbers down clearly in his notebook. He wished he could remember what the measurements had been the first time he recorded them, but they were no longer certain in his head.

Next the weight. He would have to pick the thing up. He didn't want to touch it with his bare hands. In fact, the feeling of reluctance was growing stronger in him. There was something about it that he had forgotten. Some danger.

Edward stood there feeling torn. Perhaps he should just return to his molds. Or he could go downstairs and see if there were any muffins. Behind him, from somewhere in the vicinity of the bed, he heard a low snorkish croak. He jumped and turned around. There was a toad crouched on his rumpled jacket. It blinked at him with dark liquid eyes. Danton's *Bufo americanus*. It must have been riding around in his pocket since Danton had given it to him to hold.

Now, as Edward stared back at it, the creature's throat expanded outward like a tiny pale balloon. It gave three quick snorts in succession, and then its throat rapidly deflated.

Edward walked toward the bed, speaking softly. "It's okay, little fellow. I won't hurt you." He reached his hand out, and unexpectedly, the toad took two hops and landed in his palm, like it had been waiting at a bus stop and Edward's palm was the bus it had been waiting for.

When it shifted against his skin, the toad felt as cool and slippery to Edward as a handful of olives. He carried it over to his desk and put it down under the desk lamp. As he pulled out his phone to take a photo, the creature turned its head.

Edward followed its gaze and saw that it was looking with great interest at the cocoon.

"No!" cried Edward. But it was too late. The toad took a single unerring leap and landed smack on top of the little tear-drop-shaped hole. The next moment it was gone.

Forgetting himself, Edward crossed the room and grabbed hold of the cocoon with one hand. Desperately, he stuck a finger inside of it, feeling around for the toad.

Ed experienced a curious sensation, as if he was dissolving and expanding, as if his atoms were rushing apart and he was being released into an uncountable number of loosely connected bits traveling downward and upward and in all different directions. For how long this went on was a question that couldn't really be answered. Either time had stopped or Edward was moving at too many different speeds for it to be measured.

It was hard to think clearly, because Edward found himself full of Edwards, all of them thinking many different thoughts, which he wished he had more time to consider. However, all too soon a moment arrived when the dissolving reversed and reorganized itself. All the parts could feel themselves pulling together again toward a magnetic central pole.

Then *zwup*—there was one Edward (who would never again be able to think of himself as completely singular) standing in the middle of a dimly lit sort of cave. The air smelled damp and earthy, as if he had fallen into the depths of a great mountain. Dangling right over his head was the bottom of a rope ladder. He looked up to see where the ladder went, and could make out a distant light shining through a tiny teardrop-shaped opening. Was he inside the cocoon, then?

As if in answer, when he looked down at the ground, he saw several pennies and paper clips, a quarter, and the Lego fireman. He picked them up and put them in his pocket. No sign of his marble.

It seemed unlikely to Edward that what was happening here was really happening. Perhaps he was dreaming, or perhaps it was that his molds were emitting some sort of gas that caused hallucinations. On the other hand, if by some enormously unlikely chance it all actually was real, then it was an unparalleled scientific opportunity, one he should approach with as much logic and attention as he was capable of.

Cautiously, he turned around and examined the space more closely. It was not enclosed, for there was an opening in front of him that appeared to lead into a gently curving downward tunnel. The walls and the floor of the tunnel looked to be made of some kind of warm reddish rock that had been sanded smooth, maybe long ago by water or wind. It wasn't dark, and at first, he couldn't understand where the light was coming from. Then he saw, here and there, embedded in the clay-colored walls, translucent pancake-shaped stones. Each one gave off a soft rose-colored light.

Phosphorescence! He walked into the tunnel to examine the stones more closely. Mr. Ross had talked about this a bit in science class, how some stones could emit light when they were heated or put under pressure. But Edward remembered nothing that looked like these from the pictures Mr. Ross had shown them.

He needed to bring one back. It would be proof of where he'd been.

Wherever that was.

He gently tapped one of the stones, testing to see how difficult it might be to pull loose. To his astonishment the stone bunched itself up and appeared to swim away into the tunnel wall. As he watched this, transfixed, he heard a familiar *snork!* The toad, a few feet down the tunnel, was hopping rapidly away. It went round the bend and disappeared.

Edward considered quickly. He knew from his studies (and movies he had seen) that it was not a good idea to bring non-native elements or animals into alternate universes (if that was what this was) and leave them behind. Plus, Danton would most likely be upset if Edward didn't return the toad. He forgot about the phosphorescent stones for the moment and hurried forward along the tunnel, which continued to slope downward.

When he reached the place where the tunnel turned, Edward stopped. Caution was obviously what was called for here. Who knew what could be around the corner? He poked his head out carefully.

Nothing. Just more softly lit reddish tunnel. And there was the toad, not far ahead, hopping along intently, as if it knew exactly where it was going. Edward stepped out and hurried after it, but the toad moved faster. In a short while, the toad turned around another bend in the tunnel, and again, when Edward reached it, he slowed and stuck his head out first.

To his dismay, he saw that here the tunnel split into two widely diverging pathways. The toad had chosen the right-hand one and was hopping along without a backward glance. Edward, worried that he might forget which way to go when he returned, pulled out the little Lego fireman and dropped it as a marker on the pathway he was leaving behind. Then he took off after the toad.

Twice more, the toad brought him to places where the tunnel split itself into two new paths. The second time, the toad chose to go right again; the third time, it chose to go left. At each fork, Edward left a marker to remind himself which way to go on the way back. There was a dreamlike quality to this chase, and again, he considered the possibility that he was actually lying in his bedroom, fast asleep. He pinched himself, although he knew this was not really a logical thing to do. Why shouldn't a dream pinch hurt? But in this case, the pinch was so painful he cried out.

He continued after the toad, never quite catching up.

The toad led him around another bend, and here Edward came to a stop. The tunnel had come to an end at the bottom of three polished marble steps. At the top of the steps, the tunnel, which was no longer a tunnel, became a long, richly carpeted hallway. A really long hallway. There were no windows, but the hall was lit by chandeliers from which dangled chains of teardrop-shaped rubies.

The toad had already climbed the steps, but now it stopped a few feet along the hallway to wait for him. Edward hesitated only briefly and then followed. The carpeting was dark red with a design of creeping ivy along its borders. His feet made no sound as he went forward. Naturally, as soon as he began to walk, the toad started to hop. Edward cursed silently to himself.

He wondered if he was in someone's mansion. Or perhaps it was a hotel. Here and there were doors along the hallway. Each door had a crystal doorknob. There were paintings and sculptures here and there. Tall wooden cabinets with glass fronts mostly seemed to hold boring collections of fancy silver spoons or old snuffboxes. But one was full of papier-mâché masks painted in shiny lacquer colors, the frozen faces beautifully sculpted with every kind of expression, serene or angry or terrified. Another cabinet was full of beetles of every kind, carefully labeled—dung beetles, fire beetles, click beetles, violin beetles. Just as Edward stopped to look at this cabinet, the toad gave a loud *snork!*

Edward looked around quickly. "Where are you?" he whispered angrily.

Snork!

There was a door just a little way farther down the hall. Had the toad slipped beneath it? Ed put his ear to the wood panel. Silence. He turned the crystal knob cautiously, and the door swung open.

He caught himself just in time. One more step and he would have fallen out of the hallway and dropped into endless space. Before him was a vast floating cosmos of stars and dark emptiness. Was it our universe? Or another? He saw no constellations that he recognized, but that did not mean much. The stars he was looking at seemed much bigger and closer than ours, but maybe this was because he was viewing them from a completely new angle?

The problem was that no one was ever going to believe him. He took his phone out to try for a photo, but, of course, no reception. He tried to memorize a section of what spread itself in front of him, but it was impossible to do. Too many fiercely burning suns, and they all looked alike. If only he could bring some evidence back with him. Evidence that would prove he had actually been here.

Surely it was a coincidence, but at this moment an object separated itself from the background of stars and floated toward Edward. As it came closer, he saw it was a rock of some kind, glinting as it tumbled and turned. Perhaps it was a piece broken off from a distant planet or sun. Perhaps it had been traveling in this direction for thousands of years. It might be made of elements never before seen on earth. A wonderful find and a perfect piece of evidence! Edward knew full well that he wasn't a great catcher, but he leaned out, holding on to the doorframe with one arm. With the other, he reached into space.

The meteoroid was headed toward him, but he saw now that it was going to go a little high. He pushed himself out and up on his toes, still grasping the doorframe. He reached up with his other arm until his shoulder screamed for mercy. He imagined Feenix's voice in his ear. *Stretch it! Stretch it! Are you a man or a mouse or a rubber ducky?*

He stretched an inch higher.

The rock skimmed his fingertips and shot by. Edward fell back into the hallway. The door swung inward and shut. There was the toad, only a few feet up ahead. It snorked loudly and took off again. Edward got up and followed.

They passed perhaps another dozen doors, and Edward burned with curiosity, imagining what worlds might be on the other side of them. He was tempted to give up on the toad and do some exploring on his own. But for reasons he did not entirely understand, he felt a sort of responsibility to the creature. When it paused in front of a door that was slightly ajar and then hopped through it, Edward let out a cry of panic. What if it got sucked out into the void?

He hurried to the door as fast as he could and peered through the crack. What he saw was not what he'd expected—no black space, no stars, but a large room, dark and old-fashioned, with fancy wallpaper, a gray velvet sofa, and an empty fireplace. There was a second door on the far side, and in the middle of the room was a table with two chairs. The table was covered by a dark-red cloth, which hung down so far over the sides that it nearly touched the floor. On top of that were a pile of books, a deck of cards, and a half-finished jigsaw puzzle.

Except for the toad, who was sitting on the floor, the room was empty of life. Edward took a breath and stepped in quietly. "C'mere, you," he whispered fiercely. But the toad, not tired of this game yet, hopped a few steps and disappeared under the long tablecloth.

Edward crouched down. He lifted the cloth and peered into the dimness. There was the toad, over on the other side.

Snork! it said sharply. It sounded like a command. Edward had reached a point of extreme annoyance with the creature, but he crawled under the table. He slid his arm out, opened his hand, and brought it down.

He almost couldn't believe his luck. The toad hadn't moved, just watched him coming with its unblinking black eyes. It allowed itself to be picked up without a peep. Edward slid the creature into his left-hand pocket, zipped it up, and started to crawl backward.

It was then that he heard a click and the sound of the second door creaking open. He retreated back under the table-cloth and waited. There was a sliding noise. Not footsteps, not voices, but a rustle and a slither. With great caution, Edward peered under the edge of the tablecloth.

The thing was huge. He thought it was a snake at first, but then he saw the spindly legs folded up against its sides, and the paper-thin wings. Its scales were a yellowed ivory color, like old unclean teeth, and its eyes were red. In the middle it might have been as wide around as a small tree trunk, but it tapered off into a thin whiplike tail. Edward wished he could get an idea of how long it was, but it moved in waves, never fully expanding itself.

Now it paused. Its head, wide and shovel shaped, came curling around on the end of its thick boneless neck. The mouth opened, and a forked tongue darted out to taste the air.

Edward assumed it was noticing an unusual scent in the air of the room. Namely him.

22

The Bee Lady

The thing began to slide in slow sickening waves across the floor, toward the table under which Edward was hiding. He wondered if possibly he could outrun it. One way or another, he'd have to try to make a break for freedom before it got any closer.

His heart was pounding in his chest. He dropped the toad into his pocket and crouched in a running position and leaned forward. Then, just as he was about to leap out from under the table, he stopped. Another sound had entered the room. A faint humming, buzzing noise.

The great serpent creature paused and turned its head toward the second door. A pair of bare brown feet came quietly into the room and stopped. Edward could see the hem of a rippling watery blue skirt.

"What are you up to, Old Jail Keeper?" It was a woman's voice, or perhaps a girl's. A rich, bright voice, but the speaker sounded impatient. "You know you are supposed to keep ten feet away from me. Move over to your post right now."

The creature answered with a long hiss. It flicked its tongue again.

"What? You smell something delicious? Well, I took something for you from the kitchen. And I may give it to you if you keep your crawling scaly self at a distance. Go! Settle yourself now."

The creature fixed the woman with its little red eyes and then headed to the other side of the room. Ed's heart dropped as he saw it curl itself up right in front of the door he'd come in by, like an enormous jumbled dirty-white garden hose.

The woman sighed deeply and then pulled out a chair and sat down at the table, the same table under which Edward was hiding. Edward became aware, again, of the humming and buzzing. It grew louder and then settled itself into a soft drone. The woman was shuffling the deck of cards. It wasn't long before she began to slap them down impatiently onto the table. He wondered if it would be safe to speak to someone who kept a pet like that thing over by the door. Then, even as he was making up his mind, one of the cards came fluttering to the floor and landed half under the table. The jack of hearts. He waited, holding his breath.

He heard her shift the chair backward. The humming grew louder again. Should he speak? Should he move away? She stuck her head under the tablecloth to see where the card had gotten to, and their eyes met. Hers were blue with a bright fractured light, like when the morning sun comes up over the sea and throws its first rays across the horizon. He had to look away.

When he looked at her again, he saw where the humming was coming from. Her hair was piled up with dozens of silver pins in a blazing mop on top of her head. And woven all through the pins and the mop of hair was a garland of white clover and yellow dandelions. Helicoptering in and out of these flowers was a throng of bees.

He let out a sharp breath, but she put her finger warningly to her lips. "Now where did that infernal card fall to?" she asked loudly. Across the room, the creature hissed and began to uncoil.

"No, no, you detestable worm," the bee lady called out. "Do not trouble yourself! I do not want your help. You know your eyes are worse than useless. You would just be in my way. Stay where you are."

The serpent must have settled itself back down, for it made no further sound.

A moment later the lady crawled under the table. Immediately the little space was filled with an almost over-powering scent of clover and cut grass. She sat on her heels and studied Edward intently. The bees seemed to be interested in him, too. Was it possible that she actually kept a hive in that tangle of hair? He wasn't afraid of bees. They were fascinating insects, and if you stayed still, they wouldn't sting you. But this was a lot of bees. They floated all around him, flying up and down, checking him out.

"What has taken you so long?" she demanded in an agitated whisper.

He stared at her.

"Speak," she ordered. "He has sent you with a sword or a spell of some kind?"

"I don't know what you mean. Nobody sent me. I got in by accident."

"Accident? That is not possible. You must have had assistance."

"I'm telling you. I didn't have any assistance. I just fell in. I was chasing a toad."

"A toad!" she exclaimed. "Where is it?"

In spite of her bossy manner, he took the toad from his pocket. "Be careful," he told her. "I mean it. I went through a lot to get hold of this little guy, and I've got to bring him back."

He opened his hand. The toad slipped from his fingers and jumped directly onto her palm. The bees fell quiet. Now the bee lady seemed to forget all about him. She bent over the toad, and the toad gazed back up at her.

There was no conversation that Edward could hear, except for an occasional whispered *snork*. But at last the lady lifted her head, a fierce expression on her face. "It appears that things are far worse than I feared. What a mess you people have made. You're certain you didn't bring an invisibility cloak or some such device?"

Edward looked at her, baffled. "An invisibility cloak?"

"To get me out of here."

"I don't own an invisibility cloak," he answered.

She shook her head with impatience. "Well, in any case, you have found me, which is better than nothing. We mustn't lose hope. Now you will go back and find my Green One. He is surely delayed or caught somewhere. You must discover some way to bring him to me."

Edward had no clue what she was talking about. "Well, I'd love to go back, and if I can find you some help, I'm happy to do it. But if you can't get past that snake or whatever it is, how do you expect me to do it? Is it poisonous, by the way?"

"No . . . It merely kills its prey by squeezing it so tight it stops the creature's heart. It is always hungry. Lord Lopside keeps it that way on purpose, of course. It will go after anything that moves. But you have nothing to fear. Its wings are useless, and I have a large raspberry tart. It loves sweets above all other things. If I leave this room, it will follow me. That is its charge. I will take it on a little walk through this dank and sunless kingdom. As soon as we are gone, return to your world as quickly and quietly as you are able, and find my Green One."

The news that he was going to get out of there without being squeezed to death was so relieving, Edward decided not to worry about the rest for the moment. He simply nodded at her. "Okay," he said. "I'll do my best." She handed him the toad, and he dropped it into his pocket.

He waited for her to go. But now she did something alarming. She leaned toward him and she whispered, "Good. Now I will kiss you to make certain you do not forget me."

He watched in hypnotized fascination as her lips came toward his. He had been glancing at her now and then throughout their whole conversation. Although he wouldn't have been able to describe her, he was pretty sure she was one of the most beautiful people he'd ever seen. He was so nervous he felt dizzy. The bees seemed to stop and hover right where they were, as if they, too, were dying to see what would happen.

All his life he was going to wonder what it would have been like to be kissed by her, because a low, impatient hissing accompanied the sound of the serpent slithering over the floor, and the lady sat back abruptly on her heels. "He is such an incorrigible busybody," she said with a shudder of disgust. Then she called out, "Yes, you murderous bone crusher, I hear you. I am coming. I have found the card. But I grow tired of these foolish games. I would take a walk now. Let us go down to the river and smell the swamp gas and the bog rot, shall we?"

Again, the creature gave out a low whispering hiss.

"Yes, yes. I will give you the treat I brought. But stay well away from me." With an exasperated shake of her great buzzing head, she scooted backward, then climbed out from under the table. A moment later, she was passing through the second door, the serpent trailing hungrily behind her.

Edward peered out to watch them go. After he had counted to sixty, he stood up, stiff from crouching, and hobbled over to the door. He grabbed hold of the crystal doorknob and twisted it. To his dismay, it turned loosely but didn't seem to catch. There was no click, and the door did not open. He turned it the other way, and the effect was the same. He grabbed it harder and pressed and twisted and jiggled and pushed.

Was it broken? Had the serpent somehow locked it? He took a trembling breath and grabbed the doorknob with both hands and yanked as hard as he could.

The doorknob fell off in his hands, and the door clicked and swung open silently.

In the next moment he was running back down the long hallway.

He bounded over the carpet beneath the glittering chandeliers and past the other doors and the cabinets full of curiosities.

If only he could bring one small thing back with him to use as evidence of his adventure. He hesitated for just a moment in front of a cabinet full of small potted cacti. They grew in the most fantastic shapes and colors. He was sure there was nothing like them anywhere on earth. But tempted as he was, he could not bring himself to open the door. He was far too honest to take a thing that did not belong to him. He ran on.

The hallway seemed twice as long as it had been on his way in, but at last he was at the top of the three marble steps. He jumped to the bottom and hurried around the bend. When he came to the first fork, he stopped and searched for the silver paper clip. There it was. He turned right.

At the next fork, he stopped and found the quarter. He turned left.

One more fork and there was the Lego fireman. He turned left again.

Once he thought he heard a stealthy slithering, but it could have been that he had just imagined this. He ran faster.

The light grew dimmer and dimmer. If things were in the same place as before, he should be nearly to the cave room with the ladder. He put his hands up in the air to feel for it.

Edward, not a praying sort, simply made a polite request to his aunt's Forces That Be: *Please let it be there.*

Something brushed his shoulder, and he nearly cried out. The ladder! He reached blindly, batting at the air. In a moment he had it. Reaching as high as he could, he grabbed hold of a rung and hoisted himself up. His feet found their footing, and he gave a mighty push with his legs and grabbed hold of the next rung. Up he went. And up.

When he had climbed until he could climb no more, he allowed himself a pause to catch his breath and search the air over his head. He was looking for the little teardrop-shaped hole of light that should be at the top. Where was it? All he could see was darkness. Could the opening have shriveled up? Would he be stuck down here forever?

Or have his bones crushed by that thing?

From his pocket came a sharp scolding *snork!* The sound gave him a new burst of energy. He reached again and climbed ten more rungs.

When he looked once more, there it was. The hole he had entered by. But would it let him out from this side? He reached up and put his finger to the light.

23

A Cardboard Box

When Edward opened his eyes the next morning, the first thing he saw was the toad. It was sitting on the edge of his pillow, staring at him. He sat up with a jerk. "You!" he accused. "What are you doing here? I saw you in that awful dream last night." The toad didn't answer, just regarded him quietly.

Edward stared back at it. Then he reached out and picked the little creature up. Swinging his legs over the bed, he stood up. He was surprised how stiff and sore he felt. He went over to the terrarium slowly and plopped the toad in. Then he threw in some mealworms from his emergency mealworm supply. As he was doing this, he noticed the old cocoon still sitting on his desk. He shivered and reminded himself that it had only been a dream. Still, it wouldn't do to have his aunt noticing the thing.

Once again, he felt an odd reluctance to touch it. He found a crumpled paper bag under his desk and, using it as a glove, picked the cocoon up and folded it inside. He slid the bag under his bed.

When Danton got into the kitchen that morning, his mother was rushing around getting Mikey's lunch together.

"Danny," she said, "could you take him to school for me this morning? Looks like there's going to be another freeze today, and I'd better get right over to the store. I've lost enough of my stock already with this awful weather. Your dad had a rehearsal last night, and he's still sleeping." Danton agreed, although he'd been hoping he might run into Brigit on the way to school.

By the time he had dropped Mikey off and then raced to the fountain plaza, it was empty. He crossed the street and redoubled his leaps and bounds. He ran along the outside of the park, following the low stone wall that was its boundary here. He hadn't gotten very far when he spotted Brigit up ahead.

Way up ahead. "Brigit! Brigit!" he shouted, but she didn't seem to hear him. He even tried calling out the pet name he knew her family used. "Birdie!" he yelled.

But now she had stopped right in front of the narrow park entrance at Garfield Place and was pulling something out from under the neck of her coat. With a little click of memory, he thought of the bag she had shown Feenix and him yesterday. It was hard to see from where he was, but it looked like she was opening it and pouring something into her hand. A moment later she turned and disappeared into the park.

He sprang forward with renewed energy. Surely, he could catch up with her.

A few minutes later he, too, reached the narrow entrance-way, and he hurried in after her along the curved pathway, which ran between two little hills. When he came to the end of it, he was standing with the open rolling park in front of him. To the right was the little toddler playground his dad used to bring him to when he was a kid.

He looked all around as he walked forward. There was no sign of Brigit anywhere. Something else, however, did catch his eye. All along the edge of the playground, there was a parade of tall-stemmed daffodils. They weren't fully opened yet, but under the cold gray flatness of sky, they shone out like yellow candle flames. He'd seen a few near the school yesterday, but these were the first he'd seen in Prospect Park. His heart leaped up. How were they managing it in this weather? What amazing flowers daffodils were. His mother would be so happy when he told her.

But where was Brigit? Where could she have gotten to? And Hellamenopee, he was thirsty! He stopped and opened his backpack to look for his water bottle but discovered he had forgotten to refill it. He doubted the water fountains had been turned on yet. It had been too cold. But he looked around and spotted one just inside the little playground.

He walked over to it and was surprised by its appearance. It didn't look like any water fountain he remembered seeing around here before. This one had a wide dark metal bowl, and around its rim metal birds and dragonflies peeped out from dark bronze leaves. The water spout was in the shape of a frog, which reminded him of something, though he couldn't think of what. He decided to give the fountain a try and put his finger on the button. You never knew.

The water came rushing out. Gratefully and thirstily, he leaned over and drank. It was amazingly delicious water, like it was being pumped in, fresh and cold, straight from a mountain spring. When he stood back, his thirst was quenched. He filled his water bottle and returned it to his backpack.

Now it seemed to him as he looked around again that his vision had grown suddenly clearer and sharper. There wasn't a sign of anything moving, but his eye was stopped by something standing in the middle of the toddler playground. He was sure it hadn't been there back in the old days. In fact, he had the notion that it hadn't been there a moment ago, but he must just not have noticed it.

It was a statue.

He went over to take a closer look.

It wasn't big. Nothing huge or grand like the panthers. Just a small bronze sculpture of a young man with a bird's nest on his head. The young man held his hand out in front of himself. On his finger was perched a bronze bird, maybe a robin.

Danton examined the statue curiously for a few moments, and just as he was about to turn away, he noticed there was a cardboard carton at its feet. A piece of loose-leaf paper had been pinned to the top. On it were these words: *Free! Take me!*

Danton lifted a flap to see what was inside.

24

Math Class and Probability

Feenix, Brigit, and Edward waited for Danton on the school steps that morning, and he was nearly late, but he showed up just as the first bell rang. Feenix noticed right away that he had something big and knobby inside his backpack. She was immediately burning with curiosity. She poked at it.

"What's that? What you got in there?" He frowned as if he didn't know what she meant, and pulled the pack off his back to take a look. As soon as he unzipped it, he brightened.

"Oh, I nearly forgot! I found it in the park this morning. In a cardboard box." He pulled out a tarnished-looking horn of some sort, like a small trumpet. It had red ribbon tied around one of its curvy parts. "I think it might be a real antique. I can't wait to show it to my dad. There was a note on it, too."

He reached in the pack again and pulled out the crumpled piece of paper. Feenix took the paper and examined it. On the front it said, *Free! Take me!* She was about to hand it back to him when she noticed something else written on the back: *Use only in Dire Need.*

Something in those words made her stop. Where had she heard them recently? Before she could come up with an answer, Brigit whispered a warning. "Don't look up! The superintendent is at the front door. He's watching us."

Feenix froze and did as Brigit said. "Put the horn away," she said to Danton sharply. "You don't want him to see it."

"I don't?"

"Just do what I say."

As they passed by the superintendent, they felt his eyes on them, but he said not a word. The front-door security guard, Mrs. Willard, was warning everybody to keep their coats on.

"Furnace isn't working right," she said. "It's getting cold in here."

All during morning classes, Feenix kept her ears and her eyes open, expecting him to walk in the door at any moment. But he didn't. Meanwhile, the temperature in the school dropped steadily.

By the time math class rolled around, the furnace seemed to have completely given up. Everybody hunched over their desk and went to work on the Do Now problems.

Mr. Albers patrolled the aisles. He was such a chin wart. "Are you working, Edith?" he asked.

No, she answered in her head, *I'm riding my tricycle upside down on the ceiling*. "Yup," she said.

DO NOW—Review

1. Elmer Fudd rolls a single die two times. The first time he rolls a 5. What are the chances he will roll a 5 on the second roll?

2. You flip a penny nine times. It comes up heads each time. Is it more likely that it will come up heads or tails on the tenth flip?

Feenix was distracted by one of those robins tapping again at the window. It met her eye and flew off. To help herself think, she started sketching a picture of a large die lying on a table. Its top face showed five dots. She stared at it. She tried to remember the rules about how often it would turn up one number instead of another. Nothing definite came to mind. She knew it was supposed to be random, but she could never really bring herself to believe that. What if there were actually invisible forces inside of the die or the penny?

She found herself imagining that the die was a little room. She sketched a scene inside of it. There was a pot hanging over a fire in a fireplace. She added a table with three chairs and three old witches playing cards—a fat bald one, a tall skinny one with long scraggly hair, the third with a kerchief around her head.

Mr. Albers said, "All right, anybody got an answer for number one? You throw the die and roll a five. What are your chances of rolling a five if you roll it again?"

Kseniya raised her hand. "One out of six," she said. "It is the same as it is before."

"Very good. It's a trick question, isn't it? Because what you rolled the first time does not affect what you will roll the second time. There are six sides to a die and an equal chance that you might roll any of those numbers on any throw. So one out of six is always the correct answer. Now what about the second question? If you flip a penny nine times and it comes up heads each time, is it more likely that it will come up heads or tails on the tenth throw?"

Mr. Albers called on Asim, who didn't have his hand up at all.

"Uhhh. Well, I guess it's more likely that it will turn up tails."

"And your reasoning is?"

"Well, it's already turned up heads so many times. It's too weird for it to just keep turning up heads. It's gotta change at some point soon, so it seems more likely it will be tails this time."

Mr. Albers's glasses had slid down low to the tip of his nose. His brow darkened. He looked at the class accusingly as if they were all guilty of the same outrageous crime. "The trap! The trap! He fell into the trap. Someone pull him back out."

Kseniya raised her hand again.

Feenix wondered what had happened to Robert. Robert had always been a person with a perfect attendance record. Not that she would ever admit it, but she was beginning to be a little worried about him. Was it possible that she had gotten him in trouble over those juggling balls?

Kseniya was going on. "It is the same way you explain for the die. What comes before does not make a matter. With a penny it is always fifty-fifty chance that it will make the tail. One time you throw penny does not make a change to the next time. Each one is separate."

"But somehow that just doesn't feel right," someone argued from the back of the room.

Mr. Albers said, "It doesn't, does it? Why not? Because our experience tells us that *over time* the number of heads and tails will generally even out. In fact, the bigger the sample—I mean, the more tosses you make—the more likely that around half of them will be heads and half will be tails. What are the chances that if all of you, at the same time, throw a penny up in the air, they would all come down heads? Very, very small. But for each of you, individually, the chance that you will throw heads is subject to a simple, unyielding law. It can turn up heads or it can turn up tails. The chances of its doing one or the other are always fifty-fifty."

"But what about luck?" somebody else said. "Doesn't luck play a part in any of this?"

And now Feenix could feel it coming. Like the way you can feel the electricity gathering in the air before a thunderstorm and the hair on your arms stands up.

Before Mr. Albers could open his mouth, there was a knock at the door. He crossed the room with a frown. He opened the door just a crack. Then just wide enough to stick his head out. From inside the room, Feenix could hear the rumbling of a voice, but she couldn't see who was out there. Mr. Albers pulled his head back in and addressed the class. "I will return in just a moment. Please turn to page one hundred thirty-seven and continue with the work we were doing yesterday." He stepped into the hallway, leaving the door half-open. The murmuring of the voices moved away.

Brigit and Feenix looked at each other while a growing noise went through the room, hushed and sneaky at first, then louder and happier. Alberto threw a rubber eraser at the back of Tessa's head, and she threw it back at him. A girl let out a muffled scream and then a laugh. Eight-Armed Phil, who was taking drum lessons, began a solo on his desktop with two wooden chopsticks that he carried everywhere in case an opportunity for practice arose. Everybody kept an eye on the door, but when Mr. Albers didn't return, Beatrice and Alison and that crowd got up and leaned on the windowsill.

"Look!" Beatrice said. "More robins. It's like an invasion. Where are they all coming from?"

It was here that a low, amused voice rumbled out from the back of the classroom.

"Now *that* is an interesting question. I, personally, would give a lot to know where all these robins are coming from."

Silence fell.

Feenix really didn't want to turn around, but accepting the inevitable, she finally did.

There he was. Sitting in the last chair by the window. She was more angry than afraid. How had he gotten in? He had his notepad and his fancy midnight-blue pen out.

Phil put his chopsticks away. Anybody who had been standing returned to their seat. There was no longer any sound from the hallway, either. Where had Mr. Albers gotten to? The Tiltersmith was smiling, but Feenix wasn't taken in for a second.

He stood up and looked directly at her and then began to walk toward the front of the room. She turned away and stared at the board. She pretended not to listen to the little pointed boots snapping smartly closer.

When the boots drew level with where the foursome sat, they stopped for only a moment and then proceeded on to the front of the room, where the Tiltersmith turned to face the class with a nod. "How pleasant to see you all again. Unfortunately, it appears that there's a little situation going on, and your teacher has been temporarily called away. But there's no reason we can't finish this lesson together, is there? I love this cold weather, don't you? So good for keeping the mental faculties sharp." He tapped his forehead and scanned the Do Now problems.

"Ah, the infamous laws of probability." He smiled again. "Let's play a game, shall we? We can all play together. A little game of chance."

He reached his hand into his pocket and then brought out a clinking fistful of something. "Ready?" he asked. "Everybody catch one." Into the air he threw a cloud of pennies. The copper coins flew up, sparkling and spinning, and then came tumbling down.

Most of the kids laughed and dove and scrambled until everybody had a penny. Edward picked his up, too. Only Feenix, Brigit, and Danton stayed frozen where they were. The Tiltersmith came over and bent down and picked up three pennies from the floor. He put one on each of their desks.

"We're going to go around the room, and each shall toss their penny. Let's see how the laws of probability play themselves out today. And to spice it up, we'll make it Heads or Consequences, shall we?"

"What's Heads or Consequences?" Asim asked

"Ah—you do not know this game? If you toss a head upon your turn, you receive a prize."

"What's the prize?" someone else asked.

"Ah—well, let me see. Let us do as we did yesterday. If your penny turns up heads, you may leave the school now. If you toss a tail, you will pay the consequence."

"What kind of consequence?" Edward asked.

Superintendent Tiltersmith lifted his licorice-black eyebrows. "Oh, I don't know. Some little thing. A kind of booby prize. I'll even let you pick. Worth a gamble, don't you think? To be let out of your cage and allowed to join the robins at their play. We don't have robins where I come from."

"Where are you from?" someone asked.

"Oh." He waved his hand as if to brush a mosquito away. "You will not have heard of the place. A quite distant latitude. No seasons to speak of. But let's get on with our experiment, shall we? There's no time to waste."

And in the next moment he began walking around from desk to desk, watching each student toss a coin.

"Heads!" called Alberto.

"Heads!" called Tessa.

"Heads!" called Asim.

Every toss turned up heads, and every student who tossed a coin was allowed to pack up their stuff and leave immediately with a special pass.

"Somehow, I don't think this is good," Feenix whispered to the others.

Brigit and Danton nodded, but Edward merely looked interested. "I wonder how he does that?" he said.

Feenix knew with dread that the Tiltersmith was saving them for last. When he got to Kseniya, eleven heads had already been tossed, without a single tail.

"I think," she said, "it is most unlikely."

The superintendent eyed her with interest. "So what about luck? Are you one of the ones who doesn't believe in luck?"

"No. There is just probability."

The Tiltersmith put his hands out innocently. "But even if you do not believe in luck, didn't you say that a single toss is not affected in any way by another toss? Each one of you has the same chance of throwing heads. There is nothing to prevent every one of you from tossing heads from here to the end of your universe. Am I not correct?"

"Yes and no," Kseniya said stubbornly. "Over course of time, laws of probability show heads and tails will begin to come even. Maybe there is something wrong with your coins."

"Tell you what," he said to Kseniya. "Feel free to use your own coin if you do not trust me."

Kseniya considered this. "Well, I do not trust your coins, but I prefer to go home and finish my application to STEM summer camp. I think I take *your* penny." She tossed her gleaming penny in the air and caught it in her palm. "Heads," she said. As she left the room, the Tiltersmith bowed to her, grinning. She ignored him.

One by one each student tossed a shining penny, and each penny turned up heads. At last, there were only five students left in the room—Feenix, Brigit, Edward, Danton, and Beatrice the Poisonous Toadstool.

The Tiltersmith addressed Edward first.

"My scientific friend. How about you? Your own coin or mine?"

Edward said, "Oh, your coin, I think. I've got some stuff I'm working on at home, too."

Ed flipped his coin, and it also came up heads. "May I keep it?" Edward asked the superintendent.

The superintendent said, "Hmm. Well, I'll make you a bargain. You may keep it in exchange for some information. Remember that moth you were looking for?"

Edward stared in surprise. He furrowed his brow, thinking. "Yes," he said at last. "I do."

"Would you tell me what you did with its carrying case? Did you put it somewhere safe, I hope?"

"Uh, yeah. I added it to my collection."

"And where is your collection?"

"In my room," Edward replied.

"Perfect." The superintendent smiled. "Well, off with you, then."

As soon as Edward was gone, the Tiltersmith turned to Beatrice. "Your turn, I think."

"I'll use yours," she said before he could ask. She tossed it in the air, and it landed with a tiny click on her desk. She bent over to look. She frowned.

"Hey! That's not fair," she spluttered.

The Tiltersmith made a really fake-sounding *tch* noise. "Oh, tails? Bad luck!"

"I want another turn," she demanded.

"Now, now, that is not sporting." He waved his pen

scoldingly at her. "A little booby prize for you. What's your least-favorite vegetable?"

"What? My least-favorite vegetable?"

"Yes. Tell us."

"Cabbage," she said. "What does that have to do with anything?"

He clicked his tongue. "Oh my, look at that up on the ceiling, everyone!"

Everybody did what he said, but nobody saw anything of interest. When they looked back down, Beatrice was gone.

Sitting on the desk was a cabbage, a pale-green ball of tightly packed leaves.

"What did you do with her?" Feenix demanded.

"Come, come. What a question."

"Who are you?" Feenix asked. "What kind of game are you playing at?"

His mouth stretched wide into a tight, impatient grin. "I cannot deny that if there's any fun to be had, I'm the one who is all for it. But this is no game. Time is nearly up, and I have gone to a great deal of trouble to arrange this moment alone with the three of you. You each have something I need. Let's go back to you first." He fastened his pale-blue eyes upon Feenix. "The juggling balls, please. You will tell me what you did with them."

"Look," Feenix said. "I'm sorry I misled you before, but I seriously can't remember where I put them. I've looked and looked."

At these words the Tiltersmith lifted one of his tiny feet and stamped the floorboards. "Enough!" he cried, and a thin black crack opened where his foot came down. He stamped again, and now the crack spread like breaking ice and widened. "Tell me what you did with those juggling balls!"

Feenix drew herself up angrily. "Ms. Trevino is not going to like that."

"Ms. Trevino is a toad," he replied.

Feenix threw a questioning glance at Danton. But if he noticed, he gave no sign.

"Look," she said reasonably to the Tiltersmith. "I'm telling you the truth. I can't remember what I did with them."

"How would you like to become something with eight legs and six eyes until you *can* remember the answer?" He pointed his pen at her. "I'll give you to the count of three. One . . . two . . ."

Out of the corner of her eye, Feenix saw Brigit lunge forward and grab the cabbage.

She threw it straight and true at the Tiltersmith's hand. The pen fell from his grasp and rolled toward the crack he had made in the floor with his little foot. In a moment the pen dropped over the edge and disappeared under the floorboards. While the Tiltersmith was down on his hands and knees, cursing loudly and trying to find it, Danton picked up his backpack, Feenix picked up the cabbage, and they all raced out the door.

"Go, go, go, go!" Feenix yelled.

25

The Horn

In the hallway they were met by a lot of commotion. Mr. Albers was standing there trying to direct traffic.

"What were you people still doing in there?" he demanded of the threesome as they shot out of the doorway. "Didn't you hear the announcement? The furnace is completely down, and there's some kind of weather coming. If your family has been notified and has given permission, you may sign out at the front door. Otherwise, please go down to the basement to wait. Let's move it, please."

"Okay! Got it!" Danton waved and kept going. He did not lead Brigit and Feenix toward the basement or the front door.

"Where are we going?" Feenix yelled at him.

"We've got to put as much distance as we can between us and him. Let's do it fast."

The wind hit them the moment they got out the side exit. "Keep going!" Danton yelled. "Look at how weird the light's gone. It's all sort of green." Even as the words were out of his mouth, his phone went off with that brain-paralyzing alarm that signaled public danger. Brigit's went off a moment later, and then Feenix's.

"Tornado warning!" cried Danton. "C'mon. Let's get farther away from the school. Up this street and then we'll find some shelter."

As they all crossed over to the opposite corner, they felt the first slashes of rain. Soon it was hard to see even a few feet in front of themselves. The wind screamed and whipped all around them.

"It's him!" Brigit tried to warn them. "It's got to be him!" But the wind carried her voice away.

They had gone maybe halfway up the block of old brownstone buildings when the sound of the rain changed to a knocking and clattering and cracking. "Hail!" cried Feenix.

The hail slammed against the windows and the buildings and clanged against the parked cars. In no time at all the sidewalks were covered with treacherous slippery hailstones.

"I think we better hold on to each other!" Danton cried out. "Where are you guys? Is that you, Brigit?" Brigit slid over to him, and there was his familiar face, wet and glowing with the rain. It looked down searchingly into hers. "You okay?" he asked. It was a relief to know that he probably couldn't see her blush as he took her arm.

"Where are you, Feenix?" he called out.

"I'm up here," Feenix yelled. "I'm holding on to a No Parking sign. It's cemented into the ground. Come to me, and we can all hold on to each other and the pole at the same time."

They made their way to her, and they all linked arms around the pole. For a few minutes nothing could be seen because of the fury of the pelting hailstones. Then something began to take shape, whirling up the street. Something, Brigit was sure, that wanted to be seen. A thing moving like a spinning top, the color of soot and ashes and taller than a man. It grew taller as it approached, tearing up trees and bushes from the little gardens, spitting dust and leaves and shards of ice into the air around itself. It came with a deafening roar that grew louder and louder, and inside the roaring there was a noise like voices babbling to each other.

"Is that a tornado?" Feenix screamed over the wind, but nobody bothered to answer her.

"Maybe we could find an alleyway to get into!" Brigit suggested, looking around frantically. But there weren't any alleyways. On this block the brownstones were all attached to each other without a chink of space in between them to hide in.

"Just hold as tight as you can!" Danton commanded. She could feel his breath against her ear. "It's moving fast. It'll pass quickly, I think." The twister was only a few houses away now and had grown nearly as tall as the rooftops. The light around them dimmed, as if night had come early. The spinning cloud of dust and ice edged closer. Brigit hated its laughing and roaring and babbling in her ears. She would have fought it and kicked at it if she had thought it would do any good.

The twister was almost upon them, and a great whiplash of wind grabbed the No Parking sign and tore it from the pole. The pole held, but the whole world seemed to go dark. Brigit sensed that they were almost right in the middle of the thing. Danton bent to her ear again. "Don't be scared. It'll pass." She knew he was wrong. This thing wasn't going anywhere until it got what it wanted.

The spout stalled right where they were, whirling round and round them, babbling and laughing and hungry to rip them away from each other. It was then that she saw the stream of light coming from Danton's backpack. The top zipper was still a little bit open. "Stand still and hold on to me!" she ordered Danton.

If he said something, she couldn't hear it. But in a moment, she felt him grab her around the waist, and she let go of the pole and reached over to his backpack. She tugged the zipper all the way open and pulled the trumpet out. It looked nothing like it had before. Had Danton polished it? It blazed out with a golden light into the darkness. She pushed it into his hand. "Play it. Play it!" she yelled. "Feenix and I will hold on to you."

She saw him bring his face close and look at her in disbelief. "What?"

"You're supposed to play it!" she cried out into the wind. "We're in dire need!"

Feenix must have heard her and understood. "Do what she says! She must be right!"

Danton shook his head hopelessly, but he lifted the horn to his lips. He took a breath and blew. On the first try, a cracked squawk blew out over the wind. On the second, a sheeplike bleat emerged. On the third, he tilted the trumpet up toward wherever the sky should have been. He took another breath and puffed out his cheeks. Then he blew three notes up, up, up, straight through the storm. Each note was distinct and round and pure as gold.

A great babbling cry of dismay filled the air. For a few moments the twister continued to turn, but then, like some machine that had cracked somewhere deep inside itself, the twister stalled and let out a great hollow groan. It bent to one side and then to another and then collapsed inward.

They watched as the funnel lost its shape and unraveled into a thousand twisted wires of gray smoke. In the end it scattered away on the gibbering and crying wind. They let go of each other and the iron pole.

Slowly the rain and the hail clattered to a halt. Overhead the thick leaden dome of sky broke and shifted itself into clouds. There was no sign of the sun. The temperature, however, rose a little. Everything was wet and dripping, and moisture rose up from the ground, bringing a fresh smell of earth with it. When Brigit looked up into Danton's face, she saw that he was watching the sky, too. Then he looked down at her, and for a second she imagined that he was going to kiss her.

"Danny!" a deep voice called out, and a car pulled up beside them. A big man wearing jeans and a leather jacket, his hair in beaded dreads, jumped out. Danton's father. A kind-looking man, though his face was very serious today.

"You kids all right? I've been looking for you everywhere. Danton's mom was crazy to get you home before the storm."

"We're okay, Dad. But we got caught in that twister. Did you see it?"

"Was there a twister? I didn't see it, but I sure did feel that wind. I had to stop and pull over. It's a wonder none of you were injured. Come on and get in the car. You'll tell me all about it. You too, ladies—everybody jump in. I'll get you home. Your parents will probably be worried sick."

Brigit and Feenix sat in the back while Danton chattered away to his dad about the storm. Brigit noted that he said nothing about the trumpet and that it was nowhere in sight. Feenix soon jumped into the conversation. Brigit listened to the three of them all talking at once, as people do after some great calamity has been narrowly averted. Danton, particularly, was as cheerful as eggs and pancakes with orange juice.

Brigit loved this cheerfulness in him, but she knew that there was something they were meant to do, and whatever this was, it was still waiting to be done.

PART THREE

26

Danton's Water Bottle

In the morning there was a mist over everything. All the water from the earth was rising up and covering the world in a shimmering silvery gray. Feenix was really thirsty when she got to Ed's house. She was the last one to arrive. She took off her coat and dropped her overnight bag on the floor. The plan was that they would help with the baking class this afternoon and stay overnight for the May Day celebration tomorrow.

Brigit was sitting on the floor with an open book on her lap, but today she wasn't reading. She was staring out the window. Feenix could tell Brigit saw nothing of what was out there. Her mind was in another place entirely. Meanwhile, Edward was searching for something on his desk. "What'd I do with it?" he mumbled angrily to himself. "I know I put it somewhere safe."

"What are you looking for?" Feenix asked. "You lose your head again? Is that it over there on that shelf?"

"Don't touch my stuff" was his answer. He went over to his closet and started rummaging around on its floor.

Danton was attempting to feed the toad by dangling a piece of sausage on a string. The toad didn't seem interested. Every once in a while, Danton cast a glance at Brigit, but Brigit didn't notice that, either.

Just as Feenix decided to go downstairs and get a drink, Edward stood abruptly. In his hands were the two red-and-gold juggling balls. She snatched them up. "What are you doing with these? I've been looking for them everywhere!"

"They were in my hiking boots," he said. "How did they get into my hiking boots?"

"Huh! So *that* was where I put them. I forgot! But if I say so myself, it was a good spot to hide them in, don't you think?"

"Why were you hiding them in the first place?" he responded.

"None of your beeswax."

"Okay. Good. I'd really rather not know. I'm going into my aunt's study to look for something. Stay out of my stuff. I'll be back soon."

Brigit closed her book. She shut it with such a snap that they all looked at her. "Come sit next to me," she said to Feenix. "Bring those with you. Put them on the floor here."

Feenix was a little surprised at Brigit's bossiness, but she came and sat on the floor and put the juggling balls down.

"Danton," Brigit said. "Did you bring the horn?"

"What horn?" he asked.

"Look in your backpack."

Obediently, Danton picked up his backpack and unzipped it. It was full of his overnight stuff. How he had gotten it all in there was a mystery. First he took out his water bottle, then his phone charger, then an extra pair of socks, then a T-shirt, then a toothbrush, then a pair of pajama pants. As he pulled these flannel pants out, something bulky that had been rolled up inside of them fell onto the bed—the small tarnished horn with the red ribbon.

"Oh," Danton said. "I forgot I was still carrying this around. I meant to show it to my dad."

"Bring it over here," Brigit said.

When he was sitting next to her, Brigit took the little red bag from around her neck and put it on the floor with the juggling balls and the horn. "Look at them," she said.

They sat in a circle, staring at the red-and-gold objects.

"Do you see it?" Brigit asked.

Before Feenix could answer, Danton spoke. "They look nearly alive, don't they?"

That was it. They looked more alive or real than everything else in the room. "But how do they do that?" Feenix asked.

"I was looking at mine last night," Brigit said, "and I got the idea it was trying to speak to me."

Feenix reached out to touch the little bag. "What's in it?" she asked. "Does it do something?"

"I think so. But I'm not sure I should—" Brigit broke off, and then she asked, "Can you remember where you found yours?"

Feenix struggled to think about this. It was like trying to catch a fish in your hands. The answer was there, but it kept slipping away. "Hold on. I've nearly got it! Wait! I was in the park, wasn't I? There was this funny garden with a pond. And there was this boy. I mean, he was older than a boy . . . He was dressed so weirdly I thought maybe he was one of those role-playing kids. He told me his name, but I . . ."

"Was his name Jack?" Brigit asked quietly.

They locked eyes. "Yes," said Feenix. "His name was Jack."

Brigit nodded. "He told me we were supposed to do something with these." She gestured at the objects in the middle of the circle. "But I can't remember what it is. Can you?"

Feenix tried again, but the memory wasn't catchable. She looked over at Danton. "What about you, Danton? Did you meet Jack, too? Did he give you the horn?"

Danton frowned. "No. I *was* in the park, but I told you, I found it in a cardboard box. Right in front of this statue I'd never seen before, actually."

Brigit jumped in right away. "What did the statue look like?"

"It was a statue of a boy or maybe of somebody a little older than us, I guess. He had a bird's nest on his head."

"Well, that sounds like Jack," said Feenix, as if now that she'd remembered him, he'd already become an old friend.

"He was asleep when I first got there, too," Brigit told them. "But then he woke up."

The other two waited for her to go on.

"Look, we've *got* to remember what it is we're supposed to do with these things before it's too late or somebody else gets ahold of them. Something very important depends on it. I'm sure of it. What good luck it is that we're not in school for a few days, so we're safe from that superintendent! Now, everybody think!"

Wow, Brigit was getting bossier by the second. Feenix tried rapping herself on the head with her knuckles, but it did no good. Then her eyes fell upon Danton's water bottle, which must have rolled to the floor.

Oh, Blue Mercy, she was thirsty. She grabbed the bottle, popped open the top, and took a long drink. A bright, delicious sensation filled her mouth. Oh joy, oh bliss. It would have been the coldest, sweetest water she'd ever tasted except for the fact that she knew she had tasted it before. And in a swift blowing away of cloud and fog, she remembered almost every detail of the morning she'd met Jack, including drinking from the water fountain and climbing through the brambles and the thorns and finding the garden.

And Jack offering to kiss her.

"Where'd you get this water from?" she demanded, waving the bottle at Danton.

"Ummm . . . well . . . Oh—I filled the bottle up in the park last time I was there."

Feenix couldn't help it. She laughed.

"What's so funny?" Danton asked.

She handed the water bottle to Brigit. "Take a sip."

Brigit took a sip. She closed her eyes, and when she opened them again, there was a look of wonder on her face. She took another sip.

At this moment, Edward came back into the room and shut the door. Whatever it was he had been looking for, he didn't seem to have found it, but nobody paid any attention to him.

"*The Lady*," Brigit said in almost a whisper. "I remember now. We have to find the Lady and give her these." She pointed at the juggling balls and the horn and the little red sack. "We have to give them to the lady with the bees."

Edward stopped right where he was and stared at her oddly. "What lady with the bees?" he asked.

"Well, that's just it," Brigit said. "We don't know. Somebody gave us these things to deliver to her. They're her tools or something. Do you know of any beekeepers in the neighborhood?"

Edward didn't answer. He seemed to be thinking hard, already off to one of his distant places.

"Maybe Kit can tell us," Feenix said. "It's the kind of thing she would know."

Just then they heard a loud rap on the door, and Kit called out, "It's time!"

They all looked at each other.

"Danton, you're taking the class, right?" Kit called through the door. "And you others have promised to help. You haven't forgotten, have you?"

"No, of course we haven't forgotten," Feenix answered back. "We'll be down in a minute."

"Good," Kit said. Then she seemed to pause. "And listen, I wanted to warn you—we have a guest visitor today. So . . . everybody on your toes." Kit often had guest visitors who were passing through town, so this was nothing new.

As soon as her footsteps were gone, Feenix pointed out that they really couldn't bring the Lady's things downstairs. There would be no place to hide the horn and the juggling balls. "We'll put them in Danton's backpack and hide it in Ed's closet till we get back," she said.

Brigit handed each item to Feenix, who stowed them in the pack, and whether it was chance or luck or an accident-on-purpose, somehow a bit of the dust from Brigit's little red bag spilled into Feenix's hand. With her back turned, she brushed it into a candy-bar wrapper on Ed's nightstand. When the backpack had been hidden in the closet and no one was looking, she folded the candy-bar wrapper up and stuck it in her coat pocket.

They all headed out the door except for Edward, who said he still needed to find something but he'd be along shortly.

Edward sat down at his desk and thought as hard as he could. *What was it?* What had it reminded him of—that business about the lady with the bees? It was like trying to catch a piece of wet spaghetti on a spoon.

He looked around the room for some clue and noticed Danton's water bottle sitting right in front of him. He was really very thirsty. He popped the lid open and finished the water.

When he was done, he sat for a long minute, gazing out the window at the mist, which was growing heavier. Then he got down on his knees and poked around. There it was. The crumpled paper bag. He pulled it out and carefully slid the cocoon out on his desk. Once more, he set his good-luck baseball hat on top of it so he couldn't forget again.

27

Munkki Doughnuts

The Saturday class was usually chatty and full of jokes. Most of the students were old regulars who had been coming to this class for a long time. For instance, there was Mrs. Wu, who owned a famous restaurant in Chinatown but liked to include an American-style dessert on her menu now and then. There was also Mrs. Chaduary, a grandmother who lived down the block, and Tom, who had been a tree keeper for many years at the botanic garden. Sometimes they talked as if they were still getting to know each other, but other times Brigit noticed them giving each other odd looks, as if they had secrets that went back further than baking class. Mr. Ross was the newest student, but everybody seemed to like him. Today, however, the conversation in the kitchen was oddly quiet and restrained. There were a lot of glances out the window toward the gathering fog.

But the smell that floated through the kitchen on this occasion was irresistible, and it nearly overpowered the forest of hanging dried herbs. It was both familiar and strange to Brigit. On one hand, it rolled through the air, yeasty and sweet and buttery. On the other hand, there was a wonderful scent of something that flickered just in and out of memory's range, something she'd maybe tasted long ago.

The surprise guest was standing with his back to them. He wore black jeans and a white button-down shirt with the sleeves rolled up and one of Kit's white aprons. Also, shiny black boots, which, with the jeans, gave his small feet an almost goatlike look. It took Brigit a moment to recognize him.

Brigit saw Feenix pinch Edward, who had just come into the kitchen a couple of minutes ago. "Ow! That hurt!" he objected loudly. "What's your problem?"

Danton flashed them all a warning look.

The Tiltersmith turned around. He drew in a long breath. He turned to Kit. "Do my eyes deceive me, dear old friend?" Then he looked back at the foursome. "Are these the beloved nephew and his companions that you were speaking of?"

"They are," answered Kit, her face unreadable.

"But I know these young people. They came to my attention at the school where I have been visiting."

"Is that so?" Kit said, still unmoved.

Brigit was sure it was pure baloney. He wasn't really the least bit surprised. But what was this between him and Kit? Could these two have really known each other in the past? It was a notion Brigit didn't like.

The Tiltersmith went on, addressing the foursome. "How delightful to run into you here. I must tell you, I was so tickled when I realized that my visit had landed me in the same neighborhood as dear Katherine. I had lost touch with her, personally, you see, although I had been keeping up with her rising career for the last several years. I have long been a student of the culinary arts, and she, of course, is one of the secret jewels of the bakers' world.

"I wondered if she would remember me, and I said to myself, 'What do I have to lose were I to give her a call?' I nerved myself up and I called her, and—lo and behold—by some improbable magic, by a stroke of great, good luck, she had a cancellation for today's class, and here I am and here you are!"

Brigit wondered what kind of acquaintance he and Kit could have had and what he might have done to get himself this cancellation. She checked quickly, but there was no sign of his blue pen. Perhaps it was in the pocket of his jacket, which was hanging on the back of his chair.

The Tiltersmith turned his attention to Kit. "Kit, you have grown only more radiant in the time since I have last seen you. All those years of perfecting recipes can wreak havoc with a figure. Yet look at you."

Here he took hold of her hand. She neither resisted nor seemed to welcome the gesture. She looked directly into his pale-blue eyes. "So lovely and so graceful to be the mistress of such—*delicious*—knowledge," he said.

"Is he actually coming on to her?" Feenix whispered into Brigit's ear. "Ugh."

Brigit didn't think she knew enough of these matters to answer, but she noticed how the tips of Mr. Ross's ears had turned red.

Aunt Kit took her hand back. "Yes. It is quite a surprise to see you again, too," she said. She turned to the class. "I have indeed a real treasure to share with you today. And as always,

I have made a sample for all to try." She lifted a silver dome from a silver platter. There lay a glorious mountain of fat golden-brown rings.

Danton let out a groan of delight, which almost made Brigit laugh. In spite of all they had on their minds, Danton could still be distracted by doughnuts.

"These are not just any doughnuts," Aunt Kit said. "These are from Finland, where they are called 'munkki.' In Finland this kind of doughnut is made to celebrate the first day of May and the turning of the Great Wheel toward summer. They are wonderful wherever and whenever you eat them, but they are particularly delicious if they are made at this moment. So, everybody! Try one now. That way you'll know what we are aiming for. May they help to push the winter back where it belongs."

The platter of doughnuts was passed around. The warm kitchen was filled with *mmm*s and sighs of pleasure as they munched the sugar-dusted golden wheels. The Tiltersmith laughed merrily. "So you think doughnuts are the answer to putting things back in balance? You were ever an optimist, weren't you?"

"One small answer," she said lightly. "But sometimes it's the small things which make the greatest difference."

The Tiltersmith took another slow bite of his doughnut. He savored it.

It was at this moment that Feenix passed by him, carrying a bowl of flour to the table. He turned to flash a smile at her. "Although, I'll tell you, my favorite small thing for pushing the winter back is a nice bowl of boiled cabbage."

Feenix nearly tripped over her own feet at these words but managed to catch herself and the flour just in time. She didn't look at him, but at Brigit. Brigit sent her a silent message. *You're all right. Just breathe. Just breathe and count.*

Kit clapped her hands. "To work! My assistants, Ed, Brigit, and Feenix, will distribute your materials. First the aprons! You will be making a big mess. Then the water pitchers and the yeast."

After everyone had tied on big white chefs' aprons, she said, "And now for one of the ingredients that gives these doughnuts their particular power over spring."

As she waited for everyone to turn to her, the Tiltersmith pulled something out of the pocket of his jacket, which still hung on the back of his chair—one of his yellow memo pads and his pen. "You won't mind, will you, if I take some notes?"

Brigit was sure she felt a curious stiffening of attention among the regulars.

"Actually," Kit said. "I do. I don't allow notes, but you are welcome to use your hands and your nose and your memory." The superintendent looked annoyed, but he bowed his head and put his pen away. Kit picked up a dish of some kind of white sour-creamy-looking stuff. "The quark!" she proclaimed.

Mr. Ross, who had been unusually quiet, perked right up. "Quarks?" he asked with interest. "What do you mean?"

Brigit and Feenix scurried around the room while Ed moved more slowly, and Kit explained that the quark they were using today was not an elementary particle, but a type of soft yogurty cheese from Germany and Scandinavia. "Taste it, please. It is going to give these doughnuts their extraordinary flavor and texture."

Everyone tasted it, and after the mixing of the yeast and the quark and water, the rest of the ingredients were brought to the table. Kit held up a small stone bowl. "And here is the other ingredient particular to these doughnuts—ground cardamom. A spice that came originally from the East and is loaded with flavor and health-giving properties. It is also said to bring fertility and success in love. We'll take some of these doughnuts with us tomorrow to the Maypole celebration in the park. I know many of you will be there. According to the legend—as some of you know—on this day the Green Man and the Lady of the May are supposed to meet after a long winter apart, and this meeting starts the growing season anew. So we'll need to make plenty of extra doughnuts for them."

It took only a few seconds for these words to sink in. Brigit saw it wasn't just her. Danton and Feenix looked like they had just stepped out into midair like Wile E. Coyote and didn't dare look down. Even Edward froze where he was. But before any of them could ask any questions, the Tiltersmith broke in.

"Oh yes! Another one of those old stories. From the ancient Celts, no? But does the story tell us what happens if they don't meet up? What happens, say, if one of them is being held captive somewhere and can't make it on time?"

"I imagine we'll all be in a pickle," Kit answered, looking him right in the eye. "So everyone must do everything they can. And today what we're doing is making doughnuts." After this, everybody got busy mixing and stirring and laughing and telling other spring folktales that they knew.

Brigit was anxious for the class to hurry itself along. She had been racking her brain, trying to think where they might begin their search, but then Mrs. Wu's story caught her ear. She was telling a tale from China about the last night of the old year, when the great monster Nian comes from under the mountains to destroy the crops and eat the children. He must be killed or driven back to his home before the spring may begin again.

There must have been something about this that caught the Tiltersmith's ear, too, for he laughed loudly. He turned to Mr. Ross with a sly look. "And I suppose you, Professor Ross, a scientist, don't much hold with all those old monster stories. You, I'm sure, like to stick with the facts."

Mr. Ross stared him down coldly. "I *am* very fond of facts, but why be so sure you know what I'm thinking? We scientists come in as many different shapes and sizes as monsters do."

In the silence that followed Mr. Ross's words, Brigit could have sworn she felt something electrical crackling through the air, but now Edward slipped up beside her and whispered in her ear.

"I've figured it out," he said. "I'm pretty sure I know where she is."

28

The Tiltersmith Leaves Early

Did Edward mean the Lady? Why would he know anything about the Lady?

Brigit watched him go around the work counter and whisper in Feenix's ear as Aunt Kit continued with her instructions. "Now, you're going to need to make sure your dough has just enough flour so that it will begin to pull away from the side of the bowl. If necessary, add more, a bit at a time. When it begins to pull away, you may shape it into a ball. Remember, you need to be gentle but firm."

The Tiltersmith spoke up. "Would you be kind enough, Katherine, to give me some guidance over here? Have I perhaps added too much? So much depends on the balance, does it not?" He grinned at her.

Kit walked over to his side.

Brigit saw how Mr. Ross's stirring had picked up speed.

"No, it looks about right," Kit said to the superintendent. "Watch what happens as I stir around the edges." She took the spoon from the superintendent's hand and began to run it around the inside of the bowl. "You can actually feel the dough pulling away."

"Ahhh, let me try," he said, and instead of waiting for her to release the spoon, he covered her hand with his own and stepped a little closer to her. Mr. Ross, Brigit saw, gave his dough an annoyed jab.

Aunt Kit allowed the Tiltersmith to hold on to her hand for one circle around the bowl, then she took a step away. Mr. Ross glared at the Tiltersmith. "I suppose your responsibilities must be pulling upon you and you'll be leaving us soon?"

"Oh yes. My work here is nearly done. Just a few more loose ends to tie up." He finished patting his dough into a nicely shaped ball and held it up proudly for all to see. "Not bad for an amateur, eh?"

Soon everyone else was holding up a ball of dough. Mr. Ross's was a bit crumbly, and the Tiltersmith said to him, "Dough is very temperamental, you know. It will pick up on your moods." He smiled slyly and turned to Kit. "Isn't it true, Katherine?"

Kit did not answer, but Mr. Ross spoke up, clearly annoyed. "My mood is just dandy, thank you. But perhaps I used a bit too much flour."

"No worries," Kit said. "By a well-planned sleight of hand, these balls of dough will now disappear."

Brigit knew the class would move along quickly now. Whenever a recipe called for a dough-rising period, Aunt Kit would prepare some risen dough ahead of time so the class wasn't left just hanging around.

For the next few minutes Brigit and Feenix and Ed were kept busy whisking the first bowls away and replacing them with already risen dough. Aunt Kit showed the students how to shape their dough into rings, and before they knew it, everyone was standing around the stovetop, watching the rings turn golden brown in the hot bubbling oil.

Brigit began to wash up. Hopefully people weren't going to stay around chatting for too long once the doughnuts were done. She kept looking at Edward to see if she could read his face. What could he mean about knowing where the Lady was? Edward looked worried, but he was giving nothing away.

Now and then, Brigit checked on the class standing by the stove. The air was heavily fragrant with the scents of yeast and hot oil and cinnamon. One by one the doughnuts were dipped in sugar, and soon there was a mountain of the sparkling golden rings. The Tiltersmith, in his black jeans, with his shoeblack hair, was much too merry and too pleased with himself. He kept sort-of-on-purpose getting too close to Aunt Kit, sometimes putting a hand on her back or shoulder. And Brigit was pretty sure that he did this more to drive Mr. Ross mad than anything else. It was as if wherever he went, he took delight in stirring up trouble. It made Brigit uncomfortable. What made her even more uncomfortable was the certainty that he was here for some even deeper purpose.

When she was done with as much washing up as she could do for the moment, Brigit started gathering supplies from the table. "I'll help," Feenix offered, and together they carried things into the pantry.

They worked silently for a few minutes, putting things back on the shelves, then Feenix leaned over and whispered in Brigit's ear. "Did Edward tell you he thinks he knows where the Lady is?"

Brigit nodded.

"Did he tell you where?"

Brigit shook her head silently.

"Me neither, but he said we're all supposed to meet in his room as soon as we can. He's gonna explain."

"All right," Brigit agreed. Someone passed by the doorway that led out to the kitchen. Brigit waited, then leaned in closer to Feenix. "But we'd better not do anything until the superintendent is gone. He's up to something."

"Of course he is. I'd trust him as far as I'd trust a sewer snake that came crawling up out of my bathtub drain. I don't know how Kit knows him, but she doesn't like him, either. You can see it."

They stayed in the pantry for a while, tidying up, until Kit called them out to make tea for everyone.

Back in the kitchen, they saw that the frying was done and Kit had turned off the burners. The class was sitting around the counter, eating fruit and cheese and little sandwiches that Kit had made beforehand. Feenix and Brigit gave out cups of tea, and Edward went to work dividing up the doughnuts into small brown paper bags.

Kit announced that everyone would get to take home a bag of fresh munkki, along with a ball of dough to experiment on at their leisure. "Don't forget!" she reminded them. "If you're planning to come to the Maypole celebration tomorrow, be sure to bring some of these with you." She looked quickly out the window. "Hopefully, the doughnuts will turn luck our way and this fog will lift."

When she had just one bag of doughnuts and one bag of

dough left in her hands, she turned around, looking disturbed. "Now where did—"

"Yeah," Danton said. "The superintendent. Where did he go? He was here just a little while ago." Tom and Mrs. Wu and a couple of the others exchanged one of those odd looks that passed among them from time to time.

"Maybe he went to the bathroom to wash his hands or something," Danton suggested.

"Go check, would you?" Kit asked.

Danton checked but reported that he wasn't in the downstairs bathroom.

Tom spoke up. "Perhaps he slipped away early?" He glanced at the other regulars. "Didn't he say something about loose ends he needed to tie up?"

Brigit jumped in. "Kit, would you mind if we finished the cleanup later? We have something important we need to discuss upstairs."

Kit didn't blink. "Take some munkki with you in case you get hungry." She wrapped a few in waxed paper and slid them into a drawstring bag and handed the bag to Brigit.

29

A Plan

When they got upstairs, Danton ordered them to check all the rooms, just in case. But there was no sign of the Tiltersmith up here, either.

In Edward's room, they all found places to sit except for Ed, who stood in front of his desk. "Tell us," Brigit said.

Edward seemed really uncomfortable. "I think maybe I'd be better off showing you. You're not likely to believe me."

"You're going to *show* us where this lady is?" Danton asked.

"Sort of." He turned and looked at his desk and frowned. His baseball cap was sitting next to the big-toe thingy. "Did one of you move my cap?" he asked.

Everybody shook their heads *no*. Ed looked troubled. "I must have done it myself and forgotten. I've been forgetting so much. I even forgot about this for a few weeks." He pointed to the cocoon. "I was confused about it at first. I think it's not actually a cocoon."

"Okay," Danton said. "What is it, then?"

"I'm not sure. It seems to be some type of wormhole or, you know, an Einstein-Rosen bridge."

"A what?"

"A passageway to other sides of the universe or maybe other worlds. The idea was named after Einstein and a scientist named Nathan Rosen. Wormholes are only theoretical. I mean, nobody's ever actually seen one. But . . . well . . . Could you hand me that wooden spoon next to my green mold there?" Danton handed it over. Ed held it over the small opening at the top of the cocoon. He let go of it, and the spoon was instantly sucked inside. There was a long silence.

Then Feenix burst into noise. "Wait! What just happened? Is this some kind of joke? Do that again!"

Edward did it again, using a half-eaten apple that was sitting on the windowsill.

"But where did they go?" Danton asked, looking very worried. "Do you know?"

So Ed told them his dream in as much detail as he could. About the toad falling in and how he went after it and about the cave and the ladder and then following the tunnel that led to the hallway. About the door that opened out into the dark void with all the stars and planets, and then the door that led into the room with the table and the lady with the bees in her hair, who was being held prisoner by a serpent and some person she referred to as Lord Lopside.

"Lord Lopside!" exclaimed Danton, looking around at the others. "You don't mean—"

"Yeah," said Edward. "I do. I've tried to think of one, but there doesn't seem to be any other logical conclusion." Edward then told them what the bee person said he would need to do and how he had escaped by climbing back up the ladder. And also about how, since it now appeared that what had happened wasn't a dream, this cocoon must be one of the greatest scientific finds of all time.

At last, Brigit spoke up. "Well, I don't know about the scientific-find part, but *of course* it wasn't a dream. Clearly, we're meant to find her and bring her the tools and get her free. Your dream is part of it."

Danton stood. He began pacing with excitement. "If this is really true and we have to go in, we're going to need a plan." He nodded toward the closet, where the backpack was hidden. "We'll all go in together, and we'll bring her the tools. But we're going to have to think of a way to neutralize the serpent thing while we get her out. Did you notice if it had any vulnerable points, like a soft spot under the neck or something?"

"You mean as in you're planning to bring a sword along and fight it?" Edward asked.

"Well, I don't own a sword."

"Which is probably a good thing," Edward said dryly. "In any case, what I know is that it has useless legs and wings, doesn't see well, suffocates its prey, and likes sweets."

"I'll bring the doughnuts," Brigit said, holding up the bag.

"That ought to do it," Edward said.

Brigit ignored him. "But I don't think we should spend a lot of time planning. I think the Lady needs to be freed by tomorrow morning. At least that's the way the story goes. So we'll have to improvise."

"But wait!" Feenix said. "What about Jack? We can't just leave him. He's stuck, too. They're supposed to meet up, aren't they?"

"You're right," said Brigit. "We can't just leave Jack."

"Can I throw my two cents in?" Edward said.

"If you must," answered Feenix. "Go ahead."

"We can't all go in together, anyway, because then we'd have to leave the cocoon here unprotected. If anything were to happen to it, it would become impossible for whoever goes in to come back out."

There was a moment of silence while everyone paused to contemplate the awfulness of this possibility.

"All right, then," said Feenix. "We'll split up. Brigit and Danton will go into the cocoon-wormhole thingy and find the Lady and slay the serpent or whatever it takes to get her out. Me and Ed will have to find Jack and see if we can't get him unstuck. We'll figure something out, won't we, Ed? You're the one with all the great big universe-jumping ideas."

"I don't even know who this Jack person is," pointed out Edward.

"I'll fill you in on the way," Feenix promised.

"I have no idea why I let you people get me into these things," Edward grumbled. "But me and Feenix will have to carry the cocoon with us. If we keep it on us, that way, when Brigit and Danton come back, we'll all be sure to end up in the same place."

"And we'll take the toad," Danton announced. "It sounds like the toad knows the way."

Brigit went over to the terrarium and lifted the toad out gently.

"You want to hold hands, maybe, so we don't get separated?" he asked her.

"All right," she answered. "Maybe that's a good idea."

He took her hand.

"Just a second, you two—aren't you getting ahead of yourselves a little?" Feenix said.

"What do you mean?" Danton asked.

"Aren't you forgetting something?"

"Like what?"

"Your backpack. With the Lady's tools."

Danton looked faintly embarrassed and let go of Brigit's hand and crossed the room to the closet.

The backpack was gone.

30

Brigit and Danton Inside

I t was Edward who understood first. "*He* took it, don't you see?"

"*He* who?" Feenix asked.

"The Tiltersmith, of course. That's why my lucky hat wasn't on top of the cocoon when we came in. He moved it. He left here early, all right, but he didn't go out the front door."

There was a long silence.

"This is bad," Feenix said. "Very bad. Maybe we need to rethink the plan."

At that, the toad, who had been sitting calmly in Brigit's hand, took advantage of the distraction. It slipped between her fingers, hopped onto Edward's desk, and headed straight for the cocoon. It was gone in the blink of an eye.

Brigit and Danton looked at each other. Danton took Brigit's hand. She reached out to touch the wormhole.

They both experienced the same curious sensations that Ed had told them about—a feeling of dissolving and expanding and being released into countless different Brigits and Dantons, all moving along in different directions. When this dissolving began to reorganize itself at last, they landed with a double *thwunk* on the cave floor. They were both relieved and comforted to find they were still holding hands. Without saying anything, they did not let go, but stood there gazing around themselves.

Just as Edward had described it, the light was dim and the rope ladder swung over their heads. When they gazed straight upward, they thought they could just make out the light from Edward's room shining through the little teardrop-shaped exit. The toad let out a *snork* and began to hop forward.

"This way," said Danton, and he squeezed Brigit's hand.

The going was easy and the tunnel was quiet, just as it had been for Edward. Had they not been so anxious about what they would find up ahead, they would perhaps both have been delighted by the rosy phosphorescent lights, which swam away in the red stone walls when you tried to touch them.

At each fork in the tunnel, the toad took them confidently right or left, until at last it led them to the three marble steps. There it hesitated, as if it were watching or listening for something. Then it hopped up. A moment later they were all standing in the long hallway. They saw before them the carpet, the chandeliers with their dangling rubies, the glass cases full of antiques and oddities and dead beetles. And, of course, the doors with their crystal doorknobs.

"Do you hear that?" Brigit whispered.

"Hear what?" Danton said.

"A saxophone. Someone's practicing a saxophone. C'mon." She pulled Danton along.

It was one of her favorite things. To stand outside a room where someone was practicing a piano or a recorder or another instrument. It wasn't that she didn't love a polished performance in a concert hall or on the radio, but when you listened to music this way, it sounded so personal and hopeful.

She wanted to get closer to it. "Listen!" she said and let go of his hand.

"Wait up!" said Danton, who didn't seem to hear a thing.

The toad was hopping forward, and Brigit and Danton followed behind. But when Brigit reached the doorway where the music seemed to be coming from, the toad kept going while Brigit stopped. "What is it?" Danton asked, keeping an eye on the toad but pausing with Brigit.

"Don't you hear it? The music. It's here. Behind this door." She heard a complicated curling and turning of notes that the player could not get just right. The musician tried again and then again, and then at last the notes came unsnarled and followed one another in a sweeping upward flight of freedom. Brigit could not resist. She put her hand on the doorknob.

"What are you doing?" Danton whispered urgently. "You shouldn't open that."

"Only a crack. I promise. I just want to hear it without the door between us."

"Hear what?" he cried to her, but she had turned the knob. The door swung open.

Brigit saw a comfortable little room with curtains drawn against the night. Inside the room were a music stand and an armchair and a lamp. The lamp threw a circle of light upon the musician, who stood with his back to her, white gloves, white shirt, black jeans. The saxophone was lifted to his mouth. And now he blew a slow swinging run of such lonely and sorrowful notes that she took a step forward to see him better.

The instant she did, the lamp blinked out. She found herself in complete darkness. The music stopped as if it had never been. "Hello?" she called out, and she took another step forward. *"Hello?"*

When she tried to take another step, she found there was nothing to put her lifted foot down upon. Quickly, she drew it back and threw her arms out to catch her balance, but when she tried to move backward, she discovered there was no floor behind her, either. She wobbled in the blackness, standing on what now seemed to be only a little island of solid ground.

"Danton?" she whispered, but there was no answer from him. What she heard instead was low laughter rising up from somewhere far below. With the laughter came a rush of wind. The wind blew around her, laughing and pushing.

"No!" she screamed as she teetered. She began to topple forward.

As the solid ground slipped away, a powerful hand took hold of her arm, and she screamed again. But the hand did not let go. It gave a tremendous yank and she found herself falling backward, and now there was light again. In the next moment she landed on her butt with a terrific thud and found herself in the carpeted hallway. She heard the door click shut and saw Danton bending over her. He was still holding her arm.

"Are you all right?" he asked. "What were you trying to do in there?"

Brigit took a breath and felt ashamed because she'd allowed herself to be tricked, but at the same time she was a little bit regretful at having lost the music. She'd never heard anything like it. "Was that you laughing?" she whispered to Danton.

"Laughing?"

She shook her head. "I'm very sorry," she said. "How stupid I am. I heard something, and it sounded so real and so beautiful. But it must have been a trick."

He helped her up and let go of her arm. "Brigit, never say you're stupid. You always seem to see what's most important and true inside of things. The thing is, we just have to be careful not to rush ahead of ourselves. This guy is very clever, but if we watch out for each other, I think we'll be all right. C'mon, the toad is waiting for us."

He was right, of course. There it was up ahead. Brigit could almost have laughed. She never would have thought that a toad could so clearly express impatience. It glared at them and almost seemed to be tapping one of its feet. It reminded her of someone, but she couldn't quite think who.

When the toad saw they were headed in the right direction at last, it gave out a faint *snork* and continued along the other corridor. "It seems very sure of itself for a toad, doesn't it?" Brigit said, trotting along beside Danton. She wished she dared to take his hand again, but she was too embarrassed. It would seem too obvious. "Tell me again, where did you find it?"

"I found it in Ms. Trevino's office," Danton said. "But I don't believe it's a toad."

Brigit glanced at him in surprise. "No? Why not?"

Danton didn't answer. He had lifted his face and was inhaling the air deeply. "Do you smell that?" he asked.

Brigit sniffed the air. "No, I don't think so," she said.

Danton remained intent on following his nose, sniffing the air until he came to an abrupt halt right in front of one of the curio cabinets. It was a beautiful wooden cabinet like the others, but it was divided into a dozen or so glass-covered compartments with food in them. Brigit knew immediately that they were in big trouble.

In each compartment there was a shiny shelf with a red plate on it. On each red plate was a delicious-looking serving of something or other. On one there was a hot, perfectly toasted-looking grilled cheese with a bit of cheese oozing out the side. On another there was a bright tomato, mozzarella, and pasta salad. Another was filled with coconut-battered fried shrimp. There was a shiny brown roasted chicken leg with pineapple. There were also desserts: a plate with a slice of cherry pie, a bowl of banana pudding topped with whipped cream, a hot-fudge brownie. These were all foods that Danton loved. "This is so cool," he said. "Doesn't it smell amazing?"

Brigit couldn't smell a thing. There was something very wrong here. "No," she told him. "It doesn't."

But he didn't hear her. His eyes were glassy with desire. "It looks like one of those old-fashioned Automat things. They used to have them in the city back in the day. You'd put your money in and choose what you wanted, and then there was a dining area with tables."

He crouched down now to read a neatly lettered sign on the side of the cabinet. "Look," he said in excitement. "It says it's free to all visitors! You just press the right buttons and—" He reached out and pressed a button.

"No!" she warned him. "Please don't touch it!"

But he didn't seem to hear her. He pressed another button.

A faint whirring could be heard. A little conveyor belt

began to move, and all the plates moved along with it. First over to the right. Then slowly downward like in a glass elevator. When the red plate with the grilled cheese on it reached the bottom, the glass window on the front slid upward.

Danton extended his hand to reach into the Automat, but Brigit saw what he had not. Running along the bottom of the glass window was a razor-sharp metal edge. "Don't!" she screamed. She pushed Danton aside as hard as she could, and he toppled over onto the carpet, withdrawing his hand. In the same instant the glass window dropped down out of the machine like the blade of a guillotine.

Danton looked at the Automat and he looked at his fingers. He turned to Brigit, who was breathing heavily. "Sorry," she said.

He shook his head at her, laughing a little. "What are you apologizing for? You just saved my fingers." When they stood up, he took hold of her hand again. They started back down the hallway toward the toad, who was waiting with an exasperated look in its little toad eyes.

They passed as quickly and quietly along the carpet as they could. They hadn't gone far when their corridor intersected with another. Here the toad paused for a moment and seemed to consider. At last, it made up its mind and took a right.

"Hey," Danton said. "Didn't Ed say we would be going straight all the way?"

31

Feenix and Ed Go to Look for Jack

After Brigit and Danton and the toad disappeared, Ed and Feenix stared for a few minutes at the cocoon.

It was Feenix who broke the silence. "Edward, where do you find weird stuff like this?"

He glared at her. "That's a ridiculous question. As if anybody'd ever found anything like this before. This is going to change everything. But meanwhile, we're going to need to find some way to carry it around with us safely."

He started rummaging through the things on his shelves. "A little box, maybe. We don't want it to get broken, and we don't want our skin to come in contact with it by accident, either. Look around. See if you see anything. But don't mess with my collections or my experiments."

Feenix went over to Edward's dresser and poked around at all the miscellaneous stuff—a saucer with a crust of toast, a paperback book entitled *Red Mars*, a spiraled conch shell (which she held to her ear when his back was turned so she could hear the sea), a broken shoelace, a scattering of coins, a blue-jay feather, two Lego figures—a fireman and an astronaut. She wondered if he still played with Legos and how she could find out. She was about to turn away when her eye was caught by the sparkle of something jammed between the back of the dresser and the wall. She reached across and worked it free.

She gave a little sigh of pleasure. A crystal doorknob. It was gorgeous. She was just examining the rose carved in its center when she realized Edward was turning around. She shoved the doorknob into the back waistband of her leggings so she could look at it more closely later.

"Aha!" Edward said, approaching his desk with something in his hand. "This oughta work." He was holding an empty glass spice bottle labeled *Cinnamon*. He twisted the lid off and then, using tweezers, picked up the wormhole-cocoon thingy and slid it in so it stood snugly upright, the exit hole near the top.

"See," he said. "I'll just leave the lid off. That way, if I keep it in my jacket pocket, there ought to be enough light for them to see their way back." They slipped quietly down the stairs together.

Feenix stopped at the bottom. "Shouldn't we let Aunt Kit know we're going out?"

Edward wasn't thrilled at the prospect. "I guess. But don't be getting into one of your big yakety-yaks with her, and if she asks where we're going, keep the info to a minimum."

"Pishposh," she replied, flicking her fingers at him.

It wasn't until they were drawing close to the kitchen that they realized it was just Aunt Kit and Mr. Ross alone in there, talking. Feenix smirked at Edward, but he ignored her.

"So where do you know him from?" they heard Mr. Ross say.

There was the sound of the water being turned on and off

and the rattle of a dish being placed in the dish drainer. Then a sigh. "Our circles have crossed from time to time," said Kit.

"You're friends, then?"

"Not friends." More rattling of dishes.

"Something else, then?" Mr. Ross asked.

"Yes, something else."

There was a long silence after that. At last, Mr. Ross spoke up. "You don't want to tell me?"

"Actually—I don't. It's a subject better left untouched."

"Well, I don't trust him, Kit. I suggest you be very careful."

"I'm quite capable of looking out for myself, Franklin, but he's necessary."

"What do you mean?" he asked sharply. "Necessary how? Does he have some sort of claim on you?"

"Claim?" She seemed to be thinking this over. "No, of course not."

"Well, then—" Feenix thought she could hear Mr. Ross moving toward Kit.

"No, Franklin, no. I told you, I'm too busy for this." First she sounded stern. Then she laughed. Feenix was dying to see what was going on, but Edward grabbed hold of her so she couldn't look.

"Kit—" Mr. Ross said in exasperation and stopped. Then he started again. "Kit—what's going on?"

"What's going on? What's going on? Look out the window, Franklin. It's been weeks since the equinox passed, hasn't it?"

There was a pause while, presumably, Mr. Ross looked out the window. "Well, yes, but now we have fog. At least it's not snow, and maybe it means things are warming up. Maybe the spring is coming at last. And did you know"—he paused and a hopeful tone came into his voice—"there's going to be a blue moon tomorrow night?"

"Of course I do. I know much more than you give me credit for. But that does little to further your case. You know the problem isn't mere weather. And one extra moon isn't going to make the difference, either. Right now, I cannot afford to allow myself to be distracted. I cannot spend my best energies arguing with you about whether dough has feelings or if I should be using a carefully calibrated food scale when I'm baking. I have a lot of work to do and promises to keep. You've got to allow me to keep them."

There was a pause. "To him? You have promises to keep to him?"

"Franklin," she said with a note of anger, "did you hear me say that?"

"Maybe not. But you've made yourself clear. I'd better be going, and I think it would be best if I didn't come back."

"Franklin—" she called out in exasperation.

But he ignored her or didn't hear her and came stalking out of the kitchen. Feenix saw that the tips of his ears were burning red. He nodded at them as he went by, but said nothing.

Feenix and Ed waited a long minute, for the dust or whatever it was to settle. Then Ed said, as Feenix knew he would, "I told you so. Why you think they would be in any way compatible is a great mystery to me." Before Feenix could put him back in his place, Kit emerged from the kitchen. She seemed briefly startled to find them there, but except for the fact that she, too, looked pink (although her pink was not on her ears, but right in the middle of her cheeks), she quickly resumed her unreadable look.

"Ah, here you are, then."

"Me and Feenix are going out for a bit."

She nodded and looked them up and down for shoes tied, all buttons buttoned, and so forth. Like a general inspecting his troops before a battle.

"We're gonna take a walk in the park," Feenix explained.

"Yes, I guess you are," Kit answered. She glanced out the window. "It's getting foggy out there. You should be careful. Don't get separated."

"You're thinking we could get lost in a fog here in Brooklyn, where we've lived all our lives and know every inch of?" Ed asked.

"That would depend on the fog," Kit said. "And speaking of which, what's happened to Birdie and Danton?"

"Oh, they said they had errands and stuff to do," Feenix explained quickly, "but I don't think we need to worry about the two of *them* getting separated. We'll all meet up somewhere later, and then we'll be back for dinner, okay?"

Kit just raised one eyebrow at this. "All right. But take some doughnuts with you just for luck," she said smoothly.

"I think we've had enough doughnuts," Ed said. She ignored him and handed a little bag to Feenix, who took it politely.

Once they were outside on the front stoop, Ed asked, "So what do we do now?"

"We go up to the park, of course."

As they walked, Edward asked her to fill him in on this Jack person they were looking for. Feenix told him what she remembered. And then, somehow, she couldn't help herself. She told him how Jack had offered to kiss her. How he had said it would help her remember.

"And so, did you let him?" He sounded unusually curious about this.

"No," she said. "But I keep thinking I should have. My memory's been just terrible lately."

After that, they were silent for a while, watching the way the mist thickened and moved slowly around the houses and brownstones, changing the outlines of things. Normally, it wasn't far from Ed's house to the park, but today it seemed farther. Finally, Feenix spoke. "So, what was that business about there being a blue moon tonight?" she asked. "Do you know?"

Edward perked up. "As it happens, I do. It doesn't really mean a moon turns blue. It's an astronomical term. It happens when there's four full moons in a season. As you *should* know, every season has three months, so there's usually only three full moons in a season, but when there's four of them, they call the third one a blue moon. That only happens every other year or so."

"It's truly amazing how many weird facts you've collected."

"You never know when weird facts are going to come in handy."

"I've noticed that your aunt likes weird facts, too."

"I'm not sure what you're referring to are really facts."

"I've been developing a theory about your aunt. You want to hear it?"

"What if I said no?"

"I was reading about this in some book."

"You read books?"

"Very funny. Listen. I think she's a Hedge Jumper."

"Excuse me?"

"I don't know if you could classify them as witches, exactly, but they're very big into herbs and stuff, and they can jump over the boundaries between one world and another. Or, at least, they can see between them. That's why they're called Hedge Jumpers. She's probably not allowed to talk about it, and I think that's why she knows the Tiltersmith."

"Feenix, I don't think that's real. My aunt knows a lot of weird people, and she is a complete wackadoodle. But I've never seen her jumping over any hedges."

"I didn't mean hedges *literally*. Don't be such a dunder-snap. Hedges stand for the dividing places between worlds. In any case, I think she knows what we're doing. I think she *wanted* us to go up to the park."

"Really?" Ed laughed. "You think she wants us to go in there and hunt down Jack the Kisser?"

"I'd be careful, if I were you, how I talked about him."

"Why's that?"

"Well, he's not exactly . . . one of us."

"What does that mean?"

"That lady you met in your cocoon, was she one of us?"

Ed blinked and frowned, as if he had forgotten all about her again until just this moment. "I don't know what you mean when you say 'one of us,' but actually, she did seem really different."

When they reached the top of the hill, Feenix was surprised to find they had overshot Ninth Street somehow. The fog *was* more confusing than you'd expect. "All right," she said decisively, "we'll go in at Third Street. That's where Brigit said she found him. Somehow, that little garden he's stuck in seems to keep getting moved around."

"You know that doesn't make any sense, right?" Edward pointed out.

"Does a cocoon that lets you travel from one world to another make any sense?"

He remained silent on that one.

When they got to Third Street and stopped in front of the panther statues, Ed looked at Feenix. "Well? What's the big plan?"

"Just give me a second. I'm trying to remember . . ." She snapped her fingers. "Okay! Very important. First of all, we need to take a drink from the water fountain. That's what each of us did, apparently, before we met him."

"Jack the Kisser, you mean?"

"Stop saying that."

But when they looked around, peering through the slowly swirling mist, there wasn't a sign of any water fountain. "Well, that's weird," Feenix said. "Maybe Brigit was mixed up about where she got her drink from."

"Don't you think there's an awful lot of that 'mixed-up' stuff going around?" Edward asked.

"Yes, well, if one of us had actually been thinking, we would have brought Danton's bottle with us. The water would have helped, I'm sure." Feenix was standing at the foot of one of the fierce, brooding panther statues. She looked up at it and then past it to the path that led into the forest. The mist swirled and snaked around the pine trees. Farther ahead she could see the big messy wall of brambles and thorns. "I guess we'll just have to try to find our way in there on our own."

Edward followed her gaze. "What do you mean? Up there? Are you kidding? Why would we go in *there*? How we going to get through those bushes?"

Feenix reached into her coat pocket to find a doughnut to comfort herself. As she lifted the little bag out, a sprinkling of fine red-and-gold dust came with it. The stuff that had fallen out of Brigit's little red bag! Feenix had forgotten all about it.

As luck would have it, a runaway gust of wind blew past. It stayed only long enough to pick the dust up and fling it into the air over the panther. Then the wind was gone, leaving the stuff to float to the ground.

Feenix watched with nervous interest. Brigit hadn't said what the dust was supposed to do, had she?

Nothing.

Feenix took a bite of the doughnut and stuck it back in her pocket. Then she brushed herself off. "Okay. Let's go." She entered the park. It was when she turned to make sure Edward was following that she noticed the daffodils. Several dozen of them were growing in the earth just beside the panther. Some were still in bud; some were just opening up. The ones that were opening up shone out like tiny yellow lamps in the mist.

"Hey!" she said to Edward. "Look at those daffodils. Were they there a minute ago?"

Edward looked where she pointed and shrugged. "They musta been."

"I don't think you pay enough attention to what's actually going on around you," Feenix remarked. "Now, you go first. I don't want to lose track of you."

"You don't trust me?"

"Absolutely not. You get so spaced out."

"*I* get spaced out?" he said indignantly. "You get lost just going to the girls' room at school."

She laughed. He was right. "But when I get lost, it's in a totally different world than you get lost in," she pointed out. "Now c'mon. Side by side."

Soon they entered into the trees, where it was piney smelling and sweet. And so quiet. For a while the trees were spaced comfortably apart, but then they grew thicker. In another few minutes the undergrowth started, vines crossing the path and then thickening into a wall of thorny brambles. Edward had gotten a little ahead of Feenix, and now he stopped.

"That's it," he announced. "That's as far as I go. Check out those thorns. You wanna get your eyeballs torn out, be my guest."

"But look, Edward! Bend down a little. There's a kind of passageway just up ahead." He bent a little to see where she was pointing, and then he turned to her to protest. But now his mouth fell open soundlessly, and he went pale.

He was looking at something over her shoulder.

She glanced back and froze. Not far down the path was an enormous black panther. It was stretched low and flat to the ground, as if it were readying itself to pounce. For a very long moment, Feenix had time to consider that when this cat was up on its pedestal, its gaze was cold and distant. Here, however, its gaze was very personal. It was staring directly at Feenix, and its tail flicked with an expectation that it couldn't quite contain.

32

Lily Pads

"The toad must have its reasons," Brigit said to Danton. "And what choice do we have?" So, obediently, Danton and Brigit followed the toad to the right instead of going straight, the way Edward had. After not too long, it came to a halt in front of one of the doors. "This one?" Danton asked it. "You're sure? Is this the room where the Lady is?" The toad snorted impatiently.

Danton put his ear to the door. "I don't hear anything," he said to Brigit. "What do you think?"

"I think we should trust the toad," she said. He nodded and opened the door slowly.

It was difficult to see at first. Their eyes had to adjust to the dimness, but they knew right away it wasn't a room. It was too damp and stony and drafty. Danton caught a strong scent like cotton candy. In the silence they could make out a gurgling, lapping sound.

When nothing happened, Danton opened the door all the way. Now the light from the hallway fell in a long, wide shaft across an oily, sluggish river, which appeared to be flowing through a high-ceilinged tunnel of stone. Along the banks of this river hung tree branches that dangled their blackish-green leaves in the slow current. The light also showed some large round lily pads, which floated flat on the surface of the river. They looked like giant watermelon-pink dinner plates, big enough to sit down upon. Each one had a yellow pom-pom-shaped flower smack in its middle. The cotton-candy fragrance must be coming from those flowers.

Flitting in and out of the shaft of light were a number of dragonfly-like insects. They were huge, too. As big as Danton's hand. The scene might have been pretty, Brigit thought. But it wasn't, maybe because the river itself was so oily and sluggish.

"Well, no ladies in here," Danton whispered. "What do we do now?"

Brigit remained silent, still searching the scene in front of them. The river was too wide to jump over, and there was no telling how deep it was. At last, she noticed something. "Look," she said, pointing. "Do you see that?"

Danton followed her finger and saw it, too. Another doorway, in the stone wall on the far side of the river. One of those faint phosphorescent lights hung above it.

The toad gave one of its commanding *snork*s and slipped between them. Without hesitation, it hopped down to the edge of the rocky bank.

"*Hey!*" Danton and Brigit both called out, their voices echoing hollowly through the watery tunnel. But the toad paid not the slightest attention. It took a flying leap into the air. They both held their breaths, expecting to see it plop into the oily water. Instead it landed on the edge of one of the huge lily pads. It turned itself around and looked at them expectantly.

"Is it serious?" Danton said to Brigit.

"I think it is. Let's see how strong they are." She started down the bank of the river.

Danton stood for a moment, just watching her go. From the front she appeared so mild and shy, but from the back you could tell how brave she was. It was all there in the straightness of her spine and the way her red braid bounced so proudly against her shoulders. He resolved that as soon as they got out of there, he would definitely see if she would allow him to kiss her.

He followed behind and stood beside her, peering at the lily pads. A few of them were still unopened. They stood folded up along their middles, like giant two-petaled buds. But most of them floated big and flat on the water, fairly close together, all the way across the river. He wondered how they survived without any sunlight.

The toad hopped forward onto the next lily pad and then the next. "There's something familiar looking about them, don't you think?" Brigit said.

"And that smell is really something, isn't it?" he replied. "So sweet. It gets stronger here by the water."

She bent down to pick up a stone and tossed it onto the closest lily pad. The leaves barely quivered. "You see?" she said. "I'm going to try it. The water can't be that deep here. I'll test this one to see if it will hold me."

"No, no," he objected. "Let me go first."

"I'm lighter," she countered, and before he could stop her, she had taken a step out onto the first pad. She wasn't surprised when the thing wobbled only slightly. It seemed rubbery, but stiff and thick. She brought her other foot along and balanced there triumphantly.

"You see!" she assured Danton. "It's okay. They'll hold us. And there's enough of them that I think we can get across without any trouble. Look, the toad is nearly there already." In fact, as they watched, the toad hopped onto the opposite bank. It turned. It looked at them impatiently. Who *did* that creature remind Brigit of?

"All right," she announced. "I'm going to test this one up ahead. You come along behind me." She put her foot out and stepped down near the center of the next pad, right near the flower. Again, there was a slight wobble, but she easily brought her other foot up behind and found her balance. She turned and saw that Danton had hopped on the first one and was balancing there, too. He looked a little nervous, but he nodded and waited for her to go ahead. She stretched one leg out and easily made the leap, bringing the other leg up behind. She went on to the next and the next.

"I'm good," Danton called. "Keep going."

She noticed with each jump that the smell of the lily pads grew stronger. She didn't really like the scent, but at the same time, she felt a strange urge to bend down and get closer to it.

"And the smell is unbelievable, isn't it?" Danton said.

It was at this moment that Brigit saw one of the dragonflies hovering around the next lily pad. It circled the pink dinner plate slowly, coming closer, maybe drawn by the smell. Then it landed lightly on the flower, and in the next instant—*snap*.

The two sides of the lily pad folded up along the seam down the center and came together. Now Brigit saw the long needlelike teeth that stuck out all around the circumference of the lily pad. They hadn't been visible before, because they had been hidden by the dark oily water. As the two sides of the plant came together, the teeth locked shut.

She froze. *"Danny!"* she cried out. She had never called him Danny before and didn't stop to think about why she did it now. She just swung around to look at him. He was bent halfway over, about to stick his nose in a flower. At the sound of his family nickname, he stopped and looked up and grinned at her in surprise.

"Yes, Birdie?" he answered.

She pointed. The dragonfly was no longer visible, but you could see the mighty struggle that was going on inside the folded-up lily pad. "They're traps," she said. "Like the ones Mr. Ross brought into school. Except these only take one trigger to make them go off." She told him what had happened. "It has teeth, too. Long ones. If they close on one of us, they'll go so deep into our skin, we'll never get them out."

He looked at her. He looked at the lily pad he was standing on.

"Get up slowly," she said, "and step away from the flower. The flower is the trigger button. Like the hairs were on the ones Mr. Ross brought in."

Danton did as she instructed. He stood there staring down at the flower he had almost just stuck his nose into.

They were both remembering what Mr. Ross had said about what the Venus flytrap would do when it closed up on its prey. Brigit imagined Danton's legs inside of it now, pierced by needles, rapidly being turned to ooze. She saw from Danton's face that he was thinking about this, too.

"Maybe we should turn back," Danton said with a shudder.

"No," Brigit said. "Going back will be just as dangerous, and it won't do us any good. We can do this. We're nearly halfway there, anyway. There's plenty of room on the pads. All we have to do is avoid the flowers. We know the trick now. The poor dragonflies don't."

"All right, Birdie," he said. "If you're okay with it, I'm okay with it. But please be careful."

She nodded. "I'm just going to have to go around this one," she said, pointing at the lily pad that had closed up in front of her. She took one of the lily pads to the right, making a detour around the one inside of which the dragonfly was still quaking and shaking.

Danton followed her lead. All went well. Brigit was able to avoid the treacherous flowers without a problem, and she landed safely on the far bank, next to the toad. The toad snorked in approval.

Brigit turned to watch Danton approaching. His long legs brought him along easily, and he somehow managed to keep his big feet out of the way of the yellow pom-pom flowers. It wasn't until he was about to put his leg out to jump onto the next-to-last lily pad that Brigit caught sight of the approaching disaster. Danton was too focused on his mission to see it.

One of the dragonflies was circling slowly around the pad where Danton would land next. If the dragonfly came down on the flower just as he jumped, they would both become the trap's prey.

"Not that one!" she cried out as he took off into the air.

33

Through the Brambles

Behind her, Feenix heard Edward dive into the thorny passageway. She backed up slowly, keeping an eye on the great cat. It stayed quite still. The only part that moved was its tail. Feenix backed up a step and then another.

"Now!" Edward hissed at her. "Get down now and back up. I don't think it can fit in here."

She scrunched herself in and backed up on her hands and knees.

"Get your feet out of my face!" Ed said.

"Move back! Move back," she said. "It's coming!" The cat was now slinking slowly closer along the path. The size of its paws sent a wave of nausea through her.

"Where did that thing come from?" Ed whispered. "It's huge. This is a major scientific discovery! Can you get a picture?"

"Ed, are you kidding? Tell me you're kidding."

But perhaps he had thought twice about this, too, because he didn't answer. The cat was right in front of their hiding place. It sent out an exploratory paw with its great hooked claws unsheathed, like a kitty cat feeling for a mouse under a kitchen sink. The claws caught hold of Feenix's coat sleeve and yanked backward. The cat made a happy trilling noise as it pulled. Feenix heard the ripping of her sleeve.

"Move!" she cried out to Edward. "It can reach me here."

"There's no space to move!"

"Make some space! It's gonna take my arm off next time."

Edward didn't answer, but Feenix felt him slowly squirm farther back into the brambles, and she squirmed with him. Not a moment too soon, because now the cat, perhaps infuriated at the mere scrap of wool fabric it had come away with, shoved its ginormous paw deep into the hole and whacked it forcefully back and forth, tearing at the brambles and widening the space.

"This is not good," Feenix said.

Now the cat withdrew its paw and shoved its huge head partway into the hole to look around. After sizing up the situation, it pulled back its head and then stuck the paw in again to tear some more.

"It'll be in here in a minute," Feenix said breathlessly, kicking at Edward. "You've got to push through to the other side."

"Well, that's not possible. The branches are all grown together. It's like a wall."

"Your aunt says there's always another way through. Maybe try going slideways, not straight ahead."

"Slideways?"

"That's what Kit says."

"Please don't quote my aunt to me."

"And don't break the branches. Just gently try to untangle them."

The cat stuck its face into the hole again, checking on its progress. Just before it withdrew this time, Feenix could have sworn it smiled.

"Look," Feenix said. "Do it this way. Go gently, but hurry." She pulled her long sleeves over her hands and began tugging at the branches. "Just pull at the ones that want you to pull at them."

"The ones that *want* me to pull at them?"

"I'm not going to argue with you. Don't think about it. You think too much. Just do what I say." She looked around and saw that the monstrous cat almost had its shoulders through. "Now! Hurry up!"

Feenix pulled and Ed pulled. He really did not understand how a person could stop thinking, but he did his best. In another minute there was a clear opening in front of them, and they could see the mist twisting around the trunks of the trees.

"Go, go, go!" Feenix yelled.

Edward crawled through at a speed Feenix had not imagined him capable of. He was full of surprises, wasn't he? She was right behind him.

When they stood, they did not stop to examine the open place they found themselves in, but looked behind themselves right away to see if they had been followed. Inexplicably, the hole they had made in the brambly hedge had already closed itself up. If the cat was still out there, they could no longer see it.

"Where are we?" Ed said, looking around. "What is this place? Have you been here before?"

Feenix took a deep breath. "Of course I have, ye of little faith. This is it. This is exactly where I was trying to take you."

It was pretty much the same rectangular clearing that she had found herself in before—the redbrick pathways, the empty flower beds, the muddy pond full of bracken. "This is where I met Jack."

"Jack the Kis—" Ed started to say, but Feenix put up her hand with a threatening look.

"Shhh," she whispered. "He must be here somewhere. He was over there by that tree last time. C'mon." She trotted around the pond on the slushy brick path. When she got close to the tree, she was startled to see that it had started to blossom with small fragrant white flowers and the ivy had begun to turn a deeper green. "Jack?" she called softly. "Are you here? I've come back." But there was no answer, and though she gently parted the loose twisting vines of ivy, there was no sign of him.

Ed was standing at the edge of the pond.

"What?" Feenix asked. "What are you looking at?"

"That nest on that statue's head. It looks like a beauty. I'd love to have it for my collection."

It was only now that Feenix realized there was a statue there, a worn stone figure covered in moss. Had it been here the last time? She walked around to get a better look, but she knew who it was before she even got there. She needed to get closer.

At her feet lay the end of an old tree trunk that had fallen across the water. The other end was resting up against the stone pedestal. She put one foot onto the log. It rocked only a little, and in a moment, she had tight-roped across and was gazing into the statue's face.

It was pitiful. His eyes stared out, stony and blank. It looked as if he had been standing there for years. There was moss flourishing in all the folds of his clothing. One of his hands was gone, and his nose was chipped. Bird droppings covered his shoulders.

"Jack," she whispered. "You in there?" No answer.

It took a little nerve, but she reached out and touched his face. Nothing. No warmth or movement. She placed a finger over his stone lips, but his lips were rough and hard and cold. She leaned in farther and whispered in his ear. "Wake up. We think we found your lady."

"Are you talking to that statue?" Edward asked.

"None of your big fat beeswax."

"Whatever," he said. "Would you mind bringing me back that nest?"

She didn't answer him, for she was beginning to despair. Then a thought came to her. Not wanting Edward to see her, she turned aside and reached into her doughnut pocket. Bringing out a mixture of crumbs and a last bit of the dust from Brigit's little red bag, she sprinkled it over the statue.

She stood back and watched hopefully.

It started so slowly, you wouldn't have noticed it unless you were specifically watching. Which Feenix was. It began at his feet, like a match put to a curtain, and traveled in a slow flame upward, so that at first his loose, rough woven pants grew fluid again, and then his silver-green jacket did, too. His stone gray face and neck grew smooth and took on a warm mahogany color. His nose repaired itself, and his hair turned green. Once more, she gazed at his wide ruddy mouth, which now opened into a big yawn. Then he caught sight of her.

"You're back." He smiled at her. "Did I fall asleep again? It's funny how I keep falling asleep." He looked down at himself and lifted his arm in surprise. "Could you see if you could find my hand for me?"

"Um . . . sure." She scanned the shallows of the muddy water around them and spotted it right away. It was lying, half submerged, not far from where she stood. She crouched down carefully and retrieved it. When she handed it to him, he fitted it like a puzzle piece to the place where it had broken off. In a moment the hand and the wrist had mended themselves without a trace of where the break had been. He shook his arm with satisfaction and then turned to where Edward stood on the edge of the pond with his back to them, peering nervously into the brambles. Apparently, he hadn't noticed a thing.

"You've brought a friend," Jack said. "Can he see me?"

"I don't know," Feenix answered. "You'll have to ask him."

"Can you see me?" Jack called out.

Edward swung around, startled at the voice. He stared at Jack with his mouth open.

"Can you hear me?" Jack asked.

"I can," Edward answered, though a trifle huffily. "I thought you were a statue at first, standing there like that. I suppose you're Jack?"

Quite how he did it, Feenix wasn't sure, but Jack managed to step around her on the log, and in a moment, he had walked across it so lightly it made no stir in the water. He stood in front of Edward. "You may call me that," he said. "Now what do they call *you*?"

"Edward."

Jack tipped his head to one side, causing the nest up in his hair to slip a little. A robin flew out, making tuts of annoyance. It landed in the gnarled, white-blossomed tree.

"You are not quite what I was expecting," Jack said to Ed, shaking his head. "But that's all right. It's always better when things find their own shape."

Feenix had joined them now. "You were expecting him?" she asked curiously. "What shape were you expecting him in?"

Jack laughed. "That's not important now. What's important is the key." He addressed Edward. "May I have it?"

Edward merely raised his eyebrows. Feenix flushed in embarrassment.

In all the excitement, she had totally forgotten about this particular problem. "Listen, I'm so sorry," she said. "We haven't gotten hold of it yet. Edward *did* find your lady, though, and the others went to bring her back, so maybe when she arrives . . ."

But Jack was totally ignoring her. He was staring hard at Edward. "If you found my lady, I'm sure she gave it to you." Edward couldn't take his eyes off Jack. Feenix found this all a bit annoying.

"Think about it. She must have given you *something*," Jack persisted.

"No," Ed said. "She didn't give me anything."

The robin chose this moment to fly back out of the tree and land on Jack's shoulder. It stared at Edward accusingly.

"Think about it once more," Jack said. "Did you come away with something you had not left with?"

Edward blinked, and Feenix saw that a troubled thought had dawned on him. "Well, yes, actually, I did," Edward said. "Not that it would do you any good. I broke a doorknob off when I was leaving. I think I must have put it in my pocket, but I have no idea where it went."

Jack looked stern but not worried. He waited the way Ms. Trevino sometimes did when you hadn't given her the right answer and she knew you were holding out on her.

Cheeryup! Cheeryup! sang the robin.

For a moment Feenix wondered what she had done with the knob, then she unzipped her Hello Kitty purse and rummaged around until she felt the fluted glass edge. She pulled it out.

"Hey!" Ed protested. "Where'd you find that?"

"I found it behind your dresser."

"Didn't I specifically tell you not to touch anything? Didn't I?"

What a dinklewart he was. "I was going to give it back to you."

"What is wrong with you? You can't just go lifting other people's stuff like that."

"Must you be such a crankypants? You should count yourself lucky that I found it at all."

Jack now burst into laughter. "I knew one of you would have it, but it is more likely that the key found *you*. My hour is nearly arrived, and *your* time, which burns so fast and bright, must not be wasted." He held out his hand for the doorknob.

Feenix found it was not so easy to let go of. There was something in its weight and shape, but she let him take it and wondered if it might make him think to offer her what he had offered her before.

"Now," Jack said joyfully. He shook his green curls loose, then straightened the nest on his head. "Where did that door go? I think I saw it over here the other day." He stepped lightly along the brick path, peering into the brambles. The robin stayed on his shoulder, maybe so it could keep a better eye on things. Feenix and Edward followed.

On the other side of the pond, Jack stopped and thrust his arms into the thick tangle of vines and thorny branches. He pushed them aside, and there it was, half hidden, a door, pale blue and smelling freshly of paint. You could see the hole where a doorknob would fit.

He turned to them, smiling his wide ruddy smile. "I'm excited. Are you excited? It feels like it's been forever. And tomorrow, with luck, I will find my lady again."

"Okay," said Edward. "But you'd better watch out for that cat. There's a really big one out there."

Jack laughed at this. "No fear!" he said. "It was the cat who brought you to me. We know each other well. Now tell me, Edward, did my lady set us a meeting place?"

"Uhhh . . . not that I know of."

"No matter, I know all the old places. Now then, Edward, may I kiss you? I offer this as a thank-you for finding her."

Edward, no big surprise, was startled. He took a step away and laughed nervously. "No thanks necessary. Glad to help."

"It will help you remember."

"Remember what?"

"Why, all that's happened today."

"I don't think I'm likely to forget any of this."

"Really?" Jack laughed. "Are you sure?"

"No, it's okay, really."

Feenix felt the blood beating in her ears. Now it would be her turn. Jack smiled slyly. He leaned in to whisper to her. "We'll meet again one day when you are grown. When that happens, I'll offer you what you wish for once more. Let's see if you remember me then."

She stared at him in confusion, but Jack had already turned back to the blue door and was sliding the spindle of the door-knob into the hole. He turned the knob with a click. The door swung open without a sound. They could all see the narrow passageway that had been cut through the thick hedge of brambles and thorns and mist. Jack stepped forward.

He walked ahead along the winding path so quickly and lightly, Feenix had to hurry to keep up with him. She could hear Edward following behind slowly, grumbling to himself.

When she emerged from the brambles into the more open space of the piney woods, she stood and looked around in bewilderment. There was no sign of Jack anywhere.

34

Do We Knock?

Just as Brigit cried out "Not that one!" Danton looked down and saw the dragonfly about to land on the trigger flower. In midair, just for a few seconds, gravity let go of him. He was able to lift himself a little higher, and he passed right over the first lily pad and instead came down on the next one. He leaped to the shore, and he threw his arms around Brigit. She hugged him back and was sure he was going to kiss her. The toad, however, snorked a warning that this was not the time.

They stepped away from each other a little awkwardly and turned to look at the door in the wall. "Do we knock?" Danton asked.

"No, I think we open the door a crack and we listen."

Danton opened the door the narrowest of cracks, and a bar of strong white light appeared. But there was no sound. He opened the door a little wider and peered in and then made a funny face and stepped aside so Brigit could see, too.

They were looking into a large, extremely well-appointed kitchen, the kind that someone who liked to throw big fancy dinner parties might have. Its shelves were stacked with brightly colored tableware and linen napkins and crystal drinking glasses. One wall was hung with spoons, knives, meat cleavers, and other utensils. Copper frying pans and saucepans dangled from racks. Several huge pots sat on a lower shelf, each one big enough to boil an entire pig in. It was neat as a pin, and somehow, for all its expensive kitchenware, it had a lonely, unused feel.

They stepped inside quietly. The toad came with them. "Look," whispered Brigit. The kitchen led into another room. From where they stood, they could catch a glimpse of the wallpaper with peacocks and twisting vines and the rich carpet spread on the floor. They could see an armchair, as well, and a corner of a table with a long red tablecloth.

"C'mon," said Brigit. "That must be the room where Edward found the Lady." She headed toward it, her braid bouncing against her back.

"Hey, slow down," Danton whispered and took hold of her arm. "We've got to scout it out first." He pulled her behind the half-open kitchen door, and they peered through the crack where the hinges were.

Danton's hand tightened on her arm.

The Lady sat in the middle of the room, tied to a kitchen chair. Her back was to them, but her hair buzzed and swarmed with bees.

The second thing they saw was the Tiltersmith. He sat at her feet on a low footstool.

The third thing they saw was the huge slippery serpent curled up against the exit door. Its glittering eyes watched the scene happening in front of itself.

"Well, my queen, my lady, have you not missed me at all?" the Tiltersmith was asking.

The only answer he got for a long moment was a low, angry humming of bees. Then finally, she let out an impatient gust of breath. "Why do you persist with these foolish questions?"

The Tiltersmith sighed. "I have been roaming near and far as I am bound to do," he said. "There was no hour when you were not in my thoughts. There was no world I visited, not one of my estates or palaces, where I did not wish you were at my side so we could see it through each other's eyes. There were astounding sights that would have taken your breath away. There was a place where a great green river overran its banks every time the moon came near, and drowned everything in its path for many hundreds of miles around."

"How lovely," she said.

"Ah, but when it receded, it left behind great nuggets and chunks of precious emeralds just for the picking."

"I'm sorry to have missed that one," she said.

If he heard her sarcasm, he ignored it and went on. "And you could have watched a volcano erupt out of a sea, a sight you never forget. The volcano like a genie who has waited a thousand years to be unstoppered from his bottle. First the smoke and ash and the great plume of glittering dust bowing and bending over the water. Then a great kettledrum of a thunderstorm and the mountain spitting its lava and fire and ash down into the water. Then water boiling and steaming up into the sky."

"It sounds a most entrancing sight, Lord Lopside," she said. "But was it you who unstoppered the bottle?"

The Tiltersmith gave a small cough. "Ah, well . . ."

The bees' humming rose again in volume. "As I thought," the Lady replied with some bitterness. "And was there destruction wrought? Was there a great tsunami which fell upon the lands nearby?"

"I'm sure there was destruction. It is in the nature of things. But I did not stay long. I had other business to attend to."

"And you would have me travel with you to witness such business? Perhaps tipping a world too far on its axis so all that's left is burning desert and mountains of ice? Or maybe making one of your delicate adjustments to a harmless virus. Something that will cause the new version to kill most of the life in its path? Or tearing a hole in a sky so the sun melts an ice cap and drowns all the lands? You would like a companion for this? To witness your jokes and your tricks and your farts and your tilting hallways? You think it would bring me joy to follow you around and watch you leave a trail of wreckage wherever you travel?"

The Tiltersmith sat back on his stool now and watched her sadly. "But surely you forget, my lady, these destructions and jokes, as you call them, are necessary adjustments when a world has grown too old or failed to care for itself, when it needs an ending. And just as often they bring new beginnings. A chance to start over. That little volcano I spoke of grew into a green and fertile island abounding with life."

"After many centuries?"

For a moment his face grew sadder, but they saw how he could not tear his eyes from hers. At last, he spoke again, this time more gently. "Do you forget that it was I who exploded your world out of nothing into something? I who put my finger on the scale, back there in the deep beginning of time? If I hadn't done so, matter and antimatter would have been perfectly balanced. And then what would have happened?"

She didn't answer.

"They would have canceled each other out," he told her. "There would have been no matter at all. Nothing to build with. You know this."

"All right," she said. "I will give you that. We all know what we owe you. But were you the one who did the building that came after? Were you the one who tended all the suns and the worlds and the gardens that came into being? There is an energy which always seeks to move toward wholeness. It's not your energy."

Now the superintendent finally looked annoyed. "All right, all right. You may be correct that it hasn't been *all* my doing, but still, you must admit that on your own little world, your little *earth*, they have made a fine mess of things. At the rate it's going, with absolutely no further help from me, it will finish itself off in no time at all. Why would you wish to return there when we could travel together and you could begin again?"

"What if I said it was because I don't like your tiny little feet and your bootblack hair and that tail I know you keep tucked into your pants?"

The Tiltersmith's tight gray face turned almost pink with the effort to keep himself under control. "I would say, do not be so small-minded. You know well that all of those are merely outward shapes that I take for the fun of it. I can change them to whatever you like in the snap of a green bean."

"What if I said that no matter the shape you took, you would not be the one I loved?"

"I would say your loved one is a lost cause. He has been locked out and even now has turned to stone."

"And I would say you do not have that power."

"He has despaired of you, Lady, and despair is its own power."

She was quiet for a moment. "You know the scales and what tips them, but you also know that in my world, hope bears ever the greater weight. Even now, my love seeks a way to find me through his messengers."

He gave a snort of disdain. "Well, of course. But did you think I wouldn't be waiting for him and his puny helpers? It would take great luck for any of them to find their way here, and even if they did, did you imagine I would let them through? You should have seen the fine traps I set for them. By now, I regret to say, they will be at the bottom of the abyss or have been devoured by my pet lily pads."

The bees in their outrage turned themselves up to full volume.

"If the Green One has sent them with my tools, they will have protection," the Lady told him coldly.

The Tiltersmith laughed. "Oh, my dearest. You think so? And what kind of tools would those be?"

"Nothing grand enough that would please your appetite for madness and mayhem. Just simple garden tools. But they will be powerful enough if he has cared for them properly."

"Ah. Well, I have a surprise for you. As I was going round

about on my travels this time, look at these little treasures I found."

Danton had to stifle a groan as he saw the Tiltersmith pull out his own crummy backpack. He unzipped it and brought forth the two juggling balls, the little red sack, and the tarnished horn. He set them in his lap.

At the sight of them, the Lady let out a gasp. "Thief! Pickpocket! Lopsided swindler!" she cried. The bees were in a fury. They flew out of her hair and dashed themselves against the Tiltersmith's face and eyes.

He put up his hands, laughing. "Call them off, Lady. They will spend themselves for naught. My skin is too thick for their sting."

"And my messengers? What have you done with my messengers?"

"As I said, my pet. Best not to dwell upon it." He continued batting at the bees. "Call your little warriors in, my sweet, or I shall lose my patience."

The Lady bowed her head and murmured a low hum of a word. The bees returned to her hair reluctantly. When she lifted her head again, Danton saw the tears glittering in her eyes. Such a boil of fury now rose up in Danton's throat, he nearly jumped out without regard for the consequences, but Brigit grabbed hold of his arm and shook her head in warning.

"Radiant Queen of the May, don't weep. I will strike a great bargain with you. I will give you back your beloved tools, and I will make as many new worlds as you wish for. I have a great knack for it, you know. You'll be able to garden to your heart's content. All I ask is that you consent to be my own companion."

There was a long silence.

At last, the Lady spoke. "Why is it you wish for my pledge so dearly?"

"Because I am lonely?" he answered.

"I expect you could have a hundred wives if you wanted. What do you want with me?"

He tipped his head to the side and looked at her. "There is something in you, with your bees and your unbearably brilliant eyes and your dirty feet, that charms me."

She lifted her feet and inspected them and made a little face. "And if I accept your bargain, what becomes of my own little world?"

"That is not for me to say. If your people love it enough, they will change their ways." He waited for her answer, watching her face closely.

"I don't think it's really me you long for, you know."

"No?" he asked. "Then what?"

"You long to change your own nature, but I cannot do that for you. And I will never pledge myself to you."

The look of yearning on the Tiltersmith's face changed, and he let out a breath of angry impatience. He picked up the juggling balls, the red bag, and the golden horn and threw them in the backpack. "Your foolish stubbornness is not part of your charm. When I return, before morning, I will hear your answer once more. If it is still no, then you will sit here until you, too, turn to stone." He stood and walked toward the serpent.

"Here, you great slug," he said. "You will guard this with your life. Do not move from the door. No one is to come in or go out. I must check my traps now, and if I am hungry enough and angry enough, perhaps *I* will eat what I find in them. Then I will take a few well-deserved hours of rest." He started to move toward the door to the kitchen.

Danton whispered urgently in Brigit's ear. "Quick. We've got to hide. Pick a pot. Hurry. Hurry."

She followed him to the line of big pots on the lower shelf nearby. He climbed into the biggest one and scrunched down. She climbed into the pot next to his. The toad vanished under a cupboard.

35

The Ouroboros

Danton and Brigit crouched in their hiding places and heard the angry little footsteps clickity tap past them. They listened for the sound of the door that led to the river. It opened and then shut a moment later with a bang. They counted slowly to twenty and then, as if they had read each other's mind perfectly, poked their heads up and looked around.

The gleaming kitchen was silent and empty except for the toad, which sat in the middle of the floor. *Snork*, it whispered impatiently.

Without any further waste of time, they climbed out and tiptoed over to look into the other room. The Lady sat with her back to them, still tied to her chair. The ivory-colored serpent lay curled in a mountainous tangle of coils. Its great shovel-shaped head rested on top. It appeared to be sleeping.

Danton searched the kitchen for inspiration. He tiptoed over to the wall hung with utensils and examined what was there. He could feel Brigit's eyes watching him unhappily. Which one would give him the best chance? He picked up a long carving knife with a pointed tip. This might have worked if he'd had the slightest idea where a snake's heart was located. He put it back. Then he took down a heavy meat cleaver. It was as big and heavy as a small ax. This would be better. With some luck, maybe he could cut the thing's head off. He swung it experimentally through the air.

"Danton, you can't be serious," Brigit whispered.

"You know the stories better than I do. I don't see what choice we have." He could hardly believe he was saying this, but he knew half the battle with being brave was making yourself sound that way. "Now, listen, if I miss, the creature will at least be distracted while it swallows me down. You'll have time to undo the Lady and get yourselves out the door. Don't forget the backpack. Okay?"

"No! It's not okay!"

But he had already leaped silently forward into the room, meat cleaver raised. He passed the Lady, and as he did, Brigit heard her make a sound of surprise. The bees went crazy. Danton lifted the meat cleaver a little higher and, standing over the huge shovel-shaped head, aimed for the thick neck below it. Brigit breathed in and then forgot to breathe out.

The snake opened its eyes just as Danton brought the blade down. There was a loud metallic clang. The blade bounced off.

In the same instant, faster than the eye could follow, the head and upper body of the snake shot sideways, and it looped itself like a twist tie around Danton's waist. His scream was choked off as the snake lifted him in the air and waved him back and forth, showing off its prize to an admiring crowd that wasn't there. Danton's arms and legs thrashed wildly.

Brigit ran into the middle of the room and stood in front of the snake's face. "Put him down!" she yelled. "Put him down! He's totally indigestible." The Lady, watching all of this from where she sat tied to her chair, cried out, "You have only seconds. It will choke off the boy's circulation in a moment or two, and then his heart will stop. Give the creature something sweet. It has a terrible sweet tooth."

"Sweet?" Brigit cried in despair.

Snorrrk, snorrrk! grunted the toad.

"Doughnuts!" the Lady translated. "The toad says you have doughnuts."

It took Brigit only a second to remember. They were still hanging against her side in the little drawstring bag. Oh, blessings upon the head of Aunt Kit! Brigit got hold of the bag and yanked it open and pulled out a big, fat munkki doughnut sparkling with sugar. It was, by some miracle, still completely round and intact.

"Do as I say!" the Lady cried. "Stand close in front of the worm and wave the doughnut about."

Brigit did not hesitate but walked right up to the snake's head and waved the doughnut in its face. Now the snake, who had been slowly but surely tightening the loop around Danton, stopped what it was doing and stuck its forked tongue out into the air. As Brigit and everyone else in Mr. Ross's class knew, snakes did not smell with their noses but with their forked tongues and the two little holes in the roofs of their mouths.

Brigit waved the doughnut around more vigorously, and at the direction of the Lady, she started to walk backward, still holding the doughnut out at arm's length. The snake did not let go of Danton, but it loosened its grip a bit and started to make a U-turn slowly across the floor in order to follow the scent. Danton dangled in the air, eyes wide open, gasping for breath.

"Go to the rear of the serpent and wait for its tail to come free," the Lady said.

Brigit did as instructed, and the snake began to follow her. It had to unfurl itself a bit to do this, and just as the Lady predicted, its tail, which was pointed and quite narrow at the end, popped free.

"Wave the doughnut in the air some more," the Lady said. Brigit did that. The Lady called out to the snake. "This person will give you the doughnut, but first you must let go of the boy!"

The snake flicked the air with its tongue and gave a hiss. Then, with a quick heave, it released the knot around Danton. Danton fell heavily to the carpet, like a bag of sand.

"Now hurry. You will know what needs to be done."

Brigit darted forward and slid the doughnut onto the narrow tip of the serpent's tail. She gave the doughnut a gentle but firm push so it slid several inches upward and lodged there securely. She stepped away.

The serpent's head drew closer and closer to its own rear end. The forked tongue was, all the while, tasting the air. Finally, the snake stretched its jaw wide and slid its open mouth over its tail. It had a little way to go before reaching the doughnut, but it was determined. Up the tail its mouth went. In a moment the doughnut was reached, and the serpent was swallowing with a look of bliss in its tiny red eyes.

"Quick, unloose me," the Lady said to Brigit.

Brigit did as she was told. As she worked at the knots, she called out to Danton. "You okay?" Danton was on the floor, coughing and catching his breath.

"Perfect," he managed to choke out.

"My tools!" the Lady called to him as she threw off the last of the ropes that tied her. "Get my tools. They will be needed."

Danton got up and stumbled to the backpack. He pulled it over his shoulders.

The serpent had now completely demolished the doughnut, but instead of backing up, it continued onward, swallowing its own tail. Perhaps it thought there were more doughnuts farther ahead.

"Pity that Lord Lopside should miss this," said the Lady. "He will be much disappointed. It's just the sort of sight he relishes. I wonder where he found this creature in the first place. The Ouroboros is exceedingly rare."

"What's an Ouroboros?" Danton asked.

"Later," she said. "We must find our way out of here before Lopside decides to return." The snake was shrinking rapidly. "Now," the Lady said. "Hurry. Just climb over the creature and have no fear. It is much too busy to pay attention to us right now."

Brigit lifted the toad up, and one by one, they climbed over the serpent. There was a moment of panic at the door because of the missing doorknob, but Danton asked if he could borrow a hairpin from the Lady. She handed him one with clover flowers twisted all around it, and he inserted it into the hole where the doorknob had once been. It was but the work of a moment before he had found the catch and they were all out in the hallway.

"Now, put the toad down," said the Lady. "She knows the way. We will follow her."

Brigit wondered about the "her," but, of course, there was no time to ask questions. They sped along, following the hopping toad. Down the carpet they hurried. The chandeliers glittered overhead. They ignored the cabinets full of their wonderful and grotesque treasures. Behind the doors, the mysterious worlds remained quiet. When they came, at last, to the top of the three marble steps, the toad paused. They waited.

"Do you hear something?" Brigit asked. It was soft and far away. A tappity tapping, coming rapidly closer. But when they all stopped to listen, the sound stopped, too.

The toad gave a soft *snork* and hastened down the three steps. Now, without hesitation, it led them along the tunnel to the first fork. Here it paused, once again, and once again, Brigit heard the tappity tapping. "Can you hear that?" she asked. But again, the sound had stopped.

"Hurry," the Lady said. "Hurry."

The toad took the right turn. At the next fork, it took them left, and at the third, once more, left again. It was only a short distance then before the lights began to fade and they could feel a drafty change in the air. The tunnel opened up and became the cavern. "Okay," Danton whispered. "This is it. This is where we came in."

Brigit listened, but what she heard now was only the sound of the toad, who snorked impatiently. "Yes, old friend," the Lady said. "We have done well." She picked the little creature up and handed it to Brigit, who slipped it into her sweatshirt pocket and zipped the pocket up.

"Does anybody see the ladder?" Danton asked.

"Here it is!" Brigit answered. "But I can't quite reach it." Her arms were stretched over her head.

They all saw it dangling in the air, and the Lady laughed with excitement, and the bees zoomed all around her head. "It's been so long. It feels like forever. There will be sun, won't there? And birds. It will be best to close this doorway up once we're out of here. Tell your friend—he'll know what to do. If luck stays with us, tomorrow I will find my Green One again. But there's no time to waste, so let us hurry."

Danton took charge. "I think Brigit should go first. She'll need a boost. Then you, Lady." He lifted Brigit into the air so she could grab on higher and then get a foothold. Immediately she began to climb.

Brigit had gone up only a few rungs when the Lady began to climb up behind her. Then it was Danton's turn. "Now, keep your eyes open for the wormhole," Danton called up to Brigit, "and let us know as soon as you can see the light."

"I will," she called back. "But I don't see anything yet."

She climbed on as fast as she could, her eyes straining against the darkness. For a while there was no sound other than the noise of their breathing. She wondered how far they would have to go. How much distance had they fallen when they first came in? It could have been miles. But she didn't want Danton to see her worry, so she did not allow herself to slow. Sweat began to trickle down the back of her shirt. Her eyes strained upward.

And then she heard the sound again. Not far away this time. And louder. In fact, it had become more of a pounding than a tapping. Coming closer.

"What's that?" Danton asked.

"Pay no attention!" the Lady commanded. "Move quickly."

Now the pounding was rhythmic and coming faster. *Boomp, boomp, boomp!* It echoed in the walls around them. Brigit went on climbing, but then the Lady stopped for a moment and leaned down to hand something to Danton.

"Here, take this," she said to him. "We will need it soon. Do not unsheathe it till I tell you. Use great care. It's sharp."

He took the knife. The handle felt smooth like ivory. He put it in his pocket.

"Climb faster!" the Lady urged them. The muscles in Brigit's arms and legs were beginning to tremble, but she kept on as best she could.

The sound was drawing closer. *Kaboom, kaboom, kaboom!*

Small stones began to break loose from the walls around them. "Is it an earthquake?" Danton asked.

"It is, indeed, an earthquake of sorts. It's Lord Lopside. He's discovered our escape."

"But how can it be him?" Danton objected, even as he continued to climb. "How can he make a noise like that with those little tiny feet?"

"Because his feet aren't always that tiny. He has shaped himself into something better suited to his ends," the Lady answered him. "But do not give up hope. We'll keep our wits about us."

Kaboom, kaboom! Kaboom!

"Do you see any sign of the doorway?" the Lady called to Brigit.

"Not yet!" Brigit panted back.

It was no more than a few minutes later that the great booming feet came to a halt. The three of them could see nothing in all that darkness, but they felt the ladder tighten and sway in their hands. Whatever shape was down there had grabbed hold of the rungs and begun to pull itself up.

"You will cut the ropes off beneath you when I tell you," the Lady whispered to Danton. "But not yet. It is best if he falls as far as possible."

Below them the giant Tiltersmith could be heard laughing as he used his long arms and enormous legs to propel himself upward. He was gaining quickly. The fleeing threesome tried to go faster, but Brigit felt herself beginning to fail, and as she slowed, so they all slowed.

Where could that light be? Brigit wondered.

Danton, who had been trying not to, looked now and saw, several rungs down, an enormous boulder-sized head peering up at him. Its features were distorted and crude, as if a child had pinched the nose and mouth out of clay. Danton almost didn't recognize him, but then he saw the pale-blue eyes gleaming greedily.

"I see it! I see the light!" Brigit called. "I'll be able to touch it in a moment."

"Cut the ladder!" the Lady cried to Danton.

Danton pulled out the knife and unsheathed it. Then he bent, holding on to the ladder with one hand. With the other hand he put the knife to the rope.

The giant was only two rungs away now, but the knife was wonderfully sharp. It was only a matter of seconds before Danton had sliced through on one side. The ladder immediately gave way, and the rungs collapsed uselessly. The hideous creature let out a furious yell. Danton twisted himself around and sliced the other side of the ladder free.

Lord Lopside let out a great thundering roar as he fell and fell and then crashed to the floor.

"Now!" called the Lady. "Make a chain so we will go through all at once!"

They made a chain, reaching up to grab each other's ankles. Brigit put her finger to the light.

36

In the Piney Woods

Edward came forward into the piney woods, looking around. "What happened? Where's your funny friend?" he asked.

Feenix shot him a look of annoyance. "I don't know. I came around the bend, and he was gone."

"So he musta run off somewhere, huh?"

"Or maybe we can't see him here," she replied. "I bet he's not easy to see when we're on this side of the hedge."

Edward was about to remind her that she was a deluded cream-puff head, but he was distracted by an odd thumping coming from somewhere very nearby. "What's that?" he asked.

"What's what?" she answered.

"That weird sort of kabumping. Where's that coming from? It almost feels like—" He patted at his side and then shoved his hand in his pocket. In a moment, he had pulled out the jar labeled *Cinnamon*.

They both stared. Inside the jar, the leathery cocoon was shaking and vibrating. Edward held it out in front of himself nervously. In the next moment there was a sound like a champagne cork popping, accompanied by an explosion of sparks. When these cleared away, there stood Brigit and Danton. They looked a bit bedraggled and worse for wear, though probably no more so than Feenix and Edward.

"Where is she?" Danton demanded. "Did you see her?" He was looking all around.

"Where's who?" Edward asked.

"The Lady, the bee lady. She came up with us. We made a chain. She was in the middle. I had her by the ankle."

"Well, we just got here, and we haven't seen anyone but ourselves," Feenix said. "However, if it's any consolation, we got Jack out. Only we lost him, too."

There was a long silence while Danton, Feenix, and Brigit all stared at one another. Edward was examining the glass jar in his hand with fascination.

"You've got to close that doorway!" Brigit remembered. "The Lady said you'd know what to do."

Edward looked at her, confused. Then he stuck his hand in his pocket and pulled out the jar's cap and screwed it on. "Okay. I'll take care of it." He put the jar back in his pocket.

Danton sighed, and then he stood up taller and smiled. "Look," he said. "The fog's clearing, and we did what we had to do. We got them both free. Now they'll meet each other tomorrow and they'll do the rest, right?"

"But don't you see? They won't be able to," Brigit said unhappily.

"What do you mean?" Danton asked.

"You never gave her the backpack with the tools. It's still on your back."

37

Beltane Dinner

They found Kit sitting in the middle of the living-room floor. All around her were long lengths of ribbon. Some were stretched out like the rays of the sun; some were still tangled. There were maybe two dozen of them in many different colors.

There was a look of relief on her face when she saw them all piling into the house, but she said nothing except, "Well, it's about time. You'll come and help me, won't you? There's a lot to do before tomorrow morning."

"What is that smell of garlicky cheese and tomatoes and heaven come down to earth?" Danton asked. He started to move toward the kitchen.

"Don't you dare open that oven!" Kit ordered. "It's a soufflé for our Beltane supper. Asparagus and gruyère. If you open it, the soufflé will fall. First you help me, and then we will eat."

So they all helped her untangle the Maypole ribbons and then wound them back up carefully. After that she sent them all here and there through the house, gathering other things that would be needed—paper goods and tablecloths and platters and serving spoons and matches and a bottle of home-made hawthorn brandy. She had them put together more bags of munkki doughnuts, along with muffins and scones.

While they worked, they whispered to each other. It was agreed that they would see if they could worm more information out of Kit about the old stories. Maybe she would know where to find the Green Man and the Lady tomorrow so they could give her the tools.

When they sat down to supper, there was a salad of fiddle-head ferns and roasted pine nuts. There was the asparagus and gruyère soufflé. There was fresh warm sourdough bread, along with a large soft blob of sweet butter on a silver dish. Then there were strawberries with whipped cream. All early-spring foods to honor Beltane, Kit said.

"But I thought it was May Day tomorrow," Feenix said casually, glancing at the others.

"It is," Kit said. "Beltane is just a different name for May Day. There have been lots of names for it. It's the day halfway between the spring equinox and the summer solstice."

"That's right," Brigit agreed. "Beltane is what they called it in Ireland, where my grandparents grew up. My grandmother loved that holiday."

Kit smiled at her. "I bet she got all dressed up and put haw-thorn garlands in her hair and jumped over the bonfires."

"She did," said Brigit. "I've seen pictures."

Kit nodded. "It was always a big holiday in Ireland and other places in Europe. Here it seemed to mostly die out for a while, but now I think it's making a comeback. People have always celebrated it because it's supposed to be the time of year when the bees start pollinating the flowers and animals start giving birth and the summer crops begin to come up out of the ground."

"But why a Maypole?" Feenix asked.

Edward laughed. "And you call *me* ignorant? Don't you get it? The whole holiday is just one great big fertility ritual."

Kit shook her head, laughing. "Well, of course some people say that. But a lot of people like to think that the Maypole is a symbol of the World Tree. According to the stories, the World Tree runs right through the middle of the earth. It's the axis around which everything turns. When we put up the Maypole, it was always meant to remind us how the earth keeps turning around and around, and how every year this turning will bring back warm clean rain and new green things and young life. Nowadays, of course, it reminds us of something else."

"Like what?" Danton asked.

Aunt Kit picked up a big ripe strawberry and stared at it a little sadly. She put it back down. "Well, nowadays," she said, "the Maypole also reminds us of all that is going to get lost if we don't get our act together and get the balance of nature back."

There was a short silence, then Feenix took her chance. "But what about the May Queen and the Green Man? Isn't the Maypole supposed to be where they meet up? Or is that somewhere else?"

Aunt Kit picked up her strawberry again and took a bite and then another bite. She seemed to be thinking while she chewed. A little juice stained her lips a bright strawberry red.

She said, "Well, when us modern people *act out* that meeting, the Maypole is usually where it takes place. But I imagine that for the true meeting, those two would choose some really old place, some place where the sky still comes close enough to talk to the stones, don't you?"

Feenix glanced at the others and said, "Of course."

Aunt Kit went on: "And it would have to be very early in the morning, right? But keep in mind that those sorts of persons don't allow themselves to be seen much nowadays."

"True," agreed Feenix.

"And anyway, it's just a story, isn't it?" Kit added.

"Of course it is," said Edward.

Kit wiped her mouth with a napkin and stood up to clear the table. "Why don't you people go up to the attic and find yourself some fun stuff to wear? People love to get dressed up for this. Last year there were some great May Queens and a cartload of Green Men and Green Ladies, too. But whatever looks like fun. It's very free-form."

Edward said you couldn't pay him enough to go up to that attic. Feenix, however, was quick to jump at the suggestion. She loved costumes and she loved Kit's attic. "C'mon, Brigit, Danton, let's clean up and get going. Edward, we'll find you a pretty blouse or something."

"Yuck, yuck."

"Oh, just one thing," Kit said as casually as she could. "Don't forget we're with the setup crew, so we have to be there before the crowd arrives."

Edward was about to stand, but now he froze. "What does that mean? Wait a minute. What does that mean?"

"Well, the dancing and music and eating won't start till around eight, but we need to get there a little before sunrise. There's a lot to do."

Edward made the horrible noise a person who's just been run through with a sword makes.

38

May Day

When Kit woke Edward, Feenix, Danton, and Brigit in the morning, the fog was gone, and the streetlamps were just flickering off. It was the hour when the sky overhead is a dark translucent blue and the last stars are just leaving. The moon was nearly, but not quite full. It hung, almost transparent, near the horizon. Kit gave them each an English muffin with jam and butter and then set them to bringing the Maypole and the bags and the two red wagons down the steps.

"Move quick!" Danton said. "Kit is baking something. Let's meet on the front stoop before she comes out."

Feenix went down first. She had put together a perfect May Day dancing costume, with a long patchwork skirt and a white blouse and a snug red vest. At the corner of her eye she had painted a bright-ribboned Maypole. It was still chilly, but there was a surprising hint of warmth to come in the air and she wore her coat thrown wide open.

Danton was next. He was wearing a sharp-looking green derby hat with a bright-blue feather. Feenix had painted his face green and added some yellow primroses. Otherwise, he had on his regular clothes and a sweatshirt with his backpack over his shoulders.

Edward had made no fashion concessions to the day. He wore his jeans and a T-shirt and a jacket, and he had mashed his lucky baseball hat down on his head.

Brigit came last, and it was clear she had been crying. She was wearing an old white cotton dress with a lace collar. It was a little big and a little long, but she had tied a velvet sash around the waist and that worked pretty well. Over it was her green jacket.

Danton bent down anxiously to look at her face. "What is it, Brigit? What's wrong?"

"They're gone," she said miserably.

"What's gone?"

"The notes. Everything I could remember of what we said yesterday. I wrote it all down last night on a piece of paper and put it in my jacket pocket." She searched her pocket again. "And now it's not there." She looked like she was going to cry again, but stopped herself. "I'm so sorry. Where could it have gone?"

"Where'd you get the paper?" Edward asked. "Did you, by any chance, take it from my spiral notebook?"

Brigit nodded. "I didn't think you'd mind."

"I don't, but things keep going missing from that notebook lately. It's very weird."

"It doesn't matter," Danton said to them calmly. "It doesn't matter at all. This is what matters." He patted at the backpack hanging from his shoulder. "All we have to do is remember to find the Lady and give this to her. We can do that, all of us together, can't we?"

"Of course we can," Feenix said. "They're supposed to meet up this morning, right? Jack and the Lady. I remember that part, don't you? We go to wherever they are and hand the bag over."

"Yes," agreed Danton. "Kit told us last night, didn't she? An old place where the sky meets the stones, and we have to get there early. It'll be someplace in the park, I'm sure. Everybody, think hard. We'll figure it out."

Kit stepped out onto the stoop. The group fell silent. Kit was wearing a wreath of yellow flowers in her hair and a long warm-looking cardigan. From underneath the cardigan peered out a peach-colored mandarin-collared dress embroidered with green vines and white lilies.

Whoaaa, Feenix thought. Kit was dressing up for somebody, for sure. "Nice dress," she commented casually. "Where'd you find it?"

Kit waved her hand. "Oh, that thrift store on Fifth." She looked up and spotted the moon dangling over the earth. "Oh, my fur and whiskers! As soon as that thing sets, the sun will start rising. We're going to be late. Hurry up!"

They trundled up the hill toward the park, not speaking much. The wheels of the red wagons creaked. Once they entered the park, it was not long before they came through the trees into the meadow.

Here there was a small accident. Who was to blame was not clear, but somehow Feenix's and Edward's wagons bumped into each other, and a number of picnic items went spilling out onto the ground, along with Feenix's backpack, which she had jammed into the wagon with everything else.

"You know, if you could just move a little faster than a bottle of ketchup," Feenix said, "you wouldn't keep crashing into people."

Edward retorted smoothly, "And if you could just walk directly from point A to point B without all your wackadoodling around, maybe we could get wherever we're supposed to be going by next Thursday."

Brigit and Danton, still holding the Maypole, stood by while Kit and Ed and Feenix bent to retrieve the fallen items. When Kit stood back up, she was holding a pale-green ball of tightly packed leaves. "This fell out of your backpack, Feenix." She did not ask Feenix why she was carrying around a cabbage. She simply said, "Well, I guess it will be perfect for holding down a corner of the picnic blanket," and she laid it on top of the pile in the wagon.

The translucent blueness of the sky was fading to something lighter. But the sun showed no sign of itself yet, and the meadow still wore its night colors and shapes—hunchbacked clumps of brown and gray bushes and forbidding black sentinel trees. The hills and valleys rose and fell like shadows of shadows.

"There they are!" Aunt Kit pointed. In the middle of the meadow there was a flickering of lanterns. "It's the rest of the setup crew." She hurried ahead.

When Kit was out of earshot, Danton said quickly, "As soon as we get there, we'll make some sort of excuse, and then we'll figure out where we should go look." They all nodded except for Edward, who did not appear fully convinced that he was actually awake and walking through the park at six in the morning.

As they drew closer to the flickering lights, they saw people moving around, setting up tables and taking out blankets. Aunt Kit was talking in a huddle with a little group. "Hello," Danton called out. He and Brigit put the Maypole on the ground.

The huddle broke apart. In addition to Kit, there were Mrs. Chaduary, Tom the tree guy, and Mrs. Wu. Their faces were difficult to read in the half darkness and the flickering light of the lanterns. "Welcome," Tom said. "We're so glad you made it." There was a strange silence, as if they were all waiting for Danton to say something.

Danton, who had all along been trying to think up an excuse that would free them to go and look for the Lady and Jack, suddenly put his hand up to his neck. "Oh no!" he said. "My scarf! I must have dropped it back there somewhere. That's not good. My grandmother made it for me. I'll have to go back and look."

Tom nodded. He didn't seem at all surprised. "Of course," he said without hesitation. "Granny scarves are never to be treated lightly."

"And you others will help him," Kit added. "Danton will be more likely to find it if you're all together. Just leave the wagons here. Go on, make haste."

The foursome did not wait for further permission but turned and started back across the meadow. "Did you see that?" Feenix said when she was sure they could no longer be heard. "I think they all knew exactly what we were up to. I think they're *all* Hedge Jumpers."

"What? What are you talking about?" Danton asked.

Edward groaned. Feenix gave him the look of a thousand

daggers, but he didn't seem to notice. "Never mind," she said to Danton. "I'll explain it to you later. Just keep going."

"Does anybody have any ideas where we should look first?" Danton asked.

"I do," Brigit said. "I think that business about the sky talking to the stones means a high place, and I believe I know exactly where she meant. I dreamt about it."

She led them to Weaver's Hill, which was not far to the south. In the growing light, the outline of this hill had softened. It was an old, old hill, a tall bread-loaf-shaped rise. The trees at its top were tipped with red and gold where the sun was able to meet them.

"What was in this dream?" Danton asked.

"My brother," she answered simply.

"Your brother?" Danton asked gently.

"Yes. He would have been old enough to walk by now, and in my dream he was taking me up this hill to show me something important. I had the dream a couple of times. Come on. Let's go see."

They'd all climbed this hill in the past, but today it was higher than they remembered. The farther up its side they got, the higher it seemed to go. By the time they reached the top, all four were warm and out of breath and panting. The light was growing stronger, and the orange-gold streaks along the eastern horizon could be seen clearly now.

A path ran through the trees, with a big boulder at one end. "Could that be the stone that's talking to the sky?" asked Feenix. Of course, nobody knew the answer. At the other end of the path stood a pair of wooden benches, empty. They were alone.

"Let's sit down," Danton said, which everyone was glad to do.

They went over to the bench and hadn't been sitting long when they heard the sound of footsteps coming fast through the trees. They all turned eagerly, but it was only an early-morning runner, a woman in blue cropped running pants and a white sweatshirt. She wore sunglasses, which to Feenix seemed kind of show-offy for this time of the morning, and her hair was neatly pulled back in a ponytail. The runner did not slow down as she approached. She didn't even seem to notice the foursome. She had almost gone past their bench when the toad, which had been riding quiet and forgotten in Brigit's pocket all this time, gave a loud *snork!*

Instantly, the runner braked to a halt. She turned to look. "Who snorked?" she demanded.

Brigit unzipped her pocket, and the toad hopped out onto her lap. In the next moment, the runner was standing in front of the bench, pulling her sunglasses up off her face. The Lady. Her eyes were so bright it was almost impossible to meet her gaze. She held out her hand. The toad hopped into it without hesitation.

"What a debt I owe you, faithful one," said the Lady. She brought the toad to her face and kissed it. "Off with you, then. You will not forget and I will not forget." With one swift movement, she lowered the toad to the scrabbly winter grass, and it hopped away.

Now she looked more closely at Brigit, Danton, Edward, and Feenix. "It's you! Where have you been? I hope you brought my Vernariums? We're nearly too late. Quick, give them to me."

Everyone was too dumbfounded at this point to speak, but Danton stood and pulled the backpack off his back and handed it to her. As she fumbled with the zipper, she spoke in agitation. "What a fine mess this place is in. I hardly recognized it. Why are you all just sitting there like that? I can't do this by myself anymore, you know. We've gone beyond that. You'll have to help." She pulled out the little red sack and opened it. "Your hand," she said to Brigit and poured a little of what was inside into her palm. "You may choose. But be quick about it. We're so behind. Remember, don't look."

Brigit didn't stop to think but went to the edge of the hill and tossed the dust into the air. She turned her back quickly, so as not to see where it fell, and hurried back to the others.

The Lady had already pulled out the two red-and-gold juggling balls and was handing them to Feenix. The Lady glanced up into the trees. "Once more," she said. "But be quick about it." Feenix threw them awkwardly into the air, one after the other. As before, the juggling balls seemed to know exactly what to do. Up and up and around and around they flew. The robins came first, calling *Cheeryup, cheeryup*. Next came the blue jays, yelling *Jaaay! Jaaay! Jaaay!* in full-throated screechiness, and then a great cloud of starlings, whistling and clicking and chuckling. Soon the woods all around the meadow were alive with the rise and fall of wings and a hundred competing birdsongs.

Feenix reluctantly gave back the juggling balls.

Now the Lady pulled out the horn and handed it to Danton. "Once more," she said.

"Now?"

"Now."

Danton put the horn to his lips. The first time he produced a loud squawk. The second time an ear-piercing bleat. But the third time the note came out pure and clear and rang in ever-widening circles of gold before it finally faded away. Danton handed the horn back to her.

The foursome waited, hardly breathing, to see what would happen next. Nothing.

Then the rim of the sun rose just a few inches above the treetops. Light spilled in, and the world, which had lain so flat and dull for so long, grew rounded and rolling, and all the hidden colors flooded back into things, and the earth and the stones and the sky sprang joyfully to life.

Once again, they heard a sound coming up from the far side of the hill, twigs breaking and a slap-slap-slapping noise.

A young man appeared, breathing hard. His skin was a shiny wood-bark brown, and his hair was a wiry, bird's-nesty mess. He wore flip-flops and plaid drawstring pajama pants and an unzipped green sweatshirt over a T-shirt, like he'd just gotten out of bed.

"I'm late! I'm late!" he cried. "I know it! I'm so sorry, Flora! I fell asleep again." He ran straight toward them, and they all stepped aside for fear of being run over. When he reached the Lady, he lifted her off the ground and looked up into her face. She looked down at him, laughing.

"I thought perhaps I had lost you for good this time," she said.

"Not this time," he answered and set her down.

They held their hands up and pressed their palms together,

and in a ringing voice she called, "May all shapes be returned to their true natures!"

"May it be so," he seconded.

"Look," Feenix whispered. "The bees are back."

She was right. The Lady must have pulled her ponytail loose, for now her hair was all curling and tangled with primroses and clover. The bees were mad with excitement, flying in and out of the flowers.

Jack and the Lady drew close and put their arms around each other. Whatever went on in that embrace was not clear, for the sun just then succeeded in lifting itself fully free of the treetops and blazed upward into the blue silk of the sky. In those first moments of full blinding light, the foursome had to turn away. This made it difficult to know if Jack and the Lady were kissing or what.

When they looked back again, the pair was walking off into the trees.

39

The Dance

Danton, Brigit, Edward, and Feenix stood at the edge of Weaver's Hill and looked down. The meadow did not seem nearly as far away as it had before, and they were startled to see how green the hill and the lawn had become. Rivulets of jade-green grass and patches of emerald-green grass contained spreading islands of clover.

"Did you do that?" Danton asked Brigit.

"Did I do what?" she asked.

"The grass."

She shook her head and laughed. Edward looked at him oddly. "I think that was probably photosynthesis," he pointed out.

"Well, whatever it was," Danton said, "I think we did what we needed to do, didn't we? And this is going to be fun, don't you think?" He gestured down toward the meadow.

Edward made a face. "Sure, if you enjoy hanging around with a lot of people dressed up like trees and fairy godmothers."

People were wandering into the meadow from all directions now. Some were dressed in normal clothes, but others were dressed like queens going to their coronations. Then there were those dressed in green tights and Robin Hood jerkins and the ones wearing elaborate constructions of leaves and branches so they looked like walking trees. They carried blankets and picnic baskets and musical instruments of all sorts— pipes and recorders and bells and tambourines. Some people had brought Maypoles of their own as well.

"Holy blue-footed boobies!" cried Feenix. "Is that who I think it is? Do you see her? The person talking to Mrs. Wu!"

"It is! It is! It's Ms. Trevino!" sang out Brigit. "And there's Beatrice standing next to them! And look at her dress!"

Beatrice's dress was full and many-layered, the color of a pale-green cabbage. Brigit and Feenix put their arms around each other, laughing. "But we have to be nice to her," Brigit said. "She'll be stressed."

"What? Aren't I usually nice?" Feenix asked.

"'Nice' isn't really the word I would generally use for you," Brigit said. "But you're a good friend. Come on! Let's go talk to them." The girls started running down the hill.

"Wait!" called Danton. "I left my jacket on the bench!" But Brigit and Feenix were running the way you run when your feet are flying faster than the rest of you and you're laughing too hard to stop.

Danton was glad to see them so happy, but he was also a little disappointed. He had had the idea that maybe Brigit would know what was on his mind and stay behind for a bit while the other two went on ahead.

"Go get your jacket," Edward said. "*I'll* wait here for you." Danton went back along the beaten-down path and through the dappled shade and light of the woods and found his jacket where he'd left it.

As he was returning, Danton was startled to see a familiar figure off to the side, poking around in the leaves. He froze for a moment, wondering. He put his hand in his pocket and felt for the little glass figurine. It was gone. "Robert!" he called out. "Is that you?"

When Robert came out of the trees, he looked even more rumpled up than usual. His hair, of course, was in his eyes, and his brown corduroy pants were too short, but more than that, he looked a little sticky and seemed to have bits of pocket lint stuck to him here and there.

"Hey," Danton said, "what are *you* doing here? Did you come for the Maypole thing?"

Robert looked as if he wasn't quite sure *where* he was. Then he seemed to realize he was holding something in one of his hands. "Oh!" he said. "I got distracted for a second. I was just fungus hunting." He held out a truly gross wrinkle-topped mushroom of some sort.

Danton made a face and backed up a little.

Robert actually laughed. "I know. Weird looking. But, really, it's a very interesting field of study. Mushrooms can do fantastic things. Did you know? They can digest toxins, and scientists are starting to use them to clean up soil. They can even break down oil spills. I've been doing some little experiments on my own with them."

"Seriously?" Danton responded politely. "I didn't know that. You should come over and show it to Edward. I bet he'll be interested. Come on. He's over here."

By the time the three of them reached the picnic area, Ed and Robert were deep in conversation about oyster mushrooms and the fact that they could eat plastic.

Danton wasn't paying much attention. He was amazed at how many people had shown up. A wild band of children ran past him, including his own brother. They were whacking at each other with sticks and fairy wands. His mother was deep in conversation with Tom the tree guy. He waved to her and then to his dad, who was playing a set of bongo drums, accompanied by some flute people.

Off to the side, Brigit and Feenix were sitting on a picnic blanket with Beatrice the Poisonous Toadstool. And although they had been mortal enemies as recently as yesterday, Feenix was painting Beatrice's face with little blue butterflies. How strange. Brigit looked up at him and waved, and he waved back. He wondered if he would ever have a chance to be alone with her again.

For a moment his spirits dropped, but then they picked right up again. There was the food table. Ms. Trevino was standing next to it, chatting away and eating one of Mrs. Wu's spring dumplings. Although her eternal black trousers were wrinkled and her white shirt looked like she'd slept in it near a muddy pond, she appeared as happy as a lark on the first morning of May. How glad he was to see her. It felt, for some reason, like a great weight off his shoulders.

"Danton!" she exclaimed as he drew near her. "Nice to be out of school, isn't it? And what a gorgeous surprise of a day it is, isn't it?"

"It is," Danton agreed.

Behind him a voice he recognized said, "I think perhaps we've finally turned the corner, don't you?"

It was Mr. Ross. Oh, that was an excellent sign. Danton scanned the crowd for Aunt Kit, but before he could spot her, he heard her voice calling over the crowd.

"All right, one and all. The moment has arrived! All dancers come and find a ribbon!"

Brigit wondered where Danton had gotten to. Would he dance? Before she could decide what to do, Feenix was pulling her up off the blanket and gesturing to Beatrice.

"Come on, you two! We've got to get a ribbon. It's May Day. Brigit, you know your grandmother would want you to do this."

It was true, so Brigit stood up and dusted herself off nervously. Public performances were definitely not her thing. As she walked over, she saw her parents and her grandad standing next to Danton's mother. Brigit waved at them and they waved back.

There was an inner circle of ribbons as well as an outer circle. Brigit took a yellow one on the inside, and Feenix and Beatrice took inside ones, too.

And there was Danton. He took an orange one on the outside.

When every ribbon was claimed and fully stretched out, silence fell over the dancers and the watching crowd. In the center, next to the pole, was a wooden crate. Tom the tree guy came over and stepped up onto it. He was going to be the caller. Next to him was a fiddler with his fiddle at the ready. "To begin," Tom explained in a deep, clear voice, "the outside goes clockwise and the inside goes counterclockwise. Then, when I give the signal, each circle will change directions. Got it?"

There was a chorus of yeses.

Tom turned to look at the fiddler and then started the beat with his foot on the hollow box. *"One, two, three, four . . ."*

The fiddler raised his fiddle and began a bright and high-stepping tune. Tom sang:

Come, lasses and lads, away from your dads,
and away to the Maypole hie.
For today is the day we give thanks to the sun
and the Lady comes dancing by.

The circles began to move, uncertainly first, then faster and with more confidence as the fiddler sped up. The outside ribboners went walking one way; the inside ribboners the other. When they had completed two rounds, Tom called "Change and skip!" and the circles switched directions, and the fiddler played faster as everyone began to skip.

Strike up the fiddle and play us a tune,
for at last the Maid is set free.
Today is the day we meet on the lawn
and go dancing once more round the tree.

Brigit looked at all the faces flying past. Some of the baking-class people were dancing, while a crowd stood outside the circles and clapped in time. She saw her grandad waving as she flew by, and then there was Edward, and—was it possible?—standing next to him appeared to be Detestable Robert. What was he doing here? But there was no time to puzzle this one out, because Tom called for the fiddler to change to a jig and the music grew even livelier.

Now stop for a bow and blow me kiss,
and change your direction around.
With a hop and step and a hop and step,
now jump both your feet off the ground!

Everyone did as Tom directed, and then he had them do a stately dance, with turning and bowing and weaving in and out. When they had unwoven with some laughing and tangling, he set them a quick skipping song with some grape-vining hora steps. Gradually the fiddler picked up the pace, and soon one circle was jigging one way and the other circle was jigging the other, faster and faster. Brigit looked up and saw Danton flying by. She tried to meet his eye, but it was impossible. They were going too fast.

When Brigit tried to find Danton again, she found it was hard to even look around. Her own momentum was too great, and everyone else was moving too quickly. Now the caller had them all simply running again, but so fast it was hard to catch her breath. She began to have a queasy sensation.

It was like riding on a carousel that was going too fast for its own good.

Surely, Tom would slow them down in a moment.

But when she looked to see what Tom was up to, she saw that Tom was no longer there.

The fiddler, however, played on, with a great fixed grin on his face. He played faster and faster. It was only now that she noticed the red vest and the tiny black-booted feet.

40

The Fiddler

Brigit tried to stop and give a cry of alarm, but her feet would not obey her and no sound came from her throat. Around and around, faster and faster she went, until everything was a blur.

The fiddler began to sing along with his fiddle.

Come out, come out, wherever you are,
my dearest and own true sweet.
I know you're here; how far could you go?
Aren't we bound up together from above and below?
Come out, come out, I can smell you are close.
There's no hiding from me, who adores you the most.

His voice grew more and more wheedling as he sang, and then, just as Brigit was pretty sure that she was about to throw up all over everybody, the music and the singing stopped. The dancers came to an abrupt halt. Brigit braced herself for a fall, expecting that the dancers would land all over each other, but that wasn't what happened.

Brigit could move, but everyone else seemed frozen in

midclap or midstep. The singing of the birds, the rustling of the trees, the conversation, all had ceased.

Then the fiddler spoke in a voice that sent a shudder through her.

"I see you over there," the Tiltersmith said. "There's no more hiding."

For a terrible moment, Brigit thought he might be speaking to her, but then she saw it was someone else he wanted.

The Lady walked into the middle of the circle and stood facing the Tiltersmith. She was barefoot now and wearing a loose-fitting tunic belted over a skirt that seemed to change its shade of blue every time she moved. She had her hands on her waist. Her bees buzzed in a cloud of agitation over her head.

"What are you doing here?" she demanded furiously.

The Tiltersmith shrugged and turned. "You might ask *him*," he answered, pointing to Edward.

Brigit saw the guilty look on Edward's face. He didn't move, but she could tell he wasn't frozen. Brigit wondered if the others were awake, too. She looked around quickly. Danton nodded to her from across the outer circle, and Feenix reached out and took Brigit's hand. No one else moved.

The Lady gazed at Edward in disbelief. "You didn't take care of the doorway, did you? I told them to tell you. I told them that you would know what needed to be done."

"I . . . I . . . forgot," Edward stammered.

"He forgot!" the Tiltersmith laughed.

The Lady turned back to him, steady and radiant in her defiance. "Well, what does it matter? You know you are too late. We have been freed."

Brigit saw him now. Jack had stepped quietly out from the circle of dancers. He went to the Lady's side and stood.

The Lady spoke again. "Our time is ripe. And we are where we are supposed to be. You have no power over us here. Go back where you belong!"

The Tiltersmith laughed. "It may be so that I have no power over you for the moment, but you forget—I have power over *them*." He waved his hand at the crowd. "And all the others out there." He waved beyond the park. "You know full well all the damage they wreak on their own. Imagine if this time I simply choose to *stay here*, close to them. Imagine if I keep my whispering in their ears. They would never even know it was me."

The Lady stamped her foot in a fury of impatience and fear. "You wouldn't. You can't. You couldn't bear staying up here."

"Ah, but you underestimate me, my lady. Even as I make them foolish, they have been making me stronger. And I could bear much just to be able to be near to you."

There was a long silence while the two stared each other down. Neither one blinked.

But at last, the Lady spoke. Not to the Tiltersmith, but to Edward.

"Give me the doorway," she commanded and held out her hand.

Edward swallowed and stepped forth past the dancers and into the middle of the circle, where the Lady stood. He reached into his pocket and pulled out the glass jar. Brigit could see that the lid must have blown off when the Tiltersmith came through. The glass was jagged around the top, and the cocoon and its exit hole were poking out. He handed the jar to the Lady.

Without looking at it, she spoke to the Tiltersmith. "If I agree to the old bargain one more time, you will go back?"

A mix of triumph and sadness passed over the fiddler's face. "I will," he said.

"Now? You will go now?" she demanded.

He bowed his head and said, "I accept your offer."

"Then I agree," she replied. "Put your finger here."

She held out the glass jar. He met her eyes one last time, and then he reached out and did what she'd asked.

The next moment he was gone.

The Lady wasted no time but had Edward immediately build a small mound of twigs and dry paper and slide the cocoon onto its top.

Danton found a box of matches on the picnic table and brought it forward.

"You do realize this could be a very dangerous thing to do," Edward warned her. "It could potentially explode the whole universe."

"Just do it," she told him.

He tried again. "Plus, you do realize this would have been one of the greatest scientific discoveries of—"

"Just do it!" she commanded.

Brigit and Danton and Feenix stood next to Edward and watched him light the match and toss it onto the twigs and paper. The fire licked at the cocoon. At first it did not appear to have any effect at all, and then there was a sudden loud cracking sound. Like a giant kernel of popcorn in a frying pan, the cocoon burst open, and out from it shot a cone of spinning and faintly hissing particles of light until it reached up past the treetops and then faded away.

All was quiet, and the universe, at least this one, seemed to be going about its business.

All around them the watchers began to talk and chatter. The dancers let go of their ribbons.

Tom jumped down from his crate. "Time to eat! Save me a dumpling!"

41

Stories

Danton, Edward, Feenix, Brigit, Robert, and Beatrice all filled their plates with food and sat down together on the grass. When Danton at last felt too full to get up for a refill, he lay down and half listened to them talking about movies and shoes and mushrooms and experiments and how fungi could be used to clean up the environment and what they were going to do this summer. He wondered if they would all still be friends by the time summer was over.

He was forgetting something. What was it? He turned his head and put his ear to the warm ground and heard the worms tunneling through the earth, looking for delicious rotting bits of old leaves and nematodes and fungi to munch upon. He knew from Mr. Ross that their tunneling along made it easier for water and air to pass through to all the roots of the dandelions and the trees and the grass. Sleepily, Danton thought he could hear the sound of the roots as they drank and the sound of tree leaves unfurling and the whisper of blades of grass as they pierced the soil and headed straight to the sun.

He thought about Mr. Ross's story, about how summer would come and then autumn, and if everything went right, all the trees and the plants would die back and leave a new feast for the worms and the fungi, and the circle would continue around. But what if it didn't? What then? It was really too much to think about right now with the sun warming the air and the grass and the droning of the voices.

And just as he was really and truly about to fall asleep, it hit him what he had forgotten. He came awake with a start.

Oh, Hellamenopee! He still hadn't kissed her.

When it was time to go, Danton's parents and Brigit's parents and grandad decided to walk together since they lived in the same neighborhood. And what could Danton do then? He couldn't even hold her hand. His brother was zooming in and out between them, and Danton could see that his mother was watching Brigit and him with way too much interest. But as it happened, Brigit said she needed to stop at the library for a book, and she asked Danton if he wanted to come along.

He did.

They went up the wide steps of the Grand Army Plaza library, and she pushed open the heavy door. He followed her in, and she led him through the stacks of the fiction section until they came to a completely empty aisle way in the back of the alphabet. There, she stopped and turned to him, and hardly blushing at all, she slid her arms up around his neck and pulled his face down, and she kissed him and he kissed her back.

At the end of the day, whoever was left behind pitched in with the cleanup. Mr. Ross, Feenix was very pleased to see, stayed. He volunteered to help Edward, Feenix, and Kit carry everything home.

"I saw you, by the way," Feenix said to Edward as they were leaving.

"You saw me, by the way, what?" he asked.

"With that paper cup. Scooping up those ashes from the little fire we made."

"No, you didn't."

"Yes, I did."

They left it at that. Feenix's mind was busy with many other thoughts, anyway. She could feel she was already forgetting stuff. For instance, she knew there was something she needed to remember that would happen in the future. But that made no sense. How could she remember something that was going to happen in the future? She let go of that one and turned to Aunt Kit.

"Kit," she said. "There's something I need to ask you. You know that old story where the maiden falls down a big crack and gets held prisoner by some kind of underground king or god? What's the bargain she makes with him to let her go? I can't remember."

Kit was pulling one of the wagons. She turned to look at Feenix, and then she looked away. She didn't seem happy with the question. "She promises to go back to him willingly at the end of the summer."

"But she hates him, doesn't she?"

Kit drew a breath. "Depends who's telling the story."

"Well, one way or another, there's a sadness to it, isn't there?" Mr. Ross said. "But imagine if she didn't go back with him. Then there would be no winter. What would happen then?"

This question kept Feenix's mind busy for the rest of the walk.

When they arrived back at Ed's house, Kit said Feenix could keep the costume clothes, if she'd like. Delighted, Feenix let go of her worries and threw her arms around Kit's neck and kissed her and thanked her for the wonderful day. Feenix helped Ed put away the Maypole in the attic, where they could find it next year. Then she headed for home.

Edward, not to his delight, was given several more annoying cleanup jobs to do while Mr. Ross and Kit chatted and put things away in the kitchen. As he was finishing his chores, Edward thought of a question *he* wanted to ask, one for Mr. Ross about the fungi that grew in Prospect Park. He headed toward the kitchen and then he stopped. It had grown much too quiet in there.

Edward did not want to look and see what was going on. *Let it stay a great mystery.*

He went up to his room. Very carefully, he unfolded the paper cup he had used to scoop the ashes from the fire. He poured these into a little empty chocolate-truffle tin and stuck the tin up on one of his shelves, where he was sure he would remember it eventually.

It ended up behind a stack of old board games and a couple of disintegrating birds' nests. He didn't find the tin again until many years later. What happened then is another story.

Acknowledgments

[tk]